TWISTED HEARTS

TWISTED INTENTIONS BOOK
BOOK 3

SAVANNAH RYLAN

1

———

DALIA

"Goddamn it, Dalia, you make a hell of a blue motorcycle, you know that?"

I peered over my shoulder and tossed one of my many loyal customers a playful wink. "Only for you, handsome."

He tipped the rest of his glass up. "Two more for the booth over there?"

I spun around and scooped up his drink. "You got a good tip in it for me?"

He grinned. "Don't I always?"

I dumped the ice out of his cup into the sink. "Give me five minutes and they'll be up."

He rapped his knuckles against the bar top. "You're the best, babe. Thanks."

I blew him a kiss as he walked away. "I only get this way through you guys!"

"I love it when you say shit like that!"

I barked with laughter and set out piecing together two more drinks for the tipsy duo toward the stage. Every Friday night, we had live music in the bar, and I made sure to work because it wasn't as if I could sleep through the damned thing.

Living above my place of work had its perks. Especially when my boss loved staring at the spread of my hips. I knew what I looked like, a big girl with thick tits and thighs that rubbed together. I knew what kinds of thoughts raced through their minds after a couple of drinks at my bar.

And I most certainly used it to my advantage.

"Hey, luscious!"

I snickered, slapping my rag over my shoulder. "Anyone ever tell you that I hate that nickname, Bryce?"

I sent out the two blue motorcycles with my runner for the evening before yet another loyal customer came belly-upping to my bar.

"You know what I like," he said.

"Ah, a margarita with a beer tipped up into it?"

"And float me an extra shot of tequila."

I winked at him and pulled a glass down from the rack above my head. "Sounds like a rough day on the job."

Bryce snickered. "If only my wife were as intuitive as you are."

"Maybe she should know your drink order. That might help."

He barked with laughter, but it almost sounded cynical in its origin. "She can't even figure out how to put on her lingerie half the time. I don't think she'll stand a chance with my drink order."

"Well, you can always come here."

He slapped a twenty onto the counter. "That's why I do. Two drinks, and a tip. Thanks, Dalia."

I threw the contents of his drink into a blender then blew him a kiss. "Always, Bryce."

I mean, what the hell was a high school drop-out like myself supposed to do, anyway? Work in a grocery store my entire life? It wasn't as if anyone would take a chance on my intelligence without at least a G.E.D. And a girl had to pay the bills some-how. I wouldn't have it any other way, however. The Mule was my home, especially since I lived in the studio apartment just overhead.

I loved this place, and it had accepted all of me from the very beginning.

Which was more than I could say for any physical person in my life.

Including my own mother.

"There you go," I said, handing Bryce his drink. I slammed the top of the beer bottle against the counter, using my hand to shield the crack as the bottle cap flew off. My customer clapped his hands and whooped, as if he were at a circus or some shit. Then I tipped the bottle up quickly enough to slam it down into the blended mango margarita.

I took one of my stirring spoons, turned it over, and poured a shot of tequila right over the top of the drink.

"Enjoy," I said with a smile, "and plug your ears."

He put his hands over his ears and I drew in a deep breath.

"LAAAAAAST CAH-AAAAAALL!"

Deep down inside, I was ready for the night to dwindle down. While I didn't mind closing, I hated the way my mind raced as the bar dwindled from packed to nothingness. It made me wonder things I didn't like pondering, like whether or not life had more for me than slinging drinks six times a week just to pay bills. I mean, sure, I had a good thing going with reduced rent upstairs, but it wasn't as if I didn't know why. My landlord, who just so happened to own the bar as well, loved staring at the sway of my hips whenever I came or went. I wasn't an idiot. I knew the way he looked at me. And while my mother always taught me to "use what God gave ya," I didn't want to follow in her footsteps.

I didn't want to prostitute myself for money and luxuries.

Not much for high school dropouts in this world, though.

I don't know. I did my best to try and not compare myself to my mother. But with her dropping out of high school around the same time I did, it was hard not to. I watched men come and go from our house, leaving scores of money she used to treat us to nicer wardrobes and fancy dinners. I couldn't blame her, either. She had a kid to take care of and no man in the house. No one to love or care for her. No one to give her a break or come babysit so she could go out and enjoy what it felt like to be someone other than Mom. I loved her despite her flaws and the struggles we had as I grew up, and I'd never fault her for what she had to do to keep a roof over our heads.

I simply wanted something *more.*

That was all.

"Two glass bottle beers and a whiskey neat."

The shiver that ricocheted down my spine stiffened my tits against my bra. As I stood there, cleaning the blender I had used to make Bryce's margarita, the deep, resonant voice held me hostage. I put on my best smile before I placed the blender onto the drying rack. I raised my arms and got them around the crooks of my breasts, pressing them together as I brought my arms back to a normal position. I turned around, slapping my rag once again over my shoulder and came face to face with the man who possessed a voice that could stop God Himself in his tracks.

And as my gaze landed on the man in the leather jacket, it took all I had just to remember to breathe.

"Got a preference for beer?" I asked, nodding toward our beer cooler full of glass bottles.

The jet black hair that contrasted the playful amber eyes of the man standing in front of me had absolutely nothing on the way his shoulders and arms tugged at the leather bindings of his jacket. The damned thing looked like it was crying out for mercy, and when he slid his stare down my body , I took the opportunity to do the same to him, finding the muscles of his chest damn near ripping his black t-shirt off his torso.

"Surprise us," the man purred.

I tossed him a playful wink. "Coming right up."

I stepped up to the bar as the man turned his back, and I mindlessly made a whiskey neat, watching him backtrack to a booth. He sat down with two other men who donned the same kind of leather jacket, and I wondered if they were in a club together or some shit. It reminded me of my childhood, honestly. The bike crews rumbling down the street, revving their engines and forgoing their helmets because they didn't like the way they sat against their necks.

Those men were old as fucking dirt, sure. But Mom never ceased to try and throw herself at them.

After all, a man with toys was a man with money, right?

Ah, life lessons from Mom.

I barely made it through the whiskey neat before I walked over to the beer cooler. I dropped the glass onto a runner's tray before pulling out two of our finest glass bottle beers: a couple of stouts made locally up the road. I popped their tops and placed them on the tray, and Lisa came up, ready to take the tray from me.

But I waved my hand and picked up the tray myself.

"I got this one. You start cleaning up the tables that aren't taken any longer."

She pointed at me. "On it. I'm ready to get out of here, too."

With the tray balanced in the palm of my hand, I sauntered toward the men. I swayed my hips a bit deeper and jiggled my tits a bit more as my hair swayed along my shoulders. I arrived at their booth, tossing them playful winks while I divvied out their drinks.

And the entire time, I wondered why the fuck they hadn't come in earlier.

I could have gotten them to buy drinks from me all night.

"All right, who's got the whiskey neat?" I asked.

The guy stuffed into the corner flashed me a set of sea foam green eyes that stole my breath away. "Thanks."

I put the drink down and slid it toward him. "Then, you two must be the beer guys."

The man who originally came up to the bar chuckled. "Thanks, doll."

"Mm, mm, mm," I hummed as I looked over at the other man. "I hope you enjoy."

Blond hair and blue eyes were always a classic combination, but the other man's gaze seemed to sparkle like stars in an endless night sky.

"Thanks, beautiful," he said with a wink.

I smiled brightly. "Anytime, guys."

While Ocean Green and Rumble Voice stared at me from over their drinks, the guy tucked in the corner stared way too hard into the top of his whiskey neat. Huh, a bit of a challenge I see. Nothing wrong with that.

"If you need anything else before we close in an hour," I said, tucking the tray beneath my arm, "you know where to find me."

"We certainly do," the man in the corner said, throwing back his entire drink and sliding the glass toward me.

"I'm good for another," he murmured.

I quirked an eyebrow. "Were you guys not in here when I yelled last call?"

Mr. Luscious Voice crooked an eyebrow. "Is it really last call, though?"

I winked at him. "Depends on how much you want to tip."

"Would... this be enough?" sea foam asked.

And when I watched him pull a wad of cash out from the breast pocket of his leather jacket, I did my best to keep a lid on it.

Men who carried around money like that were always trouble.

But who didn't love a spot of trouble every now and again?

"Two beers and another whiskey neat, coming right up," I said.

2

———

DALIA

The rush running straight through me as I made those forbidden drinks held me hostage. My heart leapt into my throat. I kept peering around like some mobster in a 90s movie, ready to take on whoever decided to pull a gun on me first.

Damn, I loved those movies growing up.

They were nostalgic for me. Mom loved watching them during the late hours of the night, and I'd lie in my bed down the hallway and listen to her laugh. Listen to her cry. Listen to her quote just about every single line from movies like *Scarface* and *The Godfather* trilogy. Badass men had always intrigued her, and I suppose it was a trait she had passed to me.

It was hard to resist a good bad boy every once in a while.

Though, I did my best to set my sights on men who deserved my attention.

"All right," I whispered as I walked Silent Man's drink over to the tray I had brought back with me. "Now, let's get those two—"

"What are you doing?" Lisa asked.

Raquel came up behind me. "That's a good question. Didn't you call last call already?"

I thought quickly on my feet. "Had a last-minute set of customers come in. Wanted to make sure they got served before we closed down."

"You know we're not supposed to do that," Lisa said.

I placed the two opened beers down onto the tray. "Did you lock the front door?"

"And the back," Raquel said.

I picked up the tray. "Then, we have nothing to worry—are you fucking kidding me!?"

"What?" Lisa asked.

When my gaze whipped toward the booth, it was empty. The three men in the leather jackets that had inhabited those seats had simply... vanished.

"No, no, no, no," I whispered, rushing over to the booth.

"What is it!?" Raquel called out behind me.

It had to be fake. Maybe they had all darted to the bathroom or some shit. Maybe they had been barhopping, and the seal finally broke. But as I placed my tray down, I studied the empty seats. The imprints of where their asses had once been. And when I placed my hand against the indent in one of the cushions, I cursed beneath my breath.

"Motherfuckers," I hissed.

I sighed heavily as I picked up the tray and headed back to the bar. Despite the indentation of the booth seats, their places were cold. Meaning they had probably gotten up and left the second I turned my back. I slammed the tray down, staring at the three drinks that had managed to keep themselves upright the entire time.

They'd come out of my paycheck, but that feeling had nothing on the fact that those assholes had flirted their way through a free round of drinks.

Teasing me and throwing me for a loop they knew I'd take.

"Goddamn it," I murmured, pinching the bridge of my nose.

"I won't tell if you won't," Lisa said.

Raquel squeezed my shoulder. "We'll take it out of our tips tonight. Split three ways."

I shook my head and peered at her over my shoulder. "I can't ask you guys to do that. This is my fuck-up, and I should've known better."

Raquel reached for a beer before Lisa handed me the whiskey neat.

"I think you could use the stronger of the three," Lisa said.

I heaved a heavy sigh before I took it from her. "Seriously, though. I can't ask you guys t—"

"Hey," Raquel said as she came to stand in front of me, right beside Lisa, "you did it for me last time when that entire group ran out on me on my first week. Remember?"

I groaned. "Yes, but—"

"But nothing," Lisa said before she tipped her beer back. "You've always covered our asses, and now we get to repay the favor."

"Here, here," Raquel said, holding her beer bottle out.

I relegated myself to their plan before I clinked my glass against it. "Thanks, guys."

"Anytime," they both said in unison.

And after slinging back that very strong whiskey neat, I dumped the ice into the sink.

"Let's close this place down and go get some sleep," I said.

"Damn straight," Raquel murmured.

The only good thing about closing down a bar at two in the morning was the monotonous routine of it all. After we shooed out the customers and locked the doors, we got to pull the blinds and put on music to help motivate us to clean. I mopped the floors while Raquel threw the chairs up onto the tables. Lisa washed and sanitized all the glasses we used for tomorrow's shift. I worked a double starting at noon, and I sure as fuck wasn't looking forward to it. But with the way those assholes stiffed me, it would give me a chance to recoup that money, and then some.

Maybe I'll wear that slinky little red top everyone likes so much.

I mean, who the fuck did that? Just came in for a drink and intentionally ordered more before leaving when our backs were turned? It was cowardice. It was the stuff of boys, not men. Yet, I couldn't get them out of my head. Those bulging muscles and those dazzling sea foam eyes. They held me hostage as I finished locking up and dragged myself upstairs to flop face-first into bed, with that man's voice echoing off the caverns of my mind.

"Uuuuugh," I groaned, rolling over in bed.

Part of me wondered if they'd be back. Another part of me wondered if I'd get a second chance to sit in one of their laps. But the rational part of me wanted to curse them up and down the second I laid eyes on them. No one stiffed me and got away with it. Then again, maybe there had been an emergency of some sort. Maybe they'd come back around to pay their opened tab.

But as I laid there, staring up at the ceiling with my eyes growing heavier by the second, I sure as fuck wouldn't hold my breath for it.

Men who stiffed entire bars for drinks were nothing but cheapskates, and they didn't deserve my time.

Even by my mother's standards.

BRRRNT! BRRRNT! BRRRNT! BRRRNT! BRRRNT!

I rolled over and slammed my hand against my cellphone, turning off the hellish alarm I hated hearing every single morning. It startled me so damn bad that my heart leapt into my throat, but it was the only alarm that ever got me up. Anything else simply lulled me back to sleep, and I couldn't afford to lose my job.

BRRNT! BRRNT! BRRNT! BRRNT! BRRNT!

"Jesus," I hissed as I picked up my phone and swiped the alarm away for good. "I really gotta turn off that snooze option."

An hour and a half. I had ninety minutes to prepare myself for the longest day of my week, and I wasn't the least bit ready. I heaved my tired ass out of bed and lumbered into the bathroom, ready for a steamy hot shower that cloaked me away from the world. Sure, I had three free days coming at me after my long shift, but that didn't sidestep the fact that I actually had to work first.

"Maybe being a housewife is worth it," I said breathlessly, reaching into the shower.

Peeling myself out of my work clothes from the other night made me wonder if bananas felt as free as I did whenever someone peeled their outer layers off. My tits jiggled and my hips wobbled as I eased into the shower, hissing as the searing hot water battered against my skin. Yesterday's drama melted off me, screaming and crying out as it swirled toward the drain. I hung my head, allowing the water to drench my hair as I stared down at my swollen ankles.

I'd have to wear my compression socks just to get through the day.

Skinny jeans, it is.

My muscles relaxed and my back popped. It started at the bottom as I rolled my torso all the way up, tilting my head toward the stream of water. I opened my mouth and gargled with the hot water that fell toward the back of my throat. I spat it out before I reached for my toothbrush and toothpaste. My morning routine kept me rooted in reality, especially after hard nights at work.

And as I cleaned myself up, I did my best to push all thoughts of those men to the side.

But when I walked into the backroom of the bar to clock in for work, Raquel stuck her head through the doorway.

"You'll never guess who's here."

My eyes widened as I quickly punched in my employee code into the system. I made sure it was locked by the time I arrived at work, then I forced myself to take a deep breath. Never let them see you sweat. It was yet another thing Mom had taught me. Men took advantage of weaker women more than they did women who had their heads screwed onto their shoulders.

At least, that was what she had taught me.

Time had taught me differently , though.

"You good?" Raquel asked as she came toward me.

I set my sights on the bar. "Let's get this over with."

I steadied my movements, sauntering and swaying my hips as I breached the doorway into the bar. Rumble Voice stood at the bar top, bellied up with his mountainous muscles staring me down in that same leather jacket. The shirt he donned was a crimson red, and it teased my eyes. I did my best not to stare at the etched muscles imprinted against the fabric.

I walked up to him and folded my arms across my chest. "Didn't expect to see you here."

He pulled something out of his pocket and set it on the bar. "We don't leave a tab unpaid."

He removed his hand and I found a wad of cash staring me in the face. Not quite the massive bundle the other man had in his breast pocket last night, but enough. I shot the man a look before I scooped up the cash, counting it in front of him.

I did my best not to look shocked at the fact that he had just handed me a couple hundred bucks.

"I'll keep the extra as a tip. You know, for the heartache," I said.

I stuffed the cash into my bra and watched Mr. Licky Lips stare down my movements.

"You got a name?" I asked.

His gaze darted back up to mine. "Lance."

I nodded. "Dalia."

The man grinned. "Pretty name."

"I get that a lot."

Then, much to my surprise, Mr. Platinum Hair appeared over the man's shoulder. "I'm Pike, by the way."

I tossed him a playful wink. "And the silent one? Does he have a name?"

Pike shrugged. "Yeah, but he doesn't like introducing himself. He's got a stick up his ass that way."

Someone grumbled despite the fact that there was no body to be found, and that alone made me giggle.

"Two beers and a whiskey neat?" I asked.

Lance smirked. "Already got our order memorized. I see you're good for that tip."

I reached for a whiskey glass. "Oh, honey. I'm good for much more than a tip."

Pike whistled lowly. "Be careful what you wish for, beautiful."

I grinned. "Never. You guys go take a seat. And try not to dip out on me this time, yeah? It's a bad look for my boss."

Lance rapped his knuckles against the bar. "You heard the woman. Settle in for some drinks."

As I picked up our finest bottle of whiskey to prime Mr. Silent's drink, I watched the three of them lumber back toward the booth where they had been last night. All of them slid into their same places, with Mountain Man alone on one side. Honestly, if he wanted someone sitting with him, they'd probably have to sit on his fucking lap. A place I'd happily claim for myself, if given the chance. But there was one thing that was different. As I snatched up the two beers and cracked them open against the bar top, there was one small thing that changed.

Silent Man stared me down from his perched position in the booth.

Pinning me with those sea foam eyes of his as I wondered why he hadn't spoken up yet.

I love a good mystery.

3

LANCE

"Here you go," the curvy bartender said, sliding the tray of drinks onto our table. "Let me know if you guys need anything else."

"What?" Pike asked. "No witty banter for us this time?"

She giggled, and the sound washed over my cock. "Maybe treat the bartender with respect next time, and she will."

"Fair enough," I said, nodding my head.

She wiggled her eyebrows. "Flag me down if you guys want another round."

And as I watched that ass of hers jiggle with her movements as she walked away, I had to lift my hips and give my dick room to breathe.

"So," Pike said as he dropped the whiskey neat in front of Blade, our resident mute, "what are we going to do about our little... issue?"

I grabbed my beer by the neck and slung it back while Blade played with one of his new knives. He flipped it open and closed it, watching the metal shimmer.

"Blade?" Pike asked.

I watched as our friend slid the pad of his thumb against the sharp edge of the knife. Feeling up his knives was nothing new, but for him to be lost in his own reflection?

That took some serious stress.

Still, all I did was watch. As President of my crew, it was my job to look out for the well-being of my men. Especially my core group of men. And Blade? Well, he had struggled recently with the little problem that had fallen into our laps a few days ago.

And it wasn't until he nicked the pad of his thumb that he made any sort of sound.

"Shit," he hissed, bringing his thumb to his lips.

Pike grinned. "How does it taste tonight?"

"Focus," I said as I pinned him with a look. "We have to focus, all right? We can't hold another church meeting unless we bring back results."

Pike shrugged. "The guys are tired of this shit. Can't fucking blame them for it, either."

Blade finally lifted his unfocused gaze. "The longer he's out there, the more our reputation takes a hit. We end this tonight."

Pike snickered. "You got a plan on how we're supposed to do that?"

Blade turned his gaze out the window. "No. But it doesn't stop us from knowing what has to happen."

And there was the rub. We knew what had to happen, but we had no plan for execution. It was the first time The Shadow Boys had ever been caught with their pants down, and I didn't like it. Our crew was known on the streets for being two steps ahead of everyone else. Ruthless to the core, and always part of a greater plan.

I hated this floundering around that we were doing.

It was unbecoming of the crew we had built.

"I couldn't help but notice from across the bar that you guys aren't touching your drinks," Dalia said, seemingly appearing out of nowhere.

God, what I wouldn't do to have those curves of hers against my face. "They're just fine, if that's what you're asking."

She thumbed over her shoulder. "Actually, our kitchen is open and operational now. Any of you guys want food?"

That perked Blade up. "Whatcha got on the menu?"

The smile that grew across her cheeks made my blood percolate. "Food gets me talking, too. We got All-American fare here, including funnel cakes."

That really caught Blade's attention. "You guys have funnel cakes?"

She nodded. "Mhm. Hot dogs. Cheeseburgers. Fries with all sorts of fixin's you can get. Funnel cakes, chocolate cake, hot wings—"

"How extensive is your menu?" Blade asked.

"Here we go," Pike said.

"Your kitchen's about to be very busy, Miss Dalia."

She winked down at me. "It's already busy, sunshine. So, what'll it be, Sea Foam?"

Blade blinked. " Sea Foam?"

She pointed at her face. "Your eyes. They're the color of sea foam ."

He nodded slowly. "You can call me Blade."

"I'm sure I can," she said with that smile of hers. "So, you guys hungry?"

"One of everything," Blade said. "But a funnel cake for each of us."

She blinked. "One of... everything?"

"Everything."

"Front... *and* back of the menu?" she asked.

I chuckled. "Told you your kitchen's about to be busy."

Dalia whistled lowly. "Hell of a check, guys. But I'm on it."

"Trust me," Pike said with a grin, "there's a good tip in it for you this time around."

She wiggled her eyebrows. "What was that you said about being careful what you wish for?"

Pike barked with laughter. "God, I hope so."

Dalia cleared her throat. "Do you really want the name on your order to be Blade?"

He looked her square in her eyes. "That's my name, so yeah."

She nodded slowly. "The whole menu plus three funnel cakes, coming right up. I'm assuming another round of drinks before it's all said and done?"

"And some waters, thanks," I said.

"Fair enough. I'll keep an eye on those drinks from the bar, but flag me down if I miscalculate," she said.

"Keeping an extra eye on me, I hope," Pike said with a chuckle.

"Don't you wish," she whispered.

And when she sauntered away from us, swaying those luscious hips for our viewing pleasure, a growl bubbled up the back of my throat.

"Goddamn, that ass of hers is thick," Pike murmured.

Blade rolled his eyes. "Plan. Now. What are we doing?"

My phone vibrated against my thigh, and I knew it wasn't good. For the past couple of weeks, it hadn't been good, so why ruin the streak? I lifted my hips and shoved my hand into my pocket. I pulled out the vibrating cell phone and found a multitude of messages from our guys. I opened the latest one, hoping there was nothing to it.

But after my eyes scrolled across the message, I turned the phone so Pike could see.

"Jesus Christ," he hissed.

"Let me see," Blade said, holding his hand open.

I plopped my cell into his palm, and he looked down at the screen. "Not the fucking laundromat, come on."

I ripped the phone out of his hand and tucked it back into my jeans. "They're fucking around with where we clean our money, and at this point, they've hit five of our joints. That's not a coincidence."

"But where the fuck would The Sentinels get that kind of information in the first place?" Pike asked.

"Inside man?" Blade asked.

I shot him a look. "We don't accuse any of our own without proof. You got proof?"

"Nope."

"Then can it," I glowered.

"All right, setting that off to the side for a second," Pike said, leaning back. "Where else could they get that kind of information?"

I shrugged. "This isn't necessarily a bustling town. There aren't many businesses in play for us to work with in the first place. It could just be another lowlife crew trying to push in on boundaries."

"Do you believe that?" Blade asked.

I hated that I didn't. "No."

"Exactly."

Pike sighed. "And we don't have a clue as to where these assholes came from in the first place?"

I picked up my beer and chugged the rest of it back. "You said so yourself, Pike, ain't nothin' online about any of these assholes. No papers, no blogs, no conspiracy theories. They've just poofed their way out of thin air and into our lives."

"This isn't the only crew to try and push in on this town, though," Blade said.

"Yeah," I said, raking my hands through my hair, "they're just the first ones to succeed."

"Hey, wait a second," Pike said.

My eyebrows rose. "That sounds like an idea. Spit it out."

Blade snickered. "He's wondering if 'block by block protection' is in play."

I narrowed my eyes. "I thought we ruled that out, though. The restaurant and the nail salon both said—"

"—that a guy with half a burnt face came in and offered them money for leisure," Pike interrupted.

Blade shrugged. "Sounds like some dudes trying to find easy women."

"But," Pike said, holding his finger in the air, "what if they weren't asking for *that* kind of leisure?"

I paused. "I'm not following."

Pike leaned forward and pressed his finger against the top of the table. "Think about it. You come in from off the street, walk right up to the owner of a business, and you say, 'I want to pay you X amount of dollars a month for unfettered access to your business for me and my guys.'"

"Yeah?" I asked.

"Fucking Christ," Blade hissed. "How did we not see that sooner?"

I shook my head. "Maybe the beer is getting to my head, but you're gonna have to spit it out."

Pike grinned. "What if they're wanting the unfettered access not for leisure purposes, but to eventually offer their protection when they start fucking shit up around here? That means they pull double the coin: they pay in, offer protection at double the cost, and they recoup their money without blinking an eye because they're the ones fucking shit up in the first place."

Blade started playing with his knife. "It's not a pay-for-protection scam."

My back straightened. "It's a hostile takeover."

"Three more drinks and some waters," Dalia said as she came seemingly out of nowhere.

Blade quickly sheathed his butterfly knife and I drew in a deep breath. "Right on time, as always."

She winked at me. "Can't leave my best customers in the dark. Your first round of food is coming out, by the way."

"Perfect," Blade murmured.

"Anything else I can get you guys in the meantime?" she asked.

"A helping of that ass in my lap?" Pike asked.

I kicked him underneath the table, but Dalia simply threw her head back with laughter.

"Oh, man. Catch me on my off-hours and we'll see what we can work out."

Pike smirked up at her. "Don't get my hopes up like that now. You have no idea how desperate a man can get watching an ass like yours."

She leaned toward him and giggled. "Why do you think my rent is so cheap above this place?"

Pike licked his lips. "A woman after my own heart."

Dalia stood back up and made her way toward the bar. "Food's coming right up, guys. Be back in a bit!"

Pike damn near fell out of the booth staring at her fucking ass, and I couldn't blame him. But we had to focus.

"Sit up," I glowered, kicking his shin again.

Pike hissed and bent forward. "Jesus, think you can kick any harder with those damn boots?"

"Wanna see me try?" I asked.

Blade groaned. "Enough, my God."

I swallowed hard and tried to focus my brain. "All right, now that we know what their angle is, we have to... make sure..."

Now, I didn't believe in God. Never had, never would. But if God existed, he threw us a fucking bone that day. My mind came to a grinding halt as a familiar red leather jacket strolled through the front doors of the bar. The heavy limp on the right side of his body matched the scarring I clocked on the right of the back side of his neck. And as he made his way to the bar, I watched Dalia smile over her shoulder at him.

"Guys?" I asked.

"What?" Pike asked.

I nodded. "Look who just rolled in."

Blade inched himself up and peered over the top of the booth before he slammed back down. Pike whipped his head back and forth, looking at me before looking at the man and back again.

"Holy shit," Pike hissed. "That's him!"

Blade unsheathed his knife. "Yep."

I clocked the red Sentinel logo on the back of his jacket. "Out back?"

Blade's eyes illuminated. "I finally get to break this beauty in."

"Seriously? Out back here?" Pike asked.

I shrugged. "It's our only window, and for once, we have the upper hand."

Pike peered back around the corner of the booth. "She's talking to him."

"It was only a matter of time before they made their way into this place," Blade said as he stared at his knife with those wild, crazy eyes of his.

I didn't like the fact that she had been talking to that man for such a long time. What happened to our food? Didn't she say it was coming up?

It was enough to get me onto my feet. "Pike, you get him out into the alley. Blade?"

"Yep?"

"Go check and see if anyone else is with that asshole."

"And if they are?"

I looked down at him. "Bring them, too."

"Hell, yeah," Blade said, shoving Pike out of the booth.

It's time we taught these assholes a lesson, anyway.

4

PIKE

I slung back the rest of my beer as Blade slinked beneath the booth table and headed for the side exit next to the stage. I relished the taste of it. The way the bubbles popped against my tongue teased my senses, making my stomach churn with a need for food.

"So much for that full menu," I murmured as I stood.

"I'll head out back. Be ready," Lance said, brushing past me.

And as I turned toward the bar where Dalia stood with that Sentinel, my heart sank. I watched her shove those tits together just like she did with us, her body leaned against the bar top while she flashed that pearly white smile of hers. A pang of jealousy ripped through me as Lance disappeared into the darkness of the bar. It was the middle of the fucking afternoon, yet somehow, he stuck to the shadows with those brute shoulders of his.

While Blade snuck out the side exit to go check the parking lot.

"I should've known," I murmured to myself.

Most bartenders flirted with men to get better tips. That was pretty much common knowledge. But for a minute there, I had hoped Dalia only had eyes for us. Fucking hell, I'd never seen a sexier woman in all my life, and if she gave me a chance, I'd take her on the ride of her life.

You know, before staking her on my dick.

"Here goes nothing," I said breathlessly.

I had to stay focused. Even though Dalia's tits were out for the world to see in that bullshit halter crop top she had on, the man she was talking with was ruthless. Dangerous. All he wanted was to wiggle him and his crew into this bar before completely taking it over, and they'd never survive. Crews like The Sentinels wanted only one thing: a town at their mercy. They didn't have this town's best interest at heart. They just wanted to drain this place for everything it was worth.

We couldn't let that happen.

Especially since the businesses of this town cleaned our money multiple times a year.

Wait for it.

The only upper hand we had was the fact that this lone asshole didn't know we had already claimed our turf. With The Mule being the only bar on that end of town, the guys and I had staked it out for a while, wondering if we wanted that place to clean our money or take our money for pleasure purposes. We didn't have many safe places we could go to chill out as a crew. Places that kept a lid on who we were, even in the face of the cops.

I had to wait until an opportunity arose where I could get Dalia to help us out with our plan.

I didn't know what the fuck they were saying, but when Dalia turned her back toward the man, I watched him slink off toward the bathroom. He didn't even clock his surroundings, which meant he thought he was scot-free with whatever bargaining chip he thought he had. Rule number one was never assume you were safe. Lance taught us that. Whenever you were in business mode, act like it.

Never assume your enemy didn't know what was going on.

"Hey there, sexy," I said, leaning against the bar.

"Well, lookie who it is," Dalia said as she turned around, cleaning a glass with her rag. "You guys need another round?"

I leaned forward and lowered my voice. "Actually, we could use your help."

"Oh? Do tell. I'm a sucker for a dame in distress."

I had already fallen in love with those pillow lips of hers when they tucked into a grin. And that wit of hers?

Jesus, what a woman. "The guy you were just talking to?"

She pointed to her face. "The one with...?"

I nodded. "That's the one. Mac's his name."

She paused. "I thought he said his name was Draco?"

Thank you for the info. "We've all got weird ass nicknames. I mean, Blade?"

She smirked. "Or Pike?"

I gripped my heart. "You wound me with your words, princess ."

She smiled brightly and placed the glass down, picking up another. "All right, what's the story with Mac?"

I lowered my voice even more. "He wasn't even supposed to be back in town yet."

"Back in town for what?"

"His birthday," I mouthed.

She puckered her lips. "Oooooh. Got a surprise for him or something?"

I winked. "Or something. The guys and I figured if he's trying to pull one over on us, we can get him back."

"For... his birthday?"

I clicked my tongue. "Mac's... not a fan of his birthday, really."

"I don't blame him."

I furrowed my brow. "Why?"

She shrugged. "Birthdays can be rough, that's all."

My heart sank. "I'm sorry to hear that."

She shook her head. "Don't be. Just another day. So, what's the plan? Are you guys wanting to set up something here?"

"I was hoping we could. See, since he doesn't like his birthday much, I get the feeling that he's trying to get back into town so he can hunker down and ride his birthday out without us *knowing* he's back in town."

"It's what I'd do."

One of these days, I'd figure out why. "So, how do you feel about getting him into the alley for us? We're all lining up to surprise him before we all come in and eat that delectable food."

Her jaw dropped. "I knew you guys didn't order all that food for just the three of you."

I winked. "Guilty as charged. We got the guys rolling up now. Any chance you can get him out back?"

"Well, if you really want to surprise him, out back won't work. But if you snake around the building," she pointed around behind her, "that alleyway is pretty much cordoned off from the world. You can set up there and I'll do the rest."

I pulled out a fifty-dollar bill and passed it to her. "You're amazing. Thank you for your help."

She took the bill and slid it between those delectable tits of hers. "Anything for my best customers."

"Thanks. I'll go fill the guys in. Remember, our little secret. Okay?"

She touched the side of her nose before pointing at me. "I gotcha. You're good."

"Now where's that back exit you were talking about?"

She looked around before placing her half-cleaned glass down. She slapped that rag right over her shoulder as if she'd been bartending since coming out of the womb, then she quickly raised the bar for me.

"Come on, before I get in trouble," she whispered.

I moved as swiftly as possible. "Seriously, thank you for this."

She placed her hand against my back. "Through the doorway. Go, go. Get into the darkness before you're spotted."

I slid through the doorway that had no door, and when her hand fell away from my back, I found that I missed her warmth. It had penetrated all the way through my leather jacket. All the way through my white t-shirt. And as I turned around, I backed myself into the darkness.

I watched that burnt-faced motherfucker approach the bar again.

"So," the man said, cocking only one side of his mouth into a smile, "where's that drink?"

Dalia picked up a drink she had already made behind the bar and set it in front of him. "Go ahead and sling that back. I think you'll need it for what comes next."

Don't blow it.

The guy chuckled. "And that means...?"

Dalia giggled. "It means—"

The door behind me shot open, slamming into my back. I stumbled forward before someone caught my leather jacket, and they pulled me back onto my feet before my crash completely gave us away.

"Are you fucking kidding me?" I whispered as I whipped around.

Blade eyed me with anger in his gaze. "We're ready. Let's go."

I peered over my shoulder and found Draco completely entranced with whatever Dalia was saying. Women were too easy sometimes, I swear to God. And yet, I found myself worried for her safety.

Was roping her into this really something we wanted to do?

"Come on," Blade grunted, pulling me outside. "She'll be fine. They haven't hurt anyone in any of the businesses they've approached."

I stumbled outside before I caught myself against the opposing brick wall. "Yet, anyway."

"You got your gun on you?" Lance asked as he cocked his.

I cracked my neck and rolled my shoulders back. "Never leave home without it. But I won't need it today."

Blade held two of his knives in his hands. "You wanna feel his neck, don't you?"

I cracked my knuckles. "You bet your fucking ass, I do."

Lance leveled his gun at the door. "Get ready. I hear footsteps."

I held my breath, waiting for that door to swing open. Waiting for that scarfaced asshole to come barreling out that door. I knew Dalia had this. She was resourceful, and strong. No one could push her around, that much was for certain.

But I had to let out the breath I was holding before panting for air.

"Footsteps, huh?" Blade asked.

"Shut up," Lance glowered.

I shook my head. "Just give it a second. For all we know, the man's still trying to work his way into her pants."

Blade clicked his tongue. "I'm going in after him if he's not out here in three."

"Blade," Lance warned.

"Two," Blade said.

"Shut the fuck up," I hissed.

THUDOOSH!

"All right, guys. It's not my birthday, so what the fuck gives?"

"Now," Lance commanded.

"What the—no!" Draco exclaimed.

The door crashed closed behind him as he whipped around to try and grab the knob. Blade was fast, too. The second his hand landed on the handle and tugged, Blade rushed the jacketed man and slipped one knife against his neck, slipping the other one between his legs.

"Your life, or your balls," Blade hissed, turning the man to face me, "take your pick."

"Oh, you're going to pay for this," the man warned.

"Draco," Pike said, stalking around the man, "nice to finally meet someone from the crew terrorizing the town."

His eyes widened. "How do you know—"

I walked up to him and placed the barrel of my muffled gun against his temple. "Enough talking. We want some answers."

Draco scoffed. "Fuck you and the horse you rode in on."

Blade tightened the knife against the man's nutsack. "What is your crew doing in town?"

The man curled his lips over his teeth like some petulant toddler pitching a fit. So, I looked over at Pike.

"Ready to do your thing?" I asked.

"What thing?" Draco asked.

"And here I thought you weren't talking," I growled, shoving the barrel of my gun deeper into his skin.

He hissed in pain as Pike bent down to check his shoes. He slid his finger along the side of the man's boot, then placed the tip of his finger against his tongue.

"I'll never get over that," Blade said as he grimaced.

Pike smacked his lips together. "A bit of mud. Stale water. There's sand there, though. Not gravel grit, but sand."

"Huh," I said with a nod of my head. "Sounds like some-one's been taking trips to the coast."

Draco scoffed. "Ain't no way you assholes know that."

Pike sniffed up the man's body, taking in the scent of his jeans. His shirt. His leather jacket. He got into the man's face, his nose wrinkled in concentration as Draco attempted to lean back.

And when he did, Blade tightened the knife around the man's neck.

"Jesus, what the fuck do you want?" the man hissed.

"The truth," Pike said, taking a step back. "I know where you've been, and where you've frequented. I can tell you that he stopped by the ice cream shop up the road maybe an hour or two ago?"

Draco's jaw dropped open. "How could you possibly know that?"

Pike wafted the man's scent closer to him with his hand. "The smell of sugar and milk stays with someone for a while."

Draco's stomach grumbled for all of us to hear before Blade groaned. "If you fucking fart on me, you're a dead man."

Pike chuckled. "Especially a man who's lactose intolerant."

"Who are you?" Draco demanded. "What the fuck do you want?"

"The truth," I said as my trigger finger grew itchy. "So, you've got one last chance. What are you and The Sentinels doing in this town, anyway?"

Pike smirked. "Should I tell them that the flower petal you've got attached to the toe of your left boot is alfalfa? And the only place around here that gets that kind of sun through the thicket of trees around this place is south of here? About half a mile into the woods?"

Draco started sweating. "Look, whatever you want—"

"What I want," I growled, growing frustrated, "is for you to tell me what you and your crew want."

But when Draco didn't speak, I knew we were out of options.

"Pike?" I asked.

He walked straight up to that man's face before putting on his best smile. "Happy birthday, bitch."

I pulled the trigger and splattered that man's brains against the dumpster next to the Blade.

5

DALIA

"So," the man said with his lopsided smile, "where's that drink?"

I picked up a drink I had already slung around for him behind the bar. I set it in front of him, excited and unwilling to blow the surprise. While I didn't want to be in his shoes one damn bit, I hoped he enjoyed whatever it was the guys had in store for him.

Especially since a third of their order was already up.

"Go ahead and sling that back," I said with a smile. "I think you'll need it for what comes next."

The guy chuckled and his gaze darkened. "And that means...?"

Dalia giggled. "It means you've got a surprise coming your way in a few minutes, so you're going to need your strength."

"Oh, really," he said before he took a pull from his bourbon. "Does this surprise include you?"

I leaned across the bar top and grinned. "If you can keep a secret, I'll let you in on one."

He approached me as well, his forehead almost touching mine as he lowered his voice. "I'm the best secret keeper."

I whispered. "Some of your friends are out in the alleyway waiting to surprise you for your birthday."

He blinked. "My birthday?"

I leaned up and nodded. "Mhm, and they tasked me with making sure you get out there so they can surprise you properly."

He slowly raised himself back up. "And what if I told you that it isn't my birthday?"

"Trust me, I get it. All of us that hate our birthdays aren't prone to celebrating them. But between you and me?"

He held up his fingers. "Scout's Honor, the conversation goes nowhere."

My grin faded into a soft smile. "You've got some good friends. You should go out there and see what they've got planned. Then, you can just act surprised."

He chugged back the rest of his drink. "And if I don't like my birthday present?"

I winked. "Then, I've got quite a present for you if they skimp out."

He set his glass down and slid off the stool. "I've never wanted a shitty birthday present in all my life."

I barked with laughter. "Through the doorway behind me and out the exit. Be quick, though. I'll get in trouble if someone catches you."

The man slapped fifteen bucks on the bar top and gazed around before dipping into the back. I scooped up the money and cashed him out, then stuck the rest of the cash into my bra as my tip. If these leather-jacketed men kept coming in like they were, I'd be a rich bitch in the making.

But the whole of me wanted to know what their surprise was.

"Miss?"

I peeked up at the foreign voice. "Hi there! What can I getcha?"

The man held up two fingers. "Two margaritas, no flavor, on the rocks."

I plucked two glasses from the rack above my head. "Coming right up."

Tossing around the tequila and in-house sour mix did nothing to satiate my curious mind. In fact, it only made me think harder about it. Were they singing happy birthday? Were they doting on him with gifts? Or surprising him with a trip somewhere?

They better not stick me with all that fucking food.

"Two margaritas, just for you," I said as I slid the full glasses toward him.

He pulled out his card and handed it to me. "Just open a tab for us. Thanks."

I took his card. "You got it. I'll get your card back to you after I'm done opening it. Where you located?"

He nodded toward the stage. "Off to the side. We're ready for that live music I've heard so much about."

"Well," I said, turning toward the computer, "the live music won't kick off for another couple of hours. So, pace yourselves, all right?"

"I make no promises."

I barked with laughter and opened up their tab, then I walked over to their table and handed the man his card back. I clocked his wedding ring before gazing over at the woman he sat with, and their matching rings made my heart skip a beat. I loved love, and I loved the idea of love, and I loved the idea of love even more when there were—

"Your wedding rings are so cute," I said, pointing down to hers.

She flashed it for me with a big, white smile on her face. "Anniversary gift."

The man held up his hand. "Ten years together."

I balked. "You guys look so young, though! High school sweethearts?"

They held hands from across the table before the woman nodded. "You nailed it."

"And I wouldn't want to be with anyone else," her husband said.

My heart melted. "Well, you two enjoy yourselves, and don't forget—"

"Dalia! Get this food out of my window!" the cook shouted.

"Coming, Rodrigo!" I exclaimed before my attention returned to the couple. "Don't forget, we've got an open kitchen now. So, if you guys get hungry, let me know."

The man nodded, gazing into his wife's eyes. "We will."

"Thanks," she said mindlessly.

I took one more look at them before racing toward the kitchen window. It took both Raquel and me two trips to remove all of the food Rodrigo had slung around in the kitchen, and he wasn't even done yet.

"Jesus, you feeding Noah's Ark over here?" Raquel asked breathlessly as we made our way toward the booth.

"Just set it all down over here. We got a birthday party in our midst."

"Well," she said as she unloaded plates, "let's hope they don't stiff you again. That'll be a hell of a payment for us to cover."

Worry pooled in my gut. "Don't I know it."

After unloading all of the food, I grew nervous watching our kitchen cook boss people around as plates kept stacking up. Sure, a few of them ran to the other tables, but I knew that the plates slowly piling up off to the side were for the guys. I chewed on the inside of my cheek. As I cleaned down the bar, I kept peering over my shoulder, waiting for a sign that the guys were coming back.

But my curiosity got the better of me.

"Raquel, I'm going on break," I said, slapping my rag down onto the bar top.

"And sticking me with all of those dishes?" she asked.

I rolled my eyes. "Five minutes and I'll be right back."

She eyed me carefully. "You better be."

I didn't even bother clocking out. All I wanted to do was make sure those guys were still out back. I still had a chance to cancel part of their order, and if they had pulled some bullshit on me yet again, I wanted to be given the opportunity to head off the issues at the pass. I pressed my ear against the heavy metal door. I closed my eyes, straining my hearing to see if I heard voices. Or, them singing Happy Birthday to the man. Or laughter. Anything to signal to me that they were still out there.

However, all I heard was silence before a massive thud.

"That's it," I murmured. "Enough with this shit."

I grabbed the knob and ripped the door open before I put on my best smile. But the only thing that happened was that the air got ripped from my lungs. Instead of seeing a gathering of men in leather jackets with party hats on top of their heads, I found something red splattered all over the dumpster.

Before my eyes dropped to—

"Oh, my God," I said breathlessly.

The hole. The man, he had... had a hole in...

"We got a problem, guys."

The voice snapped me out of my trance and I found all three men looking at me. I couldn't recall their names, my brain had come to a complete and grinding halt. But, there were knives and guns and hands extended. Fingers clenched. Angry eyes staring back at me.

"I'm sorry," I said quickly, "I just—"

I thumbed over my shoulder before I swallowed hard.

"I'll just go cancel that food order you guys—"

"Now," Lance commanded.

The man with the knives—Blade! Blade. Shit, was that why they called him Blade?—he lunged at me. He moved so quickly and so effortlessly that he looked more like a shadow than a moving person. I reached for the door, trying to get it closed in his face before whatever the hell was coming my way ended up right in my lap. It didn't work, though. I didn't move quickly enough.

And before I knew it, Blade tugged me out into the alleyway.

"I won't say anything, I swear," I said breathlessly.

"Wrangle her," Lance glowered.

"What!? No, don't you dare fucking—AH!"

Blade wrapped his arm around my throat, closing off my ability to breathe as something cool and sharp pressed against my inner thigh.

"Want to know how many seconds it'll take for you to bleed out once I slice your juicy little thigh open?"

Who the fuck are these guys? "Fuck you."

"Trust me, we were hoping," Lance said, standing in front of me.

I grabbed onto Blade's arm with all my might, trying to peel just enough of him away from my throat so I could catch my breath. But instead, his grip grew tighter.

Which meant my ability to draw air dwindled.

"Please," I choked out, "I won't say a word."

I refused to cry. Even though I was scared out of my mind, I refused to shed a single tear for those assholes. I had sent that man inside to his death, and that was on them. I did my best to obscure the guilt I felt. I did my best not to look down at the bleeding, lifeless man whose dead body had melded to the side of the dumpster. And as Lance tilted his head, he brought his gun up to my face.

Where I saw droplets of blood still clinging to the barrel.

"Now, what are we going to do with you?"

I wheezed for air. "Maybe you—you could—just—"

"What was that?" Pike asked, cupping his hand around his ear.

I shot him a look. "Fuck—you."

"Blade," Lance said.

"Seriously?" the man hissed.

Lance shot a look over my shoulder. "Let her speak."

"Yeah," I choked out.

Blade grumbled something beneath his breath that I didn't catch, but he released me all the same. He retracted his knife and released my neck, causing me to gasp and cough for air. Spit sputtered in front of me, causing Lance to back up. But he still kept that motherfucking gun leveled at my face.

"Repeat yourself," Lance commanded.

I snickered and massaged my neck. "Now, where's the fun in that?"

Pike chuckled as he reached out for me. "I like her, she's got spunk."

"Yeah, until she runs to the cops," Blade murmured.

I slapped his hand away. "Touch me, and you'll have to kill me to keep from killing you."

Lance cocked his gun. "That can be arranged."

I shook my head. "Can't use death as a winning tactic with someone who doesn't fear it."

Lance didn't budge, though. "What were you about to say?"

I swallowed hard. "I was about to say that I don't narc on people to the police. Not my mother, not any of her suitors, and certainly not you guys."

"Mommy issues. Typical," Blade said.

I wanted to reach out and slap him, but, you know, the gun in my face and all. "Seriously. I mean, I won't clean up your mess, but I sure as hell won't say anything. Not my place, not my circus."

"I don't think that's the saying," Pike said.

"And why the fuck do you care about any saying?"

It must've been the tone of my voice, because the instant I felt that knife against my side I turned to face Blade. I glared at him, daring him to do anything more than threaten me as he held a knife against my gut before slipping one against my neck.

"Don't tease a girl with a good time now," I said.

Lance chuckled and it turned my gaze toward him. "You have something against cops."

I nodded. "They only make things more difficult in my opinion."

Lance wafted his gun in the air, and it completely disarmed Blade. He retracted his knives once more and even went so far as to take a step back from me.

Then, I watched Lance holster his weapon.

"So, that's it?" I asked.

Pike snickered. "You wish."

When Lance moved, so did I. With every step he took toward me, stalking me with that brutal stare of his, I took a step back. I continued my journey until my back hit something cold and unforgiving, and when I peered over my shoulder, I found Blade standing there.

"Hi," he said.

My gaze whipped back toward Lance, but it was too late. He reached out with his calloused hand, wrapped it clear around my neck, and squeezed.

I started choking again. "I thought you said—"

"If you tell anyone," he growled as he dragged my face

closer to his, "we will know. If you speak of this, we will know. If you even so much as dream about narcing on us, we will know. And we won't stop until you're dead. Got it?"

I nodded quickly, but I couldn't speak. My lungs cried out for air. My body shivered with a need for oxygen. Lance continued staring at me, and for a few seconds there, I thought he was honestly going to choke me until I passed out. My vision tunneled. My legs went limp. I felt myself fading into the darkness, no longer able to fight.

Until Lance released my neck, rushing air down into my lungs.

"Jesus Christ," I choked out, dropping to my knees.

"If you tell anyone, we will know," Lance said as he hovered over me, cloaking me in his mountainous shadow, "and when we find out, you're a dead woman. Got it?"

I nodded, even though I couldn't do anything except cough and sputter.

"We're just gonna leave her here?" Blade asked.

"Don't worry," Lance said, stepping over me, "we'll be back for more drinks soon enough."

I watched as money rained down into my purview, with some of it falling into the pool of blood slowly leaking my way.

Before Pike's voice ended up against the shell of my ear.

"Money for the food," he said, patting the top of my head, "and don't worry about this mess. A clean-up crew will be by in the next few minutes. Be a doll and keep everyone out of the alley, would you, love? Thanks."

I hated how much his voice made me shiver inside. Not with the chill of their actions, either. But with an unmistakable warmth that was hard to ignore deep in the pit of my gut.

At least they paid this time.

6

BLADE

"Not smart, you guys," I said into my Bluetooth microphone as we soared down the road. "You know damn good and well that she's—"

"I know people better than you do," Pike said, racing up beside me. "And I can tell you without a shadow of a doubt that she won't say anything to anyone."

"Why?" I asked, my voice falling flat. "You lick the dirt off her boots for that information?"

"Enough," Lance said curtly. "I'm calling church. The guys are meeting us at the clubhouse. We need everyone's input before we move forward with anything else."

I shook my head. "At least someone is thinking with their larger head."

Pike chuckled and swerved in front of me, cutting me off mid-turn.

"Hey!" I exclaimed.

Pike barked with laughter. "You been staring at my dick lately, Blade? Because I'll put it out for you, if you want."

"Jesus, you two. Shut the fuck up," Lance said curtly.

"And yet, I can hear the grin in your voice," I said.

"The first person to talk before we get back to the clubhouse gets shoved into the woods going eighty," Lance said.

That pretty much did it. Not because we were concerned for our safety, but because of the tone of his voice. He was deep in thought, and Lance was the kind of president that used bike rides as a chance to clear his head. The wind whipped around us as my engine revved between my legs. We sped back toward the clubhouse, leaving town and taking a sharp left before the two-lane road turned into nothing but dirt.

The lake always came into view before the clubhouse did, and it never ceased to take my breath away.

"Goddamn it, I love it out here," I whispered.

"That makes two of us," Pike said, bringing up the rear.

"Three," Lance said and stopped his bike near the wooden porch.

My head nodded with the bike count before I pulled up beside him. "Everyone's here, minus the clean-up crew."

Pike pulled up alongside me and yanked his helmet off. "Let's get inside, then."

We wasted no time in getting inside, even though I wanted to stand on the porch and rubberneck around the lake for a little while. Some of the guys fished while others hunted. But me? I just enjoyed rocking out back with a beer in my hand while dragonflies dodged the fish jumping out of the water. Nature has always called to me. Called to us, really. It was the one bond the crew shared between our differing political opinions, honors, moral codes, and belief systems.

We all loved nature.

And we loved the fact that our clubhouse was out in the middle of the fucking woods.

"All right, everyone. Listen up," Lance said, closing the clubhouse door behind him. "The guys and I ran into an opportunity—"

"We aren't idiots," Knell said as he crossed his arms over his chest. "The clean-up crew isn't here."

Traeger chuckled. "Who's dead?"

Lance grinned. "Scarface."

The guys balked as a smile spread across Pike's face. "His name was Draco, apparently."

Knell narrowed his eyes. "Like in Harry Potter?"

"Yep," I said, nodding my head.

Lance held up his hand. "You know that bar we were scoping out? The Mule?"

The guys nodded their sea of heads.

"Well," Lance said as he slid his hand out of the air, "he waltzed right on into that bar and had no idea we were sitting right there."

"Hell yeah," Traeger said.

"That's the way to do it," Knell said.

"The clean-up crew is cleaning everything now, and once they get back here, we've got some shit to talk about. This changes the dynamic of everything, and we aren't sure how The Sentinels are going to react to one of their own disappearing."

"You think it'll bring automatic heat down onto us?" I asked.

Pike shook his head. "He's concerned it'll bring heat down onto the entire town."

Lance shot him a look. "Quit reading my mind."

Pike smirked. "Quit being so easy to read."

I rolled my eyes as chuckles ricocheted through the church meeting.

"At any rate, however," Lance said, commanding the room again, "what we need now is—"

The door slammed open, causing me to whip around as I engaged both of my knives. I whipped them out, twirling them through the air as I readied myself for whatever intrusion had decided to sneak up on us.

But when I watched our cleaning crew walk inside with their plastic tent suits still on, I quickly placed them back on my hips.

"Knock next time," I said flatly, turning back toward the guys.

"Everything good?" Lance asked.

They ripped the plastic off their bodies and discarded them in the massive burn barrel we had sitting off to the side.

"All's good on the western front," Riley said.

"Cleaned, disinfected, and taken care of," Mortar said.

The other two guys stayed silent as they stripped themselves down. I looked over at Lance, who seemed to be satisfied with their answer, but what of the girl?

Had they come into contact with her?

Was she still keeping her fucking mouth shut?

"Now that we're all here," Lance said, then cleared his throat, "we have to come up with a plan on how to handle The Sentinels once they lash out. Because they will, and it'll be on us to make sure everyone in town is safe."

"Do we even know why they're encroaching on us yet?" Mortar asked.

"Yes," I said plainly.

The guys passed by me, eyeing me carefully before Mortar spoke again. "You gonna fill us in, then?"

I looked over at Pike. "Your turn."

Pike put on his best smile. "We think they're trying to siphon businesses out of their money from dual ends. They cause a ruckus, stealing shit they want or need and freaking out the town. Then they swoop in, offer protection payment plans and shit like that, and then they keep terrorizing a town for stuff they need while extracting money from their pockets for protection from themselves."

"You have to admit it's pretty ingenious," Riley said with a shrug.

Lance's face fell. "They've already walked into four of our six businesses where we do our businesses. Remember that."

"I do, I do. I'm just saying," Riley said, holding up his hands in mock surrender.

"Well," Traeger said as he stepped up to the plate, "you'll be happy to know that I've been keeping up with my surveillance tactics. You know, seeing if they fuck up or anything like that."

Lance stared him down. "This the point where you fill us in? Because we all know your role in this crew."

Traeger snickered. "Straight to the act, got it. Anyway, I've been doing some scouting around town, keeping a close eye on our businesses, shit like that. And while they've stayed in line pretty much the whole time, it didn't take long to dig this up."

He pulled out a roll of papers from the inside pocket of his leather jacket and handed them to Lance. I peered around his body, growing curious at what Traeger had just handed him.

And when my eyes scrolled over the top of the contract, I hissed. "Shit."

"You've got to be fucking kidding me," Lance murmured.

"What is it?" Pike asked, yanking the papers out of Lance's hand.

Traeger clicked his tongue. "They've beat us out on that bid for the place we were trying to buy for our mechanic shop."

Lance's grip grew tight against the pieces of paper.

"By fifty grand," Traeger added.

"Fucking CHRIST!" Lance bellowed.

"And all cash," Traeger said.

"Will you shut the fuck up and let the man read?" I asked.

Pike snickered. "If you think he's reading, you're more of an idiot than I thought."

"Roots," Lance growled and ripped up the papers. "They're planting motherfucking ROOTS!"

He threw the pieces of paper into the air as his face turned multiple shades of red at once.

"This is war. Traeger. Take two other men with you and start scouting the area. I want all the information you can gather on those motherfuckers. All of it."

Traeger nodded. "Mortar. Get that new prospect of ours on the phone. What's his name?"

"Phil," he said flatly.

Traeger groaned. "Get him a nickname, for Christ's sake, and then tell him to get his ass here. It's time for him to learn about patrol duty."

"We were a shoe-in for that transaction, though, weren't we?" Pike asked. "I mean, we hadn't signed anything official but—"

Lance pointed at Knell. "That's what I want to find out, Pike. Knell, take Blade and go do some talking to the owners of that building we wanted to purchase. I want to know everything about that transaction. Everything that was said, agreed upon, and exchanged."

Knell drew in a deep breath. "You want to know why they went behind our backs."

Lance nodded. "And if you have to get our lawyers involved, then so be it."

"Fair enough," I said. "But my gut says that The Sentinels have something on them."

Lance whipped around and faced me. "Then I want to know what it is before the end of the week. Now, get on it. Church dismissed!"

The guys rushed past us, trying to get to their bikes as quickly as possible. I knew I needed to get out there as well, along with Pike. We all had responsibilities. We all had a stake in this fight. We had enjoyed years of prosperity underneath Lance's decisions and regulations, and these red-jacketed asshats could ruin it for all of us.

But when Pike didn't go anywhere, neither did I.

"What the hell do we do now?" Pike asked, raking his hands down his face. "Act like nothing's wrong?"

Lance nodded. "That's exactly what we're going to do. Put up a damn good front for those motherfuckers."

Pike groaned as his head fell back. "Guess it's time to get some work done before my shift at the bar tomorrow."

I nodded. "I'll pull a shift with you, too. Send home whoever is supposed to be working tomorrow. I need something to do."

Lance pinched the bridge of his nose. "I'll get the schedule rearranged and add myself to it. For now, I think it's smart that the three of us man the bar, just in case."

"You really think it's that bad?" Pike asked.

And when Lance opened his eyes, I saw the fearful fury behind them.

"I think if it's not that bad already, it's going to get a fuckton worse. So we protect what's ours, and do without what we can."

Spoken like true sitting ducks.

And I sure as hell didn't like being a sitting fucking duck.

7

———

DALIA

"Dalia?"

Blood. There had been so much blood everywhere, and I couldn't get it out of my head.

"Dalia."

Were they watching? I found myself peeking up at the security cameras we had strewn throughout the bar. They were noticeable for a reason, and it was supposed to deter people from being shitheads.

Guess they were wrong.

"Dalia, are you listening to me?"

Then again, maybe the guy deserved it?

"Do you hear yourself?" I whispered.

"Dalia!" Raquel exclaimed.

I jumped so hard that the glass I had in my hand tumbled from my grasp. The crashing of the cup against the floor seconded only the shatter that came after, and it ripped me out of my trance.

"Jesus, Dee," Raquel said, bending down. "You okay back here?"

I quickly got onto the floor with her. "I got it. It's my mess."

"Girl."

"I need drinks ran to table—"

She placed her hand on my forearm. "Girl, look at me."

My gaze found hers. "Seriously. I'm good. Just exhausted."

She nodded. "You have worked a lot this week."

I sighed. "Don't I know it."

She helped me pick up the glass. "You working this weekend?"

"No, thank fuck," I said and tossed glass into the trashcan.

"Need a broom?" a voice asked.

I looked up and saw the kitchen cook. "What are you doing over here?"

He thumbed over his shoulder. "My window is clogged with your orders. You gonna run them? Or are they supposed to be cold?"

It must've been the look on my face, but Raquel sighed heavily. "They did it to you again, didn't they?"

I shook my head as I stood and grabbed the broom. "They left money for it, but they aren't coming back in for the food."

"Seriously?" Rodrigo asked.

I shot him a look. "Offer the food to anyone in the bar. If they want it, give it to them."

"But they paid you," Raquel said, taking the broom from me, "right?"

I nodded mindlessly and gazed at a security camera just above her head. "Right."

"Well," Rodrigo said as he turned, heading back toward the kitchen, "you guys want anything from their order?"

Raquel stuck her finger in the air. "One of those funnel cakes, please."

My stomach growled with a need for sustenance. "I'll take one of them, too. And the cheeseburger with fried pickles that you threw together."

"Coming right up!" Rodrigo exclaimed before he slinked back into the kitchen.

"Seriously, though," Raquel said, grabbing my arm. "Are you okay? Do you need to go home early?"

It sounded amazing. "I can't leave you with the bar like this."

She tugged me off to the side. "The bar only has three more hours. You know we won't get any busier than this. I can handle it if you—"

"Raquel, I'm not—"

She leveled her gaze with me. "Take your food to go, grab yourself a drink, and go upstairs. Okay?"

I had to admit, having the rest of the night off sounded fantastic. "I'll leave their cash-out in the drawer. Split the tip?"

"No," she said as she slid the rag off my shoulder. "You earned every single bit of that tip dealing with those assholes."

"Did I hear her food was supposed to be to-go?" Rodrigo said, appearing with three to-go trays.

I took them from him. "Thanks."

"You want a drink?"

Raquel walked into the backroom and came out holding a large to-go cup. "Margarita for the road?"

"You know we're not supposed to—"

"You live upstairs, Dalia. Do you want it or not?"

I smiled softly. "Yeah, that would be nice. Thank you."

Then, I kissed Rodrigo softly on his cheek before he turned toward the dining area and held up his hands.

"Anyone who wants free food, come see me at the kitchen window!"

I cashed out the guys as the hoard of customers we had inside the bar already charged Rodrigo's place of peace. Or so he called it. I rang everything up and shoved the exact money into the till, then took the rest and slid it back into my bra. It was the only place most days where I knew things would be safe, so I made sure to tuck it in good in case anything squirrely happened between the bar and my apartment.

Not likely, but I wasn't sure of anything any longer.

"Here you go," Raquel said, slapping a straw into the plastic top of the cup. "One strawberry margarita, blended, with an extra shot for the road."

I took it from her and hugged her neck. "You're a lifesaver."

"And you look exhausted. Go eat and get some sleep, all right?"

"You, too."

I make quick work of getting myself upstairs. It's amazing, how well the place had been insulated. The second I closed my studio apartment door behind me, the sounds of the bar faded away. Outside of the soft pumping of the bass from the music beneath my feet, there wasn't a sound. No chittering drunks. No shattering glass. No Rodrigo practically cursing out his kitchen staff whenever he became overwhelmed with orders.

And yet, as I made my way into my bedroom to eat dinner in my happy place, I found those guys still at the forefront of my mind.

"Clean-up crew?" I asked myself.

I stripped my clothes off my body and climbed into bed. The funnel cake smelled amazing, and I couldn't wait to take a juicy bite of Rodrigo's infamous cheeseburger. But as I stared down at the food, I couldn't bring myself to eat it. I snatched my margarita off the bedside table and brought the straw to my lips. I chugged a few times, trying to get the relaxing alcohol coursing through my veins. That would surely relax me enough so that my stomach released me from its chokehold.

But as I stared at the wall in front of me decorated with pictures, a thought crossed my mind.

Keep them close, don't piss them off.

Men like those jacketed guys were people I didn't want to anger. I had witnessed firsthand what happened when you pissed someone like them off, but I also had questions. I needed answers. I had to know what the hell that guy had done to deserve having his life taken from him. Was he a terrible person? I could get behind it if he was a terrible person. Death certainly wasn't a normal occurrence for me, but I'd be lying if I said it was the first dead body I'd ever seen.

Second only to the body I found in the hallway after my mother tried to kick one of her "suitors" out.

"Guess that's what happens when you try to kill her first," I murmured.

Maybe that was what happened? Maybe the man tried to hurt them, so they were simply defending themselves. I chewed on the straw and continued taking icy pulls from my drink. Raquel made the best margaritas, and as the food grew cold in my lap, the only conclusion I came to was one that made my skin prickle against my arms.

I had to speak with those guys again.

I had to speak to the men that murdered that man.

Bzzzt. Bzzzt. Bzzzt.

"Hmmm?"

Bzzzt. Bzzzt. Bzzzt.

"The fuck?" I croaked as I rolled over.

Bzzt. Bzzt. Bzzt.

"I'm coming, I'm coming," I murmured, reaching for my cell phone.

When I saw it was Lisa calling, however, I knew exactly what was going on.

"Hey," I said groggily when I answered the phone.

"I need a favor," she said.

And when she sniffled, I bolted upright in bed. "What's wrong?"

"I'm fine, I'm fine, it's just—"

I swung my feet over the edge of the bed. "Is it Brayden? Has something happened?"

"He-he-he—"

I held my breath, waiting for the inevitable. Waiting for her to tell me that something had happened to her son.

"Brayden is—is sick. Really, really sick right now. A-a-and—and I'm supposed to work—"

"Don't worry about work," I said as I stood to my feet. "I'll take your shift. What's going on with Brayden? What do you need?"

It took her a second to gather herself and that was when I heard it.

The telltale beeping of hospital machines.

"Oh, Lisa," I whispered.

"Just cover for me tonight? Please?" she asked breathlessly.

"Only if you tell me what I can do to help you out right now."

"He just took a spill. That's all."

"What kind of a spill?"

She sniffled hard. "The kind that lands you in the hospital."

"Is he going to be all right?"

She paused. "The doctor thinks so."

"But you don't?"

"He's got a clotting disorder, Dee. Any injury is life-threatening to him."

I walked into the bathroom and turned on the light. "Keep me posted and let me know if you need anything, all right? I'll have Rodrigo bring you guys some food—"

"Please, don't tell anyone."

"It's just food. But you guys are going to need to eat, and we both know from experience that the hospital food there is shit."

She giggled softly, but not for long. "Ain't that the truth."

"So, I'll send him for lunch and again for dinner. Get me yours and Brayden's order, and don't worry about tonight. I've got you covered."

"Thank you so much."

I placed her on speaker. "You working at any other time this weekend?"

"Raquel's got Sunday."

"Good, so she knows."

"Yeah," she said mindlessly.

I splashed some water on my face. "We've got your back. You give Brayden hugs and kisses for me, and keep an eye out for food deliveries. Before you know it, you guys will be back home where you belong."

"Dee?"

I reached for my facewash. "Yeah?"

"Will you just... sit with me on the phone for a bit?"

I lathered it against my face. "I'd love nothing more."

I let her listen in as I started my morning routine. I brushed my teeth, peeled off my face mask. Hell, I even let her listen when I climbed into the shower and cleaned myself up. I sang at the top of my lungs, hoping it would bring a smile to her face to listen to anything other than the machines hooked up to her precious ten-year-old.

I'd never be able to imagine what she was going through. Having a child, loving that child with all your might, and then being told that he couldn't go run and play with kids for fear of losing his life if he got a goddamn scrape on his knee.

But when I got out of the shower and checked our phone call, at some point in time, she had hung up.

So, I shot her a quick text.

Me: Love you, girl. Let me know if you need anything else.

The afternoon passed by in a haze, and when I clocked in for work, I found myself staring at the front door. Rodrigo took the food orders off my hands, and it was pretty obvious that Raquel had been tasked with rearranging her work schedule.

"Hey, Dee," she said as she came up to me.

I poured three martinis for the group toward the front of the bar. "As long as you don't book me on Wednesdays and Thursdays, we're good."

"All right," she said, scribbling something out on her pad of paper. "Got it. You good with two back-to-back shifts?"

"You gonna be working with me?" I asked, placing the martinis on a run tray.

"I got these," Rodrigo said as he scooped up the tray.

"Hey," I said. "Aren't you supposed to be—"

"Just gotta keep busy," he murmured, moving away from the bar.

Raquel sighed. "You think he'll ever tell Lisa how he feels?"

I tilted my head as I watched him divvy out the drinks. "I don't know, but he should. She deserves a good man in her life."

"Oooookay," Raquel said, ripping the piece of paper off her pad. "Here's your new schedule for the next two weeks. I'll get it formally typed up but—"

"Yeah, yeah, yeah," I said as I took the paper from her and jammed it into my back pocket. "Thanks. I'll look at it later."

She tapped me on the shoulder, and it was then that I realized I hadn't faced her at all.

"You good?" she asked.

I drew in a deep breath. "What if something happens to Brayden?"

She snickered. "Am I supposed to be stupid enough to believe that question?"

"No, I'm serious."

She tossed the pad of paper and pen onto the back bar next to the computer where we typed in kitchen orders. "I know you're watching and waiting for those guys to come back through that door."

I shrugged. "I just—"

She placed her hands on my shoulders. "You need to focus. Lisa really needs us to focus right now, all right?"

I nodded. "I know."

"So, let's get through this shift, and if they come in? They come in. And if they don't?"

My heart sank at the idea. "Then they don't."

She patted my cheek. "Right. So let's go. We've got orders to fulfill and not a lot of time to do them."

The night dragged on with people coming and going. A bridal party slid through the front door, rowdy and hollering at the top of their lungs. They distracted me for a little while with their antics and "truth or dare" scenarios that involved things like pickle juice shots and funnel cakes slathered in ketchup.

The innocence of it all made me smile every time they came up to the bar.

But it didn't do much to divert my attention away from that front door. I wondered when I'd see those guys again. If I'd ever get the chance to talk to them. Hell, maybe I could track them down if I knew where to look. It wasn't as if our town was a big city or some shit. We were lucky if we had 5,000 people in town at any given moment. We were a spot on the side of the road, split right in half by a two-lane highway that connected one big city to another.

For all I knew, those men had simply passed through.

Then again, from what I witnessed, maybe they were from—

"Excuse me, miss?"

The voice ripped me out of my trance. "Can I get you anything?"

The kind smile on the man's face disarmed me. "A gin and tonic, if you have the time."

"Of course. Coming right up. Anything else?"

He grinned. "Maybe two, if I sit here long enough."

I giggled as I turned around and plucked our top-shelf gin off the display rack. "One gin and tonic, coming up."

And when my gaze caught the time in the corner of the computer screen that flashed at me, I drew in a deep breath.

"LAAAAAAST CAH-AAAAAAAALL!"

Raquel rushed up to my side. "I take left, you take right?"

I tossed her a playful wink. "Sounds like a plan to me. Let's get this evening wrapped up."

And after I turned around, I slid the man his drink before he scooped it up.

"Mm, mm, mm," he said after taking a long pull. "Thank you."

I leaned forward, plastering on my best smile and flaunted what God gave me. "I'll keep your second one a secret."

He took another drink , his stare never wavering from my face. "Can I ask you a question, Miss...?"

"Dalia."

"Dalia," he said with a nod of his head. "Tell me, Miss Dalia, those men in the leather jackets..."

My entire body froze. Had he just said—

"... do you know them?" the man asked.

He downed the rest of his drink before handing me the glass.

"Another one, please. You know, before last call becomes official," he said.

I cleared my throat as I took the glass from him. "Coming right up."

"So, the guys."

I peeked over at him while I busied myself with his order. "What about them?"

He rested his forearms against the bar. "Do you know them?"

I shrugged. "They come in from time to time to get their regular orders."

I handed him his second drink before I looked up at the bar. No one had come up to get another drink, which meant I was stuck with the line of questioning from some guy I didn't know about some guys I wasn't sure I wanted to see again.

No, scratch that. I wanted to see them again.

But something about this guy gave me the heebie jeebies.

"I don't know if I know them, know them," I said, cleaning down the bar, "but they come in from time to time to get their regular orders."

The man twirled with glass with his fingertips. "But they didn't come in tonight."

"Well, who's asking if they did or not?"

The man chuckled before he tipped his second glass up to his lips, and his Adam's apple didn't stop bobbing until he drained his drink. He set the glass down and pushed it toward me, and I noticed a pretty gnarly scar that stretched from his thumb all the way down to his wrist.

"Really, though," I said, picking up his empty glass. "Who's asking? Because I figured they'd come in tonight, but they haven't showed."

The man eyed me carefully. "Any reason you're expecting them?"

I snickered. "Can't help it if a girl thinks they're sexy. I was hoping to get a number. Or two."

The way the man smiled disarmed me again, and I couldn't figure out if it was genuine or if he was mocking me.

Why did it feel like he was mocking me?

"Well, you're in luck," he said as he leaned over the bar, moving closer to me, "because I know where to find them."

My ears perked up. "So, they're from around here?"

"Not quite, but essentially."

"Do you know them personally?"

The smile slid from his face. "Look, I'm not supposed to tell you this, but if you promise—"

"Whatever it is, I can keep a secret. Trust me."

The guy narrowed his gaze. "Trust you?"

I nodded. "I've kept my mother's secrets for years. I can keep yours."

He slid his gaze down my body. "Right, right."

"So," I said, mindlessly picking up glasses to clean them. "What is this secret you were about to tell me?"

The man leaned back into his stool seat a bit. "The guys sent me here to keep tabs on you because of... what happened."

My stomach sank. Did he know what they had done?

Was he there to kill me for witnessing things?

"Don't panic," he said as his voice lowered. "It's just protocol. Nothing's wrong."

I swallowed hard. "Okay. Then why do I feel like this is a loaded statement?"

"Because they also wanted me to give you this."

He pulled a folded piece of paper out of his pocket and slid it across the bar. I looked around before snatching it up, and when I unraveled it, I found an address scribbled in green ink.

"What's this?" I asked.

"It's the address of the bar their crew runs."

I blinked. "Their crew."

He nodded. "Yes. Their crew. You can find them there most nights at any given moment."

I stuck the folded piece of paper into my jean shorts pocket. "And if they aren't there?"

"Just ask for them. Someone will give them a call."

I drew in a slow, deep breath. "Thanks."

He chuckled as he slid off his stool. "They weren't the only ones that made an impression, Miss Dalia."

My cheeks blushed. "Seems like it."

"But," he said, turning to face me, "you can't get something for nothing."

My stomach sank to my toes. "The hell does that mean?"

He crooked his finger. "Come closer."

"I think I'll stand right here, thanks."

He slid his hands into his pocket. "Very well, then. I give you something, you give me something. That's usually how it works, right?"

"Not always."

"Well, that's how it works now. Right?"

I stared him down for a while before I nodded. "Sure."

"Perfect. So you'll let me take a gander at your security footage, if you have any, from that night? And before you ask me what night—"

I slapped my rag against the bar. "I know what night you're talking about."

"So? Any chance I can take a peek at it?"

"Everything okay over here?" Raquel asked, coming up to my side.

I slid my gaze down the parts of the man's body that I could see. "We have a bit of an issue."

"What kind of issue?" she asked.

The man's gaze grew hot and dark, and I wondered who he really was.

"This man here needs to see some footage from our security cameras."

"Why?" Raquel asked.

I searched the man's warning glare. "His sister's gone missing, apparently."

"Yeah," the man said as he nodded. "She has her moments when she's not medicated."

"And you think she ended up here?" Raquel asked.

The man shrugged. "Your cook, Rodrigo, said he remembered serving her that night. Said she was a bit belligerent. Not quite making sense when she talked. If she's unmedicated and wandering around town, I've got to find her before she hurts herself."

I looked over at Raquel. "Could you show him to the security room? I'd hate for something to happen to her."

"And you believe this guy?"

I peeked over at him. "Yeah, I do."

Raquel sighed. "All right, then. Take over the bar. I'll show him to the back room."

"It's much appreciated," the man said, sliding down from his perched position.

"How hard is it for someone to get a fucking glass of wine in this place?" a heated voice asked.

I watched a man rush up to the bar and I turned to face him. "What kind of wine, sir?"

"I suggest their top-shelf red," the mysterious man said, pointing to the display case behind me. "It's a good vintage, if you ask me."

The man sighed. "Fine. Just, get it for me? My wife ordered the damn thing twenty minutes ago."

I plucked a wine glass from above my head. "It's coming right up, and on the house."

"If you'll follow me," Raquel said, motioning to the man with all of the information I wanted to know.

Conveniently, on the evening I had been looking for it.

Something isn't right with any of this.

And I knew I wouldn't get any answers unless I went to them. The men that had soared into the bar and flipped everything upside down.

Especially if they weren't going to come to me.

8

———

LANCE

"Blade!"

"What!?"

"I got this," Pike said, picking up the tray full of drinks.

"Be careful," I said as I dropped one last water onto the side.

"Lance!?" Blade bellowed above our crowded bar.

"Where the hell's that food for table four!?"

He pointed in the window. "Already out! Come get it!"

"Pike!" I exclaimed.

"Gimme a second, man! I got ten dozen drinks here!"

"Excuse me, sir?"

I turned toward the flowery voice. "What can I getcha?"

"She probably wants one of those margaritas with the beers stuffed in that I keep seeing around."

Every part of my body locked up when I heard her voice. From my toes to my nose, I slowly peered over my shoulder and found that bartender bucked up to my bar.

With her tits spilling over onto the bar top.

"Dalia," I said with a grin when I turned to face her.

"Uh, sir?" the woman behind me asked.

I held up a finger. "Just a sec."

Dalia pointed at the woman, though. "Better serve her first. She may not tip you if you're a dick."

I grinned. "And what makes you think I take orders from you?"

She winked. "Just a tip from one bartender to another."

Goddamn it, she looked delicious. Her black tank top squeezed her torso, showcasing the mounds of excess I wanted to sink my teeth into. Her red bra sparkled beneath the fabric, pushing those tits up to her chin and creating hills my dick wanted to slide in between. She perched her forearms onto the bar top, leaning forward with that bright, beautiful smile of hers.

It hardened my dick as I turned back toward my original customer.

"What'll it be?" I asked, trying my best to conceal my hardening dick with my bar rag.

She pointed toward Dalia. "Two of those margaritas she was talking about."

"Flavor?"

"You gotta do the mango with those Coronas," Dalia said. "It's the best flavor with that kind of beer."

I shrugged. "She's not wrong."

The woman smiled. "Mango, then. For both."

"Coming right up."

The ripeness of Dalia's lips as they curled into a smile had nothing on the way her stomach bunched up when she climbed up onto a stool at the bar. She looked pillowy soft, perfect for my aching muscles that had been pounding the pavement behind the bar for the last ten hours. I was ready to close down and go home, yet we still had two fucking hours to go.

You know, before the two and a half hour clean-down that came after.

"By the way?" Dalia asked, flipping her hair over her shoulder. "I'll take one of those as well once you're done."

I smirked. "One mango beer-tipped margarita, on the house, coming up."

I wasted no time in getting that other woman her drinks before I turned my full attention to the woman that had stumbled in on us. With those ruby red lips of hers that matched her bra and the way her red hair sparkled in the bar light, I almost couldn't take my eyes off her. She had these steel gray eyes that were filled with force. Almost as if they were showcasing the strength that ran through those thick bones of hers. The smattering of freckles along her nose and cheeks matched the freckles cascading down her forearms, and I found myself wanting to lick every single one of them.

God, I bet she tastes divine.

"You know," she said, leaning back in her seat, "if it hadn't been for your guy coming to see me last night, I wasn't sure I'd ever see you guys again."

What did she just say?

I continued my fluid movements as I pieced her drink together. "Sounds like our guy did his job, then."

Except there was one problem.

We never sent a guy to speak with her.

"I just wanted to stop by and say that you don't have to worry," she said, studying me.

I placed her drink onto the bar before turning toward the beer cooler behind me. "Not sure what you're talking about."

I cracked it open and spun around, tipping it up quickly into her drink. But she didn't take the hint. Instead, she leaned forward and shoved her fucking tits in my face as she lowered her voice.

Like that would somehow get me to pay attention more than I already was.

"I gave him the payment he asked for, so you don't have to worry."

I leaned over, hunching my back and rested my forearms on top of the bar. "And you came all this way to...?"

She reached for her drink and slid it between us. "I just wanted to let you know in person. Some things like this are..."

She curled her lips around the straw I had jammed into the glass, and I couldn't help but wonder what those lips might feel like wrapped around my leaking dick.

"... better said in person," she finished after she had taken a few pulls of her drink.

I chewed on the inside of my cheek. "Why don't you walk me through what happened then, and I'll figure out for myself if everything is okay."

She snickered before she took another sip. "Why? Don't trust your men?"

"Wouldn't want my men taking advantage of a beautiful woman like yourself."

She blushed furiously, and I wondered if I'd be able to get her thighs to change colors as well.

You know, with my tongue between her pussy lips.

"Lance," she said, pinning me with a look, "I made sure that I gave him access to the hidden camera footage in the alleyway."

My stomach hit the fucking floor. "Hidden camera?"

She nodded. "The owner keeps it concealed for obvious reasons. Most stores in the area do. I kept it concealed, though. I told my co-worker that his sister was unmedicated and missing, and there was a chance she had come through our bar not too long ago."

"And he stuck with that story?"

"As swiftly as ever."

I wiped down the bar. "And you're sure no one saw him."

Her gaze softened. "I promise. I pulled up the footage and told him to have at it as long as he needed it."

Fuck.

I didn't let it get to me, though. Inside, I stirred with anger. But on the outside, I simply hunched over the bar and smiled.

"Good girl."

Her eyes fluttered closed for a split second. "Well, then."

I chuckled as I ticked my crooked finger beneath her chin. "Enjoy your drink. I'm gonna go get the guys. They're gonna want to see you again."

She picked up her drink and smiled. "Can't wait to see my favorite boys."

I slapped my rag over my shoulder. "You stay right there. Don't go anywhere."

Then, I moved over to the other side of the bar and pulled out my cell.

Me: Kitchen. Now. 911.

"I don't think I've seen you around here yet."

I peeked over at the sound of the voice and found our resident manwhore already bucked up to Dalia's side.

"Is that so?" Dalia asked.

The man clearly glanced down at her tits before looking back up at her face. "Trust me, I'd remember you if I saw you."

"And why's that?"

I wanted to go over there and slam the man's face into the bar. I wanted to hear his nose break before I slung him to the ground and told him to stay away from Dalia. Forever. But I couldn't resist the smug look on her face as the man reached out and slid his finger up and down her bare arm.

"Did I give you permission to touch me?" Dalia asked.

I felt my cell vibrate in my hand and looked down to see Pike's return message.

Pike: Here. Blade's still running food.

I closed my phone's screen and slid it into my back pocket. But not before catching the gigantic slap Dalia delivered to Manwhore's face.

"Get away from me. Now," she commanded.

I whistled through my teeth. "Randy!"

He groaned as he cupped his reddened cheek. "Yeah, yeah. I know."

I pointed to the door. "Get out before I throw you out."

"Promise?"

I pointed at Dirt, one of our prospects bartending with me. "Get him some water."

"On it," Dirt said, reaching for a cup.

"And make sure he leaves," I said as my gaze returned to Dalia.

She grinned before she curled those lips around that straw, and it took everything inside of me to pull away. I wanted to drag her by her hair into that back room and stake her on my dick. I wanted her to cry out into the palm of my hand while I fucked her against every surface this fucking place had to offer.

But there were bigger fish to fry.

"About damn time," Blade said when   I pushed my way into the back cooler.

I sighed and the door closed behind me. "Jesus, it feels good in here."

Pike wiped at his forehead. "Still sweating, so we've got time. What's up?"

I peered over my shoulder, making sure the door was closed before I cleared my throat. "Dalia's here."

Blade's eyes widened. "How?"

Pike grinned. "Just my luck. I've wanted to snag her number for a while."

I pointed at him. "No."

Pike blinked. "No?"

I drew in a deep breath. "She comes waltzing up to my bar claiming that one of our men came to her bar, told her where we were, and asked to see her bar's security footage on our behalf."

"But we didn't send anyone," Pike said.

Blade balked. "Ya think?"

"Now's not the time for arguments," I said. "We have to focus."

"Did she do it?" Blade asked, throwing his hands into the air. "Was she that stupid?"

I shrugged. "It's not stupid. I'm sure he was very convincing and just vague enough for her to fill in the blanks herself."

Pike nodded and crossed his arms over his chest. "It's a tactic I use myself all the time. Works like a charm."

"So, she's an idiot, is what you're saying," Blade said.

I growled. "Don't you fucking dare call her that."

Pike's eyebrows rose. "Sounds like someone's already laid claim to her."

Blade rolled his eyes. "Figures."

Pike groaned. "Are we under any impression it's anyone other than who we think it is?"

I snickered. "You're still thinking about it?"

Blade snarled. "We know it's The Sentinels."

I shot him a look. "Good, because we're in trouble."

"Why?" Pike asked. "Did Blade not track down every camera or something?"

Blade shook his head. "No chance in hell. I scoped things out well beforehand."

I stared blankly at the man. "She mentioned a hidden camera in the alleyway."

"She what?" they asked in unison.

I sighed. "She said there's a hidden camera in the alleyway, and that she let 'our guy'—"

"Who wasn't our guy in the first place," Pike hissed.

"—see all of the footage from that night."

Pike cursed beneath his breath. "Fucking hell."

"They've got evidence," Blade said flatly.

"And we have to get that footage back," I said, raking my hand through my hair. "We're sunk if they have it."

"God, get me their fucking throats!" Blade exclaimed.

Pike dug the heels of his hands into his eyes. "Do we think Dalia's compromised?"

I shrugged. "I don't have a fucking clue, to be honest."

"A hidden fucking camera? Seriously!?" Blade bellowed.

I snatched his wrist and whipped him to face us. "Shut. The fuck. Up."

He ripped away from me. "*Do* you think she's been compromised?!"

My gaze searched his. "I don't know, and that means—"

"—keeping her close is our best bet," Pike said.

I nodded. "Whether we like it or not, she's wrapped up in shit she doesn't even realize, and as long as The Sentinels can access her, she's in trouble."

Blade straightened his back. "No."

"No, what?" Pike asked.

"We don't have a choice," I said.

Blade pointed his finger in my face. "Don't even fucking say it."

Pike grinned. "Hey, I wouldn't mind keeping tabs on her in the evenings."

I wanted to wring his neck for talking about her that way. "I'm calling church tomorrow morning. We need to talk to the guys."

But Blade dug his heels in. "We are not bringing another fucking woman into our circle to—"

"Die?" I asked.

Blade swallowed hard. "You know what I mean."

I shoved his chest, causing Pike to cry out. "Hey! Lance!"

I shoved Blade's chest again before I wrapped my fists up into his shirt. "Are you fucking kidding me?"

Blade simply shrugged though, even as he stood on his tiptoes. "We can't deny what happened last time."

Pike grabbed my arm. "Let him go."

I gnashed my teeth together. "You have the fucking audacity to bring her up when—"

"Put him down, Lance," Pike said.

I slammed Blade into the wall and watched him cough to try and catch his breath. I gripped his hair and yanked his head back, watching his eyes widen as I hovered over him.

"As long as she's with us, she's safe."

"Blade, don't," Pike warned.

But Blade never heeded warnings. "Isn't that what we told Trishelle?"

Pike damn near wrapped his arms around my body. "Stop it, Lance. She's right out there. Anyone could hear us right now."

I glared at Blade, watching his face turn red as I tightened my grasp into the collar of his shirt. I wanted to choke him out. I wanted to watch the life drain from his eyes for ever thinking he could bring her up.

"I should kill you for saying her name," I growled.

Pike's angry voice sounded in my ear. "And you will if you don't fucking let him go, Lance."

I released Blade, but not before I shoved him against the wall. "Keep her here as long as possible."

Blade slid his hands down his shirt. "Like we have a choice."

"And if you don't like it, you can hand me your fucking cut," I hissed.

"Lance!" Pike exclaimed.

Blade stared me down. "Anything else, *President*?"

"No, *Vice* President."

"Good," he said, brushing   past me.

But not before he knocked his shoulder against mine.

Like he was the big man on campus or some shit like that.

"Pike?" I asked, lowering   my voice.

He scoffed. "Yeah?"

I peered over my shoulder at him. "Make sure she   stays at our bar as long as possible. I have to make some phone calls."

"Yeah, sure. Anything else?"

I turned my entire body to face his. "Make sure Blade doesn't do anything stupid."

"You know her death hurt all of us, right?"

My face fell flat. "Was she pregnant with either of your children?"

His shoulders sagged. "No."

"And don't you fucking forget it," I said as I walked past him.

We had a mess to clean up. A big one, depending on how badly Dalia had been influenced. We had a camera we didn't catch with footage we didn't know to exist now in the hands of an enemy crew hellbent on fucking us over as much as possible. We had to focus. We had to come together and figure out what in the absolute hell was really going on. I pulled out my phone and informed the entire crew that we'd have   church as soon as possible at the clubhouse after the bar closed. They needed to know what was going on. They needed all the information at their disposal so they could watch their backs.

And all the while, I had to figure out if Dalia had been compromised.

9

DALIA

As I gazed around their bar, it struck me as... old school, with a hint of stifling privilege. Wooden floors. Wooden chairs. A wooden ceiling with differently stained wooden beams. Bowls of peanuts cracked with every set of hands that plunged into the bowl and shells got spit onto the floor to be mopped up by a busboy that kept coming by every few minutes. The drinks were simple. The beer overflowed. Their tap system alone lined their back wall with only top-shelf liquors shelved above them, and I wondered if they only hired tall people to work behind the bar since someone like me would have never been able to reach them in the first place. But the second I heard his lumbering footsteps, I looked over to find Lance making his way back behind the bar.

With that cocky smirk on his face and that confident swagger of his walk.

Jesus, he's hot.

"Want another one?" he asked, pointing at my empty glass.

These men looked too damn good. "Maybe a menu to go with it? I plan on being here a while."

He chuckled as he picked up my glass. "Meeting someone?"

"Already met them. Just wanting to get to know them if they'll let me."

Something passed across his face and he dumped the glass into a sink behind the bar top. "You aren't ready for that. Trust me."

A challenge, huh?

I loved challenges.

"Well, you're in luck," I said, leaning closer to the bar, "because I'm not in the business of listening to people who think they can tell me what to do."

"Told you, Lance," Pike said as he walked up behind me, "she already knows what she wants."

The feeling of his hand as he settled it against my lower back shivered me to my core. Goosebumps fled across my back. I looked over and found those thin little lips of his curled up into the snarkiest grin. His body heat warmed my thighs as Lance grumbled something beneath his breath. I heard a glass sliding toward me, but it wasn't until the sound of a wobbling plastic menu dropped in front of me that I turned my gaze away from the chiseled man with the deep blue gaze.

Pike's fingertips curled into the small of my back and he used his other hand to point. "You want our extra crispy fries loaded down with a B.L.T."

I smiled with glee as I peeked over at him. "I do now. And why is that?"

"Because it's Blade's specialty," Lance said flatly.

I furrowed my brow and shot him a look, but Pike gripped my chin and pivoted my gaze back to his.

Practically forcing me to melt into his touch against my back.

"Don't worry about him. He's just pissed we're still working while you're here."

"Sure," Lance murmured.

But I still managed to nod my head. "I love a man that can cook."

"Trust me, we do more than cook!" Blade said before he stuck his head out of the kitchen window and yelled over the crowd.

I had to curl my lips around the straw plunged into my drink to keep from groaning out loud. I didn't know what the hell had crawled up Lance's ass and died, but these men were downright delectable. I wanted to dive headfirst into the three of them and never come back up for air. They had no right to be as sexy and as inviting as they were. It was criminal, I tell you. Absolutely criminal.

And yet, I found I didn't give a shit.

"That sounds like a great meal," I said.

Pike winked. "Coming right up. Hey! Blade!"

"I heard her!" he said, disappearing into the kitchen.

It was Lance, however, that kept staring me down. Even as people came up to order drinks—even as people came up to give their food orders—he never once moved away from his steady position. He stayed in front of me, as if he were guarding me from something, and I wanted nothing more than to come undone for him.

"So," I said, swirling my straw around in my second drink, "why do you not like me?"

His stare burrowed a hole between my eyes as he passed off a round of martinis. "What makes you think that?"

I shrugged. "The fact that you seem very eager to get me out of this bar."

"Doesn't mean I don't like you. Just means I'm—"

"Too dangerous for a woman like me?"

His gaze searched mine. "You have no clue what you're getting into with us, that's all."

"Was there someone else that got too entangled with you guys?"

His jaw pulsed. "You have no right to ask that question."

I furrowed my brow. "I didn't realize I was asking a question that had an answer. I'm sorry."

His gaze got tossed over my shoulder as he went back to cleaning down the bar top. "Then, stop while you're ahead."

"One B.L.T. and a loaded extra crispy order of fries for one," Blade said.

A hovering plate came out of nowhere, dropping down in front of me with one of the biggest sandwiches I'd ever seen in my life. The plate alone dwarfed the size of my fucking head, and as Pike climbed up onto the stool to my left, I found Blade perched near my right elbow.

With Lance in front, staring me down like some prized pup.

"Is that... candied bacon?" I asked.

Blade nodded. "It is. In-house specialty."

I picked up the triangular half of the sandwich. "I'm not sure I can even get my mouth around this."

"Lance will be disappointed in that," Pike said with a chuckle. "Won't you, Big Boy?"

"Shut up," Lance grumbled.

I snickered. "At least someone around here knows how to have a good time."

Blade cleared his throat. "Gotta keep at it. Enjoy, Dalia."

I looked over at him and reached out, patting my hand on his shoulder. "Thank you for the food. It looks amazing."

He stared down at our connection before shrugging off my touch. "Have a good night."

I watched him walk away, and he didn't even so much as look back over his shoulder at me. He slinked back into his kitchen and started barking out orders, and I found myself wondering what the hell I'd done to piss these guys off.

They were fine coming into my bar.

Was there something wrong with me coming into theirs?

"Don't worry about him," Pike said, turning my stool to face him. "Blade's just—"

"Cautious. As we all should be," Lance said curtly.

"Cautious?" I asked, picking up a loaded fry. "About what?"

Pike put on his best smile, but his eyes gave away how annoyed he had become. "When beautiful women come into a packed bar like this, there's always reason to be cautious."

I took a bite of the fry, and the crisp alone tickled something deep within my teeth. "Jesus Christ, how the hell do they taste like that?"

"Right?" Pike asked and his smile grew broader. "Blade fries them twice. We cut them fresh, they get stuck in a bowl of ice water with some salt and lemon, and then he—"

"Just giving away trade secrets like that, huh?" Lance asked.

I rolled my eyes. "You know damn good and well I'd never do that to you guys."

"We really don't, though," Lance said.

I tilted my head. "What the hell crawled up your ass and died? If you're pissed that I'm here, just say that."

"I'm not pissed that you're here," he groaned.

"Then why the hell are you acting like I'm not welcome here? Because the last time I checked, bars welcomed beautiful women because that meant men were drooling right behind them off the fucking street."

"She's right," Pike said as he perched his hand on the back of my bar stool. "You and Blade have been pretty—"

"Cautious?" Lance asked.

The two of them stared off with one another and I relegated myself to my sandwich. Taking my first bite of that candied B.L.T. catapulted me into the heavens, and I lost myself in how wondrous the food tasted. I mean, bar food was bar food. No one expected a five-star restaurant in the back of some slummed-up, beat-down joint. And yet, I devoured every single shred of food that had come on that plate.

"I love a woman with an appetite," Pike said, exchanging my second drink for a third.

"This should really be my last one," I said when I took it from him.

He nodded and winked at me yet again.

Goddamn it, I loved it when he winked at me.

"Noted," he said, turning toward Lance. "Did you hear that?"

"Yep," he said, not looking up from the glasses he was clearing off the bar top.

"Hey, Blade!" Pike yelled over everyone's heads.

"What?" he called back when he stuck his head out the kitchen window.

"We got a clear plate over here!" he said as he picked up my plate and held it up for Blade to see.

I hadn't seen Blade smile once yet. His stoic glare had become his trademark. But when he saw that empty plate, I could have sworn I saw a shadow of a grin playing upon his cheeks.

Before he inched his way back into the kitchen and continued barking out orders.

"Last call!" Lance bellowed.

My eyes widened as I grabbed my purse. "Is it really?"

Pike barked with laughter. "Time flies when you're having fun."

I jammed my hand into my purse and pulled out my phone, only to find that it was damn near three in the morning. Holy fucking hell, I'd sat at that bar for three hours and I hadn't once batted an eye. How the fuck had it been three hours? I swear, I had only gotten into the bar a few minutes ago.

"That's what you get for being so much fun," Pike murmured along the shell of my ear.

And I swear to hell on high, the goosebumps that overtook my body raced across my skin like someone was timing them at a goddamn finish line.

"Don't you have a job to be doing now that the bar is closing down?" I asked, turning to face him.

He gazed down into my eyes as his nose nuzzled mine. Our lips were mere millimeters from crashing together. His mint-laced breath pulsed against my lips. His eyes danced in between mine, as if he were drinking me all in. His warmth beckoned to me. His mouth cried out for attention. And as I held my position, my thoughts screamed .

Just kiss me! Do it!

"Be right back," Pike whispered.

Before he moved away from me, leaving an empty vacuum for the cool air of the dwindling bar to suck me backward.

"Are you working tomorrow night?" Lance asked.

I pivoted myself in that bar stool until I faced him. "Usually, my weekend is Wednesday and Thursday. But we've got a bartender experiencing some issues right now, so I have tomorrow and Monday off."

"Here," Blade said, exchanging my empty plate for a filled plate of sizzling mozzarella sticks.

"Oh, no," I said as I shook my head. "I'm not sure that I can—"

"Hand made," he said and plopped a massive bowl of piping hot marinara sauce onto the plate. "You're going to want to have at least one."

They did smell incredible. "And if I don't eat them all?"

He brandished a to-go tray from behind his back. "Already got you covered."

"You're the best, Blade. Thank you."

I took the to-go tray from him and set it off to the side, then I picked up one of the honking mozzarella sticks and hissed. I had to drop it into the marinara sauce itself before using a fork to pick it out, and the entire time, I felt his gaze on the side of my face.

"Is... something wrong?" I asked, peeking over at Blade.

Lance, for the first time in a while, chuckled. "He wants to watch you eat them. It's his thing."

"Is it, now?"

Blade shrugged. "Can't help it if a cook enjoys watching people enjoy his food."

"Then," I said as I held the dripping mozzarella stick on the fork up to my face, "let me put on a show."

I unfurled my tongue from my mouth, catching some sauce drippings on the tip. Blade's gaze locked hard onto my mouth, and as I placed the tip of that deep-fried cheese stick into my mouth, I hollowed out my cheeks.

"Mmmm, this marinara sauce is just outstanding," I whispered.

"Mom's recipe," Blade said flatly.

I slurped the sauce off one end of the stick. "I could eat a bowl of that just by itself."

Blade scooted a bit closer. "I do sometimes. It's a great dipping sauce."

I chomped off the end of the stick, but I didn't have to fake my reaction. The cheese immediately melted in my mouth, and the heat that kicked up behind it made me moan.

"Oh, God. It's pepperjack," I said as my eyes fluttered closed.

"Girl knows her cheeses," Blade said.

"Everyone knows what pepperjack tastes like," Lance said.

I shoved the rest of the stick into my mouth as my eyes fell closed. It was so good. Like, I'd have to talk with Rodrigo about changing around some things, it was so damn good. I'd never had mozzarella sticks that tasted like the ones Blade had placed in front of me. The melted cheese coated the tantalizing crispy breading that had been seasoned perfectly with all sorts of Italian flavors. Basil and oregano. I could have sworn I tasted a hint of parmesan as well. I wasted no time digging around for another. I plunged it into the sauce, damn near drowning the poor thing out before I brought it back to my lips.

I devoured them while Blade stood there, drinking in my every sound.

And the second I finished the entire plate, he gathered the dishes in his hands.

"You know, I've got dessert back at my place if you've got the stomach for it."

I leaned back and tilted my head toward him. "It takes calories to keep up these curves, handsome. What do you think I have the stomach for?"

Pike barked with laughter, and it was the first and only time I made Lance genuinely smile that night. But when he smiled, it lit up his face with such boyish complexity that I found myself staring a bit too hard in his general direction.

"A woman with confidence," Lance said, slapping his rag over his shoulder. "A rarity nowadays."

Someone spun my stool, and I came face to face with Blade. His sea foam eyes seemed much more playful than they had the nights they had come into my bar, and I found myself hanging onto his every movement. He slid the empty plates back on top of the bar. He settled his hands onto my knees and parted my legs, peeling my thighs apart. My breath caught in my throat as he moved in between them, his lean body forcing my excess to mold to his presence.

His brown hair fell into his face, giving him the look of a predator.

"Ever been on the back of a bike?" Blade asked.

I dropped my gaze down his stealthy structure before I chewed on my lower lip. "First time for everything, I guess."

And when that man licked his lips, my fucking head almost blew through the roof.

"She's mine tonight, boys," he said as he offered me his hand. "Don't wait up."

10

———

BLADE

"Ready to get going?"

The earpiece in my helmet came alive with her sultry voice. "I was born ready."

"Lovely."

I revved the engine of my bike, feeling her thighs clinging to my hips. Her arms enveloped me as she twisted her fists into my leather jacket, and the feeling of that heated pussy against the slope of my back made me salivate. Soaring away from the bar felt like finally busting out of prison, and I had the sweetest gem of a fruit hanging on behind me for dear life. Every turn we took, she clung tighter. Every stop that brought us to a halt, and those tits of hers smashed into my back. Her giggles filled my eardrums as the wind kicked up around us, attempting to hold us hostage while my bike pierced through the resistance.

She didn't say another word until I took that right-hand turn off the road and into the woods.

And when she spoke, I found myself eager to hear her crying out my name.

"Where are we going again?" she asked.

A grin spread across my face. "Nervous?"

"I mean, it's just—"

"Our crew's clubhouse is where we conduct all of our business."

"And here I thought we were going to be conducting pleasure."

I licked my lips. "Of course, once we get home."

"But I thought we were going t—"

"The clubhouse is my home. Now, hang on, this next part gets a little rough."

Turning off the asphalt onto the dirt road wasn't the issue. The muddy patch that separated the dirt from the gravel driveway, however, had always given us problems. Lance thought the solution was to keep throwing cardboard on it to soak up the ambient water. Which only made things worse once the cardboard broke down and became one with the mud beneath our tires.

I splashed through it, weaving and keeping friction beneath the tires as mud sprayed against my boots.

I couldn't resist that giggle of hers, though.

"I feel it on my calves," Dalia said.

I crooked an eyebrow. "Guess I'll have to hose you down, then."

"Promise?" she purred.

My cock leapt to life. It pressed against the zipper of my jeans, begging to be set free. I breathed a sigh of relief as my tires locked onto the gravel driveway that eased us up to the front of the clubhouse. The lake glistened in the moonlight, the crescent moon reflecting off the still water's edge.

"Wow," Dalia whispered.

"Home sweet home," I said, parking my bike.

She quickly slid off the back of my bike without help, and I had to admit, it was sexy. Twenty minutes on my bike, and she walked around like she'd been riding on them her entire life.

The things I'd do to her once we got inside were damn near unfathomable.

"Is that a river I hear?" she asked.

I put down the kickstand and pulled off my helmet. "There's a river that feeds into the lake."

"So, there *is* a river on the property."

I nodded. "Yes."

She turned back toward the water. "I just never thought a place like this existed around here."

I cut the engine and slung my leg over. "The woods hide a lot around here. It's why we like it. Very private. No trespassers."

"Right, right."

Her mindless statement gave me pause. The guys and I had gotten used to the scenery. Well, except for Pike. He fucking worshipped the place like it was his full-time job. But watching her watch the water struck a chord inside of me.

A chord that tugged me to her side before I relieved the helmet from her hands.

"Beautiful, isn't it?" I asked, gazing down at the top of her head.

She nodded, but she didn't speak. She had been silenced by the world around us.

I'd fix that, though.

Before the night was over, she'd be crying out for more of what I had to offer.

VROOM, ROOM, ROOM, ROOM.

Dalia turned around. "What's that?"

I watched her carefully. "Pike and Lance, most likely."

She casted her sparkling gray eyes up at me as her red hair shimmered in the moonlight. "But I thought you said—"

I nodded toward the porch and started walking. "The core group of the crew lives here at the clubhouse."

"So, Lance and Pike will be...?"

I made my way up the steps. "Don't worry, the walls are sound insulated."

"Oh?"

I opened the clubhouse front door and turned to her. "You coming?"

And that was when that cheeky smirk of hers ignited her stare. "I sure as hell better be before the night is over."

"Then get your juicy ass inside and let's see what we can do about that."

I'd never seen a woman move so eagerly in all my life. I watched her curves bounce for me, jiggling with every step as if to serve me with an invitation to dine privately. I wanted to feast on her deliciousness. I wanted to dive between her legs and not come up for air until my lungs screamed for mercy. Women like her deserved to be worshiped , and my knees were primed, ready for the force of her thrusts as I took her from behind.

God, I can't wait for her ass to bounce against my dick.

She soared past me, making her way into our three-story clubhouse. We each had our own floor, dedicated to whatever nefarious and whimsy deeds we decided to take on in our spare time. Lance was at the top, of course, being our President and all. Pike chose to stay on the main floor since most of his technological systems he had set up around the property were also grounded on the main floor. So, that left me with the middle of the three floors.

"So," Dalia said when I strolled on in behind her, "where are we headed?"

I pointed to the steps. "Up those, down the hallway, last door on the left."

She came over and linked her arm with mine. "And what is this dessert you've teased me with? Because I have to say, I'm a fan of anything that requires chocolate and caramel mixed together."

I ushered her up the steps. "Don't worry, you'll be full and satiated by the time you leave."

"Are we still talking about dessert?"

I decided to leave her question be. After all, nothing seduced a woman quicker than a mystery of the mind. I guided her up the steps and down the hallway, feeling the carpeted floor beneath our feet give with our steps. I gripped the handle of my bedroom door and tossed it open, readying myself for her gasp.

And when it came, it curled my toes in my boots.

"Holy shit," she said breathlessly, releasing my arm.

I watched her walk into the middle of the room, bathing herself in the moonlight. Sure, Lance had a great view and Pike didn't have to haul his shit up steps. But I had floor-to-ceiling tinted windows that looked out along the whole of the property. I watched her hips sway in those pathetic excuse for jean bottoms she donned, watching as the globe of her ass cheek started poking out from beyond the lower hem of her shorts. She placed her hand against the glass. She surveyed the world around her, taking it all in as if she were seeing it for the first time.

Which gave me a chance to close the door and flip the lock.

"This place is beautiful," she said.

I turned to face her now that I had her exactly where I wanted. "I have a question for you."

"Yeah, sure," she said, still not turning away from the windows.

"Did you think you could bat your eyes like you do and get away with it?"

That made her turn to face me, and when she did, her smile overtook me. The pure joy and happiness in her features felt like something from a bygone era. A part of my soul that had been chipped off and left in a ditch to shrivel and die. Good god, she was a gorgeous woman, and I had her in my grasp.

Mere feet from my bed, where I had scores of surprises just waiting for her.

"I'm going to be dessert, aren't I?" she asked.

The grin on my features fell. My shoulders rolled back when I locked my stare with hers. I put one foot in front of the other, inhaling her scent through my nostrils as every single one of my senses sharpened. I heard the owl cooing outside and the soft footsteps of Lance and Pike finding their rooms. I smelled her cotton candy body spray, just as trashy as ever in those peek-aboo shorts and the black tank top that barely concealed tits that could smother me in my sleep. Her red bra twinkled for my viewing pleasure. She pressed her back to the window as I stalked toward her, placing my hands on either side of her head.

And as I trapped her against the chill of that glass, I watched her nipples pucker against her sorry excuse for a bra.

"Yes," I said, licking my lips. "But I'm also going to be yours."

"Well," she said as she heaved her lungs for air, teasing me with the upward motion of her breasts, "let the games begin, then."

I lowered my lips to her ear. "Stay."

She giggled. "Yes, sir."

I gripped her chin and pinned her with a stare and ran my thumb along her lower lip. "Blade. It's 'yes, Blade.'"

She darted her tongue out and licked the tip of my thumb before gracing me with another one of those heavenly smiles of hers.

"Yes, Blade."

I wrapped my hand quickly around her throat. "Good girl."

"Oh!"

I whipped her around, leading her toward the bed before I pushed her down onto the mattress. Her plump frame bounced for me, her legs parting as she tried to stabilize herself. I slid my leather jacket off my arms and hung it up on one of the four wooden posters that sat attached to my bed's frame. I kicked off my boots and walked around the outer edge of the bed, watching and waiting. Wondering what she'd do next.

It wasn't until I bent down that she finally spoke.

"What are you doing?" Dalia asked.

I opened the door of the mini-fridge I kept beneath my bed. "Just gathering some of my favorite toys."

"So, you're a vibrator guy, huh?"

I pulled out the chocolate and caramel sauce from the back. "Not exactly."

After gathering everything that I wanted, I stood to my feet. With the fridge softly whirring to life, I placed my toys on my side of the bed. Yes, I had a specific side of the bed. Even though it was a king-sized bed and even though no one else shared it with me, one day that would change. One day, I'd have someone next to me. Someone waking up with me every morning and greeting me with her warmth.

But until she came along, I trained myself to get used to my side of the bed.

Dalia snickered. "Is that chocolate and caramel sauce?"

I set the cherries and edible pens beside the bottles before I turned to face her. "You said so yourself: chocolate and caramel is your combo."

She slid her gaze down my form. "You really are a foodie, aren't you?"

I reached for the caramel sauce and walked back toward her. "Spread your legs."

She did as I asked. "Yes, Blade."

I scooted in between her piping hot thighs and felt my

clothed dick grow another size. "Now, stick that tongue out for me."

She giggled. "Yes, Blade."

I watched that delectable tongue unfurl for me before I uncapped the caramel. I held it over her mouth, allowing it to drip naturally as she caught it against her tongue. Against her lips. Against her chin. I swirled it around and watched it splash over her mountainous cleavage.

"Mmmm, so good," she hummed.

"Now, lay back," I commanded.

And as if she had been sent to me by God himself, she did exactly as I asked.

With the caramel sauce already begging to be dripped on her wet pussy lips.

11

—————

DALIA

The mattress cushioned me as caramel slid across my skin. My toes curled against my sandals, slipping from my feet as Blade stalked around me like a lion in heat. I waited on bated breath for his next move. I waited for his hands to touch me, ready to shoot me into the heavens with whatever dessert he had planned.

Then something came down around my eyes.

"Blade?" I asked.

"Lift your head," he urged.

"Blade, I don't know if—"

"Are you scared?"

I paused. "Should I be?"

His heated breath pulsed against the shell of my ear. "Yes."

My heart stopped in my chest. Was that a warning? A signal that I needed to pick up on? I swallowed hard as I laid there, my head suspended in midair. My neck ached for relief. My pussy cried out for his touch. And as I laid there with caramel sliding between my breasts, I made a decision.

"Just don't hurt me," I said.

He kissed the shell of my ear. "Never. Now lay back."

With my eyes blindfolded and my skin sticky with syrup, I waited for his next move. Every sense seemed to heighten as my legs crawled with anticipation. Every step he took, my head pivoted in that direction. Every clunk my ears picked up had me guessing what came next. Toys? Spankings? Tie downs?

It wasn't until I felt his hands against my jean shorts that I lifted my hips.

He stripped me down without a word spoken between us. He manipulated my body, lifting it and molding it to his every whim. Not once did he grunt, either. He moved me as if I were nothing but a ragdoll at his disposal, and not an inch of him struggled with my weight. And sure, I didn't define myself by my weight. But let's not act like there were certain things all us big girls dealt with in our sex life.

Like men grunting whenever they tried to move us.

"There," he said when he had me stripped naked. "Perfect."

I giggled and shook my hips. "Like what you see?"

His hand dipped between my thighs and peeled them apart. I hissed as the cool air of the room gently graced my pussy lips. The drips started again and the scent of chocolate filled the space around my head, the delicate touch of his fingertips contrasting the growl of his voice.

"Now," he grunted as his fingers teased the sides of my pussy, "time to feast."

His mouth dropped to my tits, and I gasped. His warmth wrapped around my nipples, and they puckered so hard they damn near hurt. His tongue languidly slid across my skin with hums and groans falling from my lips so effortlessly, it was like he had me controlled with a button off in the corner. I bucked against his hand as he splayed it along my naked cunt. I gripped the sheets of the bed, allowing the sensations to overwhelm me while he slurped the caramel sauce away from my skin.

"Fucking hell," he hissed then kissed down my stomach. "So good."

I moaned. "Blade, please."

He growled as I heard him slip off the bed. "Say it again."

"Blade, please."

"Please... what?"

I parted my legs and his hands explored my thick thighs. "Please let me feel your tongue. Your fingers. Anything. Just—just touch her. Please."

The first thing I felt was his body scooting between my legs. That languid length of him , with stretched muscles over a slender frame. He fit cozily between my voluptuous curves, and his fingertips parted my pussy lips to release a smell that gave away my want for him. My need for him. My desire to be filled by him. It filled the air, leading his lips to my clit as he kissed its tip.

Causing me to jump.

"Yes," I whispered.

He flicked it with his tongue. "You mean, like that?"

"Yes, Blade," I moaned.

"What about... like this?"

Something cold fell against my clit and I jumped. Over and over, it splashed against my heated pussy and my legs shivered. His shoulders crooked beneath my knees, supporting my legs as they jumped with every spurt.

He inched a finger into my pulsing opening.

"Oh, Goooood."

He spanked the inside of my thigh. "That isn't my name, girl."

I hissed, and yet my skin broke out in goosebumps. "Oh, Blade. Fuck."

"Do you kiss your mother with that mouth?"

I scoffed. "I was raised in foster care. Haven't seen my

mother since she left me on the side of the road when I was seven."

Silence filled the air around us, and it wasn't until he crooked his finger against that pebbled spot inside of my body that I whimpered.

"Sorry," I murmured.

"Don't be," he said, licking my clit gently, "just gives me a reason to help you forget."

Feeling his tongue slide all the way up my slit catapulted me into another dimension. Relief finally washed over my body as he devoured my pussy, lapping up whatever sauce he had decided to drip all over my sensitive skin. I reached for his hair, knotting my fingers within it, and I bucked ravenously against his face. His fingers filled me with one. Then, two. Pumping, curling, and teasing me as I propped my heels against his back.

"Blade," I groaned.

"Mmmmm," he hummed, "so good for me."

My walls quivered. "Blade, I'm so close."

"Come for me," he commanded.

My back arched into the air as he swirled his tongue around the base of my clit. He flicked it at lightning speed before flattening his tongue against it, and I swear to God, I lost my head. My body took over. The need for release was all too great. And as I coated his face in my juices, that coil behind my gut tightened.

"Blade," I said breathlessly.

"Do it," he growled.

"Blade, oh fuck," I moaned.

"That's it," he said, pumping his fingers faster. "Come for me, Dalia. Take what's yours. Be the little whore you so desperately want to be."

"Oh, fuck," I choked out.

The world spiraled around me as my blindfold clung tighter than ever to my face. My body exploded, fireworks bursting behind my eyes as they rolled back into my head. Something squirted from between my legs, and the feral sound that fell from Blade's lips could only be described as animalistic. He ripped his fingers out of my pussy and I collapsed to the bed, panting and gasping for air. But when he ripped the blindfold off my face, I found myself staring up at a red-faced Blade with chocolate patched against his chin.

And tattoos strewn across his chest.

"Wow," I whispered.

He said nothing. All he did was stare down at me as he undid the belt buckle of his jeans. I turned onto my side, drinking in his chiseled abs and his thin form. He wasn't weak by any means, not if he could toss and roll me around like I weighed nothing. His muscles, while not bulging, were fraught with veins that throbbed for my viewing pleasure. His strength had been etched by the Gods. Every muscle stood taut, waiting for my next reaction. And as he pulled his cock out of his pants, the sheer length of it dropped my jaw.

"Jesus fuck, Blade," I said breathlessly.

His chuckle could have come from the Devil. "Just you wait."

I heard the pop of a top before the smell of cherries washed over my body. The squelching sound made me snicker, but when he buried his hand into my hair to turn my head back toward him, I saw his long cock dripping with red cherry juice. It dripped onto the sheets as he cupped his balls, his dick standing tall for me as I rolled back onto my side.

I wanted to trace his tattoos with my tongue.

But as he bounced his juicy dick against my lips, I realized Blade had other plans.

"Open wide, beautiful," he coaxed.

"Yes, Blade," I said before I unhinged my jaw as far as it would go.

The taste of cherries tantalized my throat, causing it to open before his intrusion made me gag. I wanted to pull back. In fact, I tried. But his hand kept my face staked on his dick.

"Don't fight it, beautiful," he grunted as my hands pressed into his jeaned thighs. "Only makes it worse."

"Mmph," I groaned and my throat continued to force gags.

"Breathe," he whispered. "Through your nose, just breathe."

I didn't know how long it took me to get over the sensation of being choked. In fact, it wasn't a sensation I had ever encountered before. I'd never once struggled this badly with taking a dick to the back of my throat, and it made me wonder about some of the other guys I had been with. Why did I struggle with Blade, but not them?

The thought made me giggle, and the sound itself released my throat.

"There we go," he sighed, inching in further. "Such a good girl for me."

I trembled in his wake. "Mmmmmmm."

I worked against my body, wanting nothing more than for him to fill the back of my throat. I forced my mouth into submission, and when his cock finally crested down my throat, I felt it bulge. Blade sighed with relief as he stroked my forehead with this thumb. I peeked up and saw beads of sweat sliding down his chest, showcasing the work it took for him to be so gentle with me.

I'd never forget it, either.

How kind he was in the face of my body rejecting his intrusion.

"Now," he glowered, looking down at me. "Stay very, very still."

He pulled his dick out and slammed it back into my mouth,

and it took every ounce of energy I had not to throw up on him. It was all so new, and as the room spun around me, the feeling of my throat bulging with his thickness crumbled me to my core. I wanted to be used by him. I wanted him to fill my stomach before complimenting me on a job well done. I wanted, so badly, to impress him, that I ignored my body. I ignored my throat closing. I ignored the churning of my stomach as I closed my eyes and relegated my breathing to my nose, no matter how much my body wanted to reject him.

And little by little, my body finally succumbed to his strokes.

"Oh, fuuuuuuck," I moaned around his cock.

"Fucking hell," he hissed. "Jesus, you feel so good."

I felt helpless, and yet in control at the same time. But more than that, I felt beautiful. Wanted. Received, and accepted. I lost myself in the taste of his cherry-slicked cock. I raked my nails up and down his thighs, wanting to receive more of him as he stood there, fucking my face. His balls clapped against the underside of my chin. My tits bounced against his legs, wishing for his jeans to simply disappear into thin air. His dick grew thicker. I felt him pulsing against my tongue as his hips stuttered.

"God damn it, Dalia," he growled, "open that pretty little throat for me."

He shoved himself down my throat one last time and I held my ground. With my hands wrapped around to the backside of his thighs, I held him against me as my nose nuzzled his tightly wound curls. Pump after pump slid down the back of my throat, with Blade sending obscenities up to the heavens that would make God Himself blush.

And when he collapsed against the bed, his dick fell out from between my lips.

"Jesus Christ," he said breathlessly.

I rolled onto my back and wiped my mouth off. "You can say that again."

He fell to the bed next to me, our bodies molding together as I rolled into him. I tucked my face into the crook of his neck, hoping he'd allow me just a few minutes of rest before I had to get up and leave. My heart kept slamming against my chest. No matter what I did, it felt like I couldn't catch my breath. My body buzzed. The room around us tilted on its own axis, as if our bodies alone had gotten us drunk.

I need a shower.

And that was the last thought I remembered having before darkness completely overcame me.

With Blade stroking his fingertips up and down my bare-naked arm.

Birds chirping were the first thing I heard before the warmth of the sunlight streaming through the windows graced my skin. I rolled over and stretched, feeling something cool and airy gliding against my skin. My legs shook as my toes curled. My arms lengthened above my head before my entire spine seemed to convulse.

"Oooooh, yeah," I groaned before I flopped back down into bed. "That's the stuff."

And yet, when I opened my eyes, I didn't see my apartment. I didn't see my bedroom. I didn't hear the slamming of doors and cursing of people that usually greeted me whenever I decided to peel my way out of bed.

Instead, I heard the sound of fish jumping up from water. Birds chirping in an attempt to find their mates. The wind rustling through trees.

I bolted up in bed as it finally clicked.

"Shit," I hissed as I looked around with tired eyes.

I had fallen asleep in Blade's bed.

I swung my legs over the edge of the bed and searched for my clothes. Surely, he hadn't meant to leave me there. I probably fell asleep on him, and he couldn't wake my ass up. Fuck, this was bad. I had to get back to my place before he came back. But when I finally stood onto my feet, I found myself facing a robe.

A robe with a sticky note that had my name on it.

"What?" I asked breathlessly.

I dug the heels of my hands into my eyes and walked toward the robe. I plucked the sticky note off and turned it over, but there was nothing written on the back. Just my name, attached to a robe that looked fluffier than heaven's clouds.

And when I pulled it off the hanger, I proved myself right.

"Oh, man," I moaned, wrapping it around my naked body, "I could get used to this kind of treatment."

Still, where was Blade? I heard no sounds as I made my way toward the bedroom door. I silenced my footsteps as much as I could in the hopes that no one would hear me creeping around like a curious little idiot. I didn't have to go far to find them, though.

Because when I found the stairs heading down into the foyer, I heard all of them talking.

"Are you fucking kidding me? Does she even know?"

I sat on the top of the steps and closed my eyes, trying to focus my ears. But I was so tired that I didn't know who the hell was talking.

I just... heard them talking, in general.

"She can't possibly know. There's no way. She didn't even know who we were, and we rolled up in our cuts, man."

"But if she does know, we can't take that chance."

"She doesn't know."

"And how can you be sure of that?"

"I just do. She doesn't know a thing. She's not part of this."

"We have to be certain. We have to make absolutely sure that we haven't just brought the enemy into our fucking house."

The enemy? Who the hell were they talking about?

Me?!

"The guy who visited her—"

"The guy who visited her is a piece of shit and we're going to find him. But right now, we have to focus on something greater. She's in danger. If they approached her the way they did, then they think she's connected to us somehow. That's not good for her."

Wait, were they talking about the guy they sent?

"She's still under the impression that we sent him. What happens when she figures out we didn't?"

My jaw hit the floor. Were they talking about the guy who told me where to find them?

He wasn't part of their crew?

My skin crawled with fear. I eased myself up onto my feet and moved as silently as possible. I wanted to hear more. I needed to know more.

Then, a thought stopped me in my tracks.

Did Blade sleep with me just to get me back here?

The thought sucker punched me in the gut.

"If she's working with them—"

"Working with them or not, she's in danger. You know that girl's got no fucking clue what's going on. I'm not worried about her knowing shit. But if they're ballsy enough to approach her in her own damn bar on her own damn shift in broad fucking daylight, then we've got a problem. She's not safe, and what's worse is that now she's a liability to us. We have to keep her close. She knows too much about us."

Tears crested my eyes, but I refused to shed them. As I stood at the bottom of the steps, I held my breath as the guys continued bickering. So, there it was. Blade brought me back and used his dick to entice me to stay so they could figure out if I was some risk for them.

Risk assessment.

That was all last night had been.

Fuck you guys, too.

I should have known they weren't in it for me in the first place.

Men never were.

Instead of following their voices, I figured I had heard enough. I turned around and made my way back upstairs, keeping as quiet as possible and didn't bother to close the door. There was nothing they could say or do that would keep me in this prison. No matter how beautiful the scenery was and no matter how comfortable the bed was, it all felt... tainted somehow.

I refused to live in their nightmare, just like I had refused to live in my mother's.

I'd abandon them first, though.

I wouldn't give them the chance to abandon me.

It took me a while to find my clothes, but when I finally found them perched on the bathroom countertop, I shed the robe. I dropped it to the floor and ignored the slimy, sticky residue that reminded me of Blade's nefarious kinks. I drew in a deep breath as I tucked my tits into my bra. I jumped with the force of God just to wiggle my way into those tight jean shorts. And after splashing some water into my face to wake me up, I relegated myself to walking home.

Because it was better than accepting any other "charity" from these assholes.

"Sleep well?"

"Ah!" I exclaimed as I jumped.

The hand towel tumbled from my grip as water dripped off my face and onto my tank top.

"Here," Lance said with a grin on his face. "Let me get that for you."

I watched him carefully as he lumbered his massive form into the bathroom. He dipped down and scooped the towel up before gripping my chin with his fingers.

"Hold still," he said, wiping my face.

I stared him down as he stroked the soft fabric along my skin.

"So?" he asked.

"So, what?" I asked flatly.

His eyebrows ticked together ever so softly. "Sleep well?"

I yanked the towel from his hand and pulled away from his grasp. "Not good enough."

"Sounds like Blade didn't do his job, then."

I wiped off the rest of my face before tossing the towel into the sink. "Now, if you'll excuse me."

But when I tried to wiggle past him, he caught my wrist in his hand, wrapping his entire grasp around it and halted me in my tracks.

"Off so soon?" he asked.

I scoffed and yanked out of his grasp. "Yeah, since apparently your rival crew bullshit is following me around."

"What?" Lance asked.

"Told you she was listening at the top of the steps," Pike said as he rounded into the bathroom.

And when Blade stepped from around the other corner, I found myself blocked in. Pike and Blade in front of me, standing in the doorway with Lance behind me, blocking my only access to the only window in the damn bathroom.

I was fucked.

"How much did you hear?" Blade asked.

I folded my arms across my chest. "Once you let me out of this room, I'll tell you."

"We can't do that until we have a talk," Lance said.

I peered over my shoulder. "Did it look like I was talking to you?"

"Now, what happened to the good girl from last night?" Blade asked.

I shrugged. "Guess you didn't really do your job right."

Pike barked with laughter, but Blade's face fell into cold, sharp stone. "Be careful with your next set of words."

"Why?" I asked. "You'll kill me just like you killed that man if I tell you that what I experienced last night was subpar compared to other performances I've endured?"

"Enough," Lance grumbled.

"My thoughts exactly," I spat. "Now, let me out."

"How much did you hear?" Pike asked.

I pinned him with a look. "Enough to know exactly why Blade brought me back here last night."

Blade growled. "You have no idea why I brought you back here."

I stalked toward him, my fists balled up at my sides. "I came back here to get to know you guys. To talk. To experience you. I think you're interesting, not to mention drop dead gorgeous. Are you really attempting to tell me, after the conversation that I just overheard, that you brought me back here for all those same reasons?"

And when he didn't say anything, my heart shattered.

"Figured as much," I murmured, holding my head high.

I turned to face Lance and found him staring Blade down as well.

"If you let me leave now, I won't go to the cops. But if you hold me here against my will, I'll have no choice," I said.

Lance finally scraped his gaze toward me. "If you walk out

that door, we can't protect you."

That statement gave me pause. "Protect me from what?"

Pike sighed behind me. "That's the thing, Dalia, we aren't sure what their endgame is. And until we do, you're not safe."

My fists finally unfurled. "I have work. I start back on Tuesday, guys. I can't just not show up."

Lance shrugged. "Are you asking us to work with some sort of timeline? Because that isn't how this works."

I felt my shoulders slump as anger bubbled up my throat. "I don't give a damn how you think something like this is supposed to work. I made my best friend a promise—"

"Ooooo," Blade said mockingly as he stalked around me like a predator analyzing its caught prey. "Is this best friend of the... male variety?"

"*Lisa*," I said curtly as I stared Blade down, "is currently in the hospital with her son, who's fighting for his life."

That got them to stop.

Huh, maybe they did have hearts somewhere deep down in the dark, black pits of their souls.

"And she needs me to cover her schedule so that she can cover her son," I said with a nod of my head. "So, staying here simply isn't an option. I made a promise. I gave my word."

Lance shook his head. "Doesn't mean it's safe out there."

"What hospital?" Blade asked.

I rolled my eyes. "Does that matter?"

He got into my face, placing his hands on his knees as he crouched down to level his stare with mine. "It matters to me."

I scoffed before I turned to Lance. "Fine. Whatever. I'll play your game for now. That means you've got until Tuesday morning to figure out how to make me safe again. Because no matter what you say, I'm gone by that point. I worked too hard to get to where I am in life to throw it all away because some assholes wanna be assholes, and I've got my best friend counting on me so that she's got a damn job when she comes back to pay for her son's medical bills!"

"Is that what you really think of us?" Blade asked as he reared up out of my face. "People who play games with other's lives?"

I snickered. "You're one to talk."

"All right," Lance said.

I blinked. "What?"

He shrugged. "We have until Tuesday, that's fine by me. You can ride with me to go pick up some of your things to make your stay here more comfortable."

I shuffled on my feet. "Just like that?"

"Just do one thing for me," he said, cloaking me in his shadow.

I had to crane my neck back to keep his face in view. "Okay?"

He gripped my chin, stilling my gaze upon his. "Pack for more than a couple of days because once Tuesday rolls around, I guarantee you're going to want to stay here longer."

"Why? You gonna try to fuck me, too?"

His gaze grew firm, and I knew he was serious. "Because when Tuesday rolls around, I believe you're going to be asking us to stay for a longer time. And when that time comes, I'm going to tell you that you're more than welcome to go back and forth to work from here instead of your place. Got it?"

And even though his warning stilled my gut in a fit of cold fear that washed through the marrow of my bones, I kept my façade strong.

After all, I'd need it while coping with Blade's betrayal.

"Whatever, let's just go. I need coffee," I said, pulling out of Lance's grasp.

Before turning and pushing through Pike and Blade to get out of the corner they had backed me into.

12

LANCE

I did my best to ignore the feeling of her tits splayed against my back. Every time we came to a stop, I looked down and found her cute little fists balled up in my leather jacket. She couldn't even get her arms around me, and for some reason, that stiffened my dick. Her curves coaxed themselves around me as if her entire body were trying to hang on for dear life. Her legs melded to mine, filling my thighs with a heat that tugged at my dick. I grew jealous of Blade having had her first. I dreamt all night of the things I'd do to her. The surfaces I'd pin her to. The furniture I'd bend her over.

She needed time, though.

And I respected that.

"Here," Dalia said as she pointed.

"You live at your bar?" I asked, parking in front of the door.

"No," she said, damn near scrambling to get off my bike. "Just above it. Come on."

It was the first time she had spoken since we'd gotten onto my motorcycle in the first place, and the heat of her voice matched the taut posture of her body. She had every right to be pissed at us, especially Blade. I mean, I didn't even think he was capable of it. Using sex to get her back to the house? It was a genius idea.

One I would have talked him out of, too, because of the scenario unfolding in front of me.

"You coming or what?" she asked, yanking a wrought iron gate open.

I put the kickstand of my bike down and pulled my helmet off my head. "Right behind you."

"Whatever," she murmured, disappearing into the darkness.

I needed caffeine. I hadn't even had breakfast, for fuck's sake. But I kept that shit to myself as I started in behind her. I took the steps three at a time, walking in behind her just in time to see her skirt through the kitchen. Her apartment was bigger than what I expected. It seemed to stretch over the entirety of the bar's roof, and as I closed the door behind me, I heard Dalia murmuring to herself.

"Stupid fucking men," she hissed as something clunked against the wall.

"Always fucking me around. " Something slammed open.

"Always thinking they know what's best. "

"Fuck men," she hissed once more.

"Yeah," I said, standing at the end of the hallway. "Fuck men. They suck."

She poked her head out of what I assumed was her bedroom. "Stay silent or get out."

I nodded. "Fair enough."

With my back to her hallway, I glanced around her studio apartment. Her kitchen had nothing sitting out on the counters. No fruit bowl. No appliances. Her living room had one raggedy couch in front of the smallest television I'd ever seen in my life. There was an empty space near a gathering of windows where anyone would have pictured a nice four-chair dining room table. And yet, all that sat there were cardboard boxes. Some of them opened and tipped onto their side, and some of them still looked as if they were lugging shit around.

I didn't need Pike with me to figure out that she didn't regard her place as home.

And it made me wonder why.

"Ready," she said, her voice hot with frustration.

I turned to face her and was shocked to find that she only carried one bag. "I told you to pack for—"

She held it up. "Two weeks' worth of stuff."

I blinked. "In one bag?"

She tilted her head. "You like them high maintenance, I see. Come on, let's get out of here before someone else comes rolling up to spill your secrets."

I smirked. "A pretty girl like you shouldn't be frowning as deeply as that."

She scoffed and tossed me her bag. "Not in a smiling mood right now."

I dropped her bag to the floor at my feet. "I could put a smile on that face if you let me."

She narrowed her eyes in my general direction. "Outside of the fact that Blade has pissed me off, you think fucking me is going to make me feel better?"

I took a step toward her. "Well, there are scientific articles out there that would argue in my defense."

She blinked. "You read scientific articles?"

I stood over her, hovering as I gazed down into those strong gray eyes of hers. "There are a lot of things you don't know about me, Dalia."

"Like what?"

I crooked my finger beneath her chin. "Like how big of a smile my body could put on your face."

She stared me down for the longest time. So long, in fact, that I wondered if she had heard me. She kept her stare locked with mine. She kept her back straight and strong, and I wondered where she had gotten all the gumption she had. People didn't just stand up to us. That wasn't a thing. She either had a death wish or something worse.

Life experience with some of the hardest things anyone could ever endure.

Then, she said those two magic words. The only magic words I needed to shed my leather jacket to the floor before I cupped her ass cheeks into the palm of my hands. Before I slammed her into the wall of her hallway. Before I thrusted my lips against hers, claiming her as mine just so I could wash away the stench of Blade's actions the night before.

Anything to make her smile.

Anything to make her forget the trouble she had gotten herself into.

"Prove it," Dalia glowered.

And the feeling of her pulling my dick out of my pants as I pinned her to the wall damn near made me explode in the palm of her hand.

13

———

DALIA

"Whoa—Ah!"

He scooped me into his grasp as if I were nothing but a sack of feathers. My back fell against the wall, his lips attached to my pulse point and my tits puckered for the occasion. His large hands roamed my body, pawing at my breasts and tugging at my shorts. I wrapped my legs around his girthy waist, barely able to lock them at my ankles as I threaded my fingers through his hair.

And as his hungry tongue devoured my mouth, the tick of a smile graced my cheeks.

Might as well get something out of this hellish nightmare.

"I hate these shorts," Lance growled, his body pressed against mine, pinning me to the wall. His hands fell to my cut-off jeans and the fabric of them ripped with every yank of his hands.

"Lance," I whispered.

"Fuck," he growled and another ripping sound tore through my eardrums.

"Lance," I whimpered.

"Just," he grunted, "one more."

And when he yanked his hands apart, the flimsy jeans fell to the floor in tatters and my naked pussy sat against his stomach.

"Such a dirty girl for me," he said, kissing in between my tits.

The warmth of his tongue as it darted between my breasts froze me against the wall. I couldn't get enough of him. His muscles pulsed against my excess. His hands gripped my naked hips and he bucked his clothed dick against my center. My clit poked out from beneath its hood, begging for friction as he buried his face into my cleavage.

He fell to his knees without once planting my feet onto the ground.

"Lance!" I exclaimed.

He wrapped my thighs around his face and chuckled. "Hang on tight, naughty girl."

"Lance, what are y—ooooooh, my Goooood."

With his hands pressed against the wall on either side of my hips, his shoulders held me up as his knees planted onto the floor. He buried himself into my pussy, licking and lapping and sucking and I clung to jet black curls for dear life. I hung there, midair, while his tongue devoured me. While my hips bucked against his face and my back pressed into the wall so hard that I knew for certain there'd be an outline by the time we were done. His tongue filled my entrance, licking my walls that throbbed around his intrusion.

But when he slid that thick, fat tongue of his all the way up my pussy, I cried out.

"Lance! Holy fuck!"

His growl rattled my ribcage and my juices dripped down his chin. My eyes rolled back, cloaking me in darkness as my wanton lust rose from its deep, dark depths. My nails raked against his scalp. My thighs quivered around his face. The sound of him lapping me up sent electric shockwaves pulsing through my body, sending my heart into a fluttering frenzy as I chanted his name like a wishful prayer.

"Lance. Lance. Lance. Fucking hell, don't stop. Don't stop. Don't you dare stop."

"Never," he growled. "So long as you're mine, I'll never stop."

His? The fuck did he mean by that? I didn't care. I shook the thought from my head and focused on the knot curling behind my gut. His tongue traced my clit. He flicked its tip at a blinding pace as I panted for air my lungs desperately needed. The world faded into darkness. His tongue filled me with a need for release. And as my back arched, I covered his face in my juices as his hands gripped my hips.

"Come for me," he growled from the depths of my cunt.

And just like that, I came undone.

"Oh—my—God," I choked out.

My legs jumped and my toes curled when Lance flattened his tongue against my swollen mound. He held his position, allowing me to use his face however I pleased. I tugged at his face only to push it away. I wanted more, and yet my body couldn't take it. It hurt so good, and I dug my heels into his back as tears crested my eyes. I'd never felt so amazing. No, scratch that, I'd felt that amazing only one time in my life.

And that had been last night.

"Oh, Lance," I whispered and my body collapsed.

He caught me effortlessly before his ass touched down to the floor. He gathered me in his lap, cradling me as if I were nothing but a child.

For a second there, I thought I had envisioned the kiss he placed against my forehead.

But the lingering heat embedded it into my conscious mind.

"Take your time," he murmured. "Gather yourself."

I swallowed hard. "But—but you don't—"

He shook his head. "Not here. Not now."

Not now?

Did that mean there was a chance for some other time?

Either way, it wasn't like I had a chance to move. The orgasm his tongue had teased out of my body drained me of whatever pre-caffeinated energy I'd woken up with that morning, and I relaxed into his embrace. He blanketed me away from the world, his massive muscles wrapped around me as if to protect me. I tucked my face into the crook of his neck. He sat there, in the middle of my hallway, holding me as if there weren't anything else important in all the world.

Why didn't Blade treat me like this?

"You can't blame it all on him," Lance said.

I peeked one eye open. "What?"

"Blade. You can't blame it all on him."

I picked my head up. "How did you know—"

"Pike has taught us a thing or two about body language. Your sigh said it all."

I scooted out of his lap and leaned against the wall, facing him with my legs spread open lazily. "I sighed?"

He chuckled. "Yeah, you did."

I snickered and tried to bury the smirk rising upon my face. "Well, I can blame him."

He shrugged. "If we had been truthful with you, would you have come with us?"

"I guess we'll never know."

His gaze danced in between mine. "Trishelle."

"Who?"

"Trishelle."

"Who's that?"

His gaze fell against the wall over my shoulder. "A girl the three of us used to... you know."

"Fuck?"

He grimaced. "Love."

I paused. "The three of you were in love with the same woman?"

He nodded. "It's not for everyone. It took us all by surprise. But, you know, under the right circumstances."

I tilted my head as my brow stitched itself together. "What happened to her?"

I could have sworn his blinking got quicker. "She died."

My heart broke for him. "I'm so sorry, Lance."

His stare dropped into his lap. "She was in trouble, like you are, and we promised to help her out. Things spiraled, like they always do—"

"Does that mean things are going to spiral with me?"

"I'm trying to tell you why Blade treated you the way he did, and you're concerned about you?"

I shrugged. "No one else is."

"We are," he said curtly.

"No, you are. I'm not so sure about him yet."

"Why do you think he did what he did?"

I scoffed. "To fuck me over."

"No, to keep you safe. We knew without a shadow of a doubt that if we were upfront with you, you never would've come with us. Blade placed himself in the line of fire—"

"Jesus, Lance, he didn't take a damn bullet. He fucked me."

"And you think he wouldn't have wanted to do that under better circumstances?"

I leaned heavily against the wall. "He didn't seem to care at the time."

Lance pressed himself up onto his feet with a grunt. "Well, he does. When Trishelle died, it fucked all of us up. Blade clings to things like that. He's more emotional than anyone gives him credit for, and he struggles with things."

I looked up at him. "Like fucking me to get me back to a place where I'd be safe."

He stuck his hand down toward me. "Exactly."

I stared at him . "How did she die?"

He wiggled his fingers. "Let's get you back to—"

"How did she die, Lance?"

He sighed. "Give me your hand and I'll tell you."

So, I took the deal. I took his hand and when he yanked me up from the floor, he pressed his lips to the shell of my ear.

"She killed herself," he murmured.

I closed my eyes and sighed. "Lance, I'm so sor—"

He released me and started toward the kitchen. "You need to make a choice, Dalia."

"What choice?"

He scooped up my bag from the floor. "You know we're not good men. So you need to make sure you know that going forward."

I shrugged. "From where I'm standing, I don't see how this world could make such wonderful things like you guys bad."

He stared at me for a while. So long, in fact, that I almost asked him if he was all right . But a roar off in the distance pulled him out of his trance.

"Get in the room," Lance commanded.

"What? Why?" I asked.

The roar grew greater as he tossed my bag back into the hall-way. "Get into your bedroom and stay there. Now!"

"Lance, if you guys are going to protect me, you have to fill me in on—"

He stalked toward me and grabbed my arm so hard that it made me yelp.

"Ah!"

"If we're going to protect you, then you better get used to

not knowing all the answers beforehand. We'll talk later, but you need to get your ass into that—"

CRASSSSSHHHHH!

The sound of glass shattering made me shriek. Well, I would have shrieked had Lance not slapped his hand against my mouth. He charged down the hallway, gliding me on the tips of my toes before he tossed me into my bedroom. I watched him withdraw a gun I hadn't even realized he had on his hip.

How the fuck had I missed the goddamn gun on his hip?

"Stay there," he growled before slamming the door closed.

Glass continued to shatter, and I scrambled to get into my bathroom. I grabbed a baseball bat that I kept in the corner and held it over my shoulder, ready to put all those years of softball in high school to good use. I forced my breathing to steady. I silenced it altogether once my heart came down from the rafters of panic that had held me hostage for what felt like forever. And as I stood there, waiting for death, I wondered what the hell I had gotten myself into.

Who the fuck were these guys?

Just as quickly as the roar had kicked up, it faded away. Was that a good thing? Were they gone? I kept an ear locked on the sound, listening to it fade into nothingness until all I heard was the sound of my own breathing. Of the blood, rushing through my ears and attempting to drown out the panicked tears that begged to surface.

I had to stay strong, though.

Because whether or not I liked it, these men were my only hope for answers.

"Dalia?" Lance asked as the door whipped open.

"Lance," I said breathlessly, dropping the bat.

I rushed toward him, ready to catapult into his arms. But before I could throw my arms out toward his neck, he pulled a brick out from behind his back.

"They tossed this through the dining room window."

I took it from him. "A brick?"

"Turn it over."

And when I did, I found writing in black sharpie on the back.

We're coming for you, Dalia.

I gasped and dropped the brick. "Holy shit."

Lance caught it before it hit the ground. "There's two more out there just like it. They know where you live. We've got to get you back to the clubhouse."

That was explanation enough for me. "Let's go, then."

He shook his head. "First, we wait."

"Wait? For what!?"

He set the brick on the bathroom countertop. "For Pike and Blade. I've already messaged them. We're taking the long way back to the clubhouse and they're going to do a patrol while they're out."

"A patrol?"

He walked up to me and cupped my cheeks. "You're safe with us, Dalia. We've got you. But you're wrapped up in something nasty, and I'm afraid it's because of—"

"—the man I watched you kill."

"Be careful who you say that to."

I swallowed hard. "Tell me you're the good guys."

"We're not the ones trying to kill you. Isn't that proof enough?"

And while I wasn't sure of anything any longer, one thing was for certain. I felt safe with the three of them. Protected. Taken care of, even if I was pissed at Blade. Even if they had tricked me into getting me back to their place. At least they had tricked me in order to protect me.

I looked back over at the brick sitting on the countertop. That was the proof. Proof that I wasn't safe without them. Proof that I had bore witness to something someone wanted to kill me over.

Which meant I had to do what they said to stay alive.

"When will they get here?" I asked softly.

When he sighed, it almost sounded like relief. "Ten minutes. Then we'll all head out together."

So as we stood there waiting for the other two to show up, I thought about all the vacation time I had racked up. All the hours I had yet to cash in because my life had been chained to the bar downstairs. I loved what I did for work, but if being with them had made me a target, didn't that mean the bar was a target so long as I was there?

Maybe it was time for me to cash in some of that vacation, if I could find someone to cover Lisa's shifts.

Because if something happened to my girls while they were working, I'd never be able to forgive myself.

14

PIKE

"Goddamn it," I spat, parking my bike beside Lance's.

"Fuck, is that—"

"Glass," I said, ripping my helmet off. "They busted the windows."

"Dalia!" Blade exclaimed as he tore off toward the staircase.

"Lance!" I followed behind him.

"Dalia! Dalia! Where are you?!"

"Blade?" she called out.

I grabbed Blade's arm and whipped him around. "She's fine. They're both fine, all right?"

The panicked look in his eye wasn't what worried me. It was the unfocused glare. I'd seen it a few times before, right after—

"Blade?" Dalia asked.

He yanked out of my grasp and whipped around but stayed rooted to his place. "Are you all right?"

Dalia looked him up and down. "Yeah, are you all right?"

Blade swallowed hard before he cleared his throat. "Where's Lance?"

Dalia narrowed her eyes and thumbed over her shoulder. "Getting my bag."

Lance came around the corner. "We have to go. Now. They know where she lives."

"Gimme," I said, holding out my hands.

Lance tossed me the bag. "You take the east side. Blade, take the middle. I'll wrap Dalia around the west side and we meet back at the clubhouse. Got it?"

But Blade hadn't unlocked his stare from Dalia. "Are you sure you're all right?"

She snickered. "Do you really care?"

"Yes, he cares," Lance said flatly.

Blade finally turned to face me. "You heard the man. Let's go."

I'd never seen someone cling to a person so badly in all my life. I rode next to Lance, ready to take my exit and patrol the streets looking for those goddamn thugs. And even from where I sat perched on my bike, I saw how white Dalia's knuckles became from clinging to Lance so tightly.

I hated that she had gotten wrapped up into all of this.

Especially with how things went down with Blade this morning.

"Blade, you good?" I asked.

"Fine," he said flatly.

"Right. Okay, well, if you get into trouble—"

"Trouble's my middle name," he growled.

"Meet back at the clubhouse," Lance said. "And until then? Radio silence."

I reached up and pressed the button on the outside of my helmet. Radio silence meant no transmissions of any sort until we got to our final destination, just in case someone was listening in. The problem with technology was that so long as it was hooked up to a broad spectrum of Wi-Fi or Bluetooth, it could be hacked. So, while the guys could stay connected on their bikes, it left us vulnerable to anyone passing by who knew anything about basic hacking.

Hence, the buttons to disengage all technological aspects of the helmets I developed for us.

It took me damn near half an hour to get back to the clubhouse, but when I did, I found Dalia still clinging to Lance. Blade's bike sat in the dirt, tipped over onto its side with the front door of the clubhouse hanging wide the fuck open. I shook my head as I pulled up to Lance's right side. I propped up my bike, discarded my helmet, and walked over to a trembling Dalia whose hands were red from hanging onto Lance's leather jacket.

"She's terrified," Lance murmured.

"Can you blame her?" I asked.

"Hey," she said breathlessly.

I placed my hand on top of hers. "Hey there, cutie."

She snickered. "You guys and your pet names. It's insane, really."

I massaged her hand. "Can you blame us? You're pretty cute."

"No woman wants to be cute."

"Well," I said, finally loosening her fingertips, "'sexy' seemed a bit strong for the moment."

"Never."

I grinned. "Noted."

I slid my free hand around her back and all the way down her opposing arm. With her one hand already disengaged from Lance's leather jacket, I cupped her other hand and massaged it as well. She sighed heavily as she released the man, her entire body flushed from head to toe. How hard she had been clinging to him and for how long, I had no idea. But when she collapsed into my arms, I scooped her up and held her against my chest.

"There we are, there's a good girl," I whispered.

She curled tightly against me. "Where are you taking me?"

I started up the porch steps. "To a bedroom at the back of the clubhouse. You'll be safe there."

"In the back?"

I turned us sideways to go in through the front door. "Uh huh. That means if anyone tries to get to you here, they'll have to go through us."

Her entire form shivered in my grasp. "O-o-o—okay."

I'd kill them. All of them. I'd pop their heads off their necks and set up their arms and legs for a fucking bowling match. How dare they spook such an amazing woman. How dare they think they wielded that kind of power in *our* town.

I wouldn't stop until we slaughtered all of them.

Until we staked their bowling ball heads on spikes for the animals of the woods around us to feed on.

"Here we are," I said, walking into the room.

Blade quietly slipped out without so much as a glance in our direction, and even though I wanted to go after him, I tucked it away for another moment. Right now, Dalia needed me. She needed us. She needed to know that she was safe. So, I walked her over to the bed and placed her against the freshly-changed sheets.

No doubt, courtesy of Blade.

"There we go," I said as I lowered her.

She didn't let go of me, though. "Is it safe? Are we okay?"

I stroked my fingers through her hair. "You're very safe. It's okay to let go, I promise."

And to my surprise, she released me.

"So," I said, taking a small step back and rolling my shoulders. "What do you think?"

She gazed around the room. "Is there a bathroom?"

I pointed to the opened door in the corner. "Right over there. Got a stand-up shower and a bath, so have at it."

"You saying I stink?"

"What? No," I said, shaking my head. "I'm just saying that some people—"

She swung her legs over the edge of the bed. "Towels?"

"In the bathroom."

Her voice grew more and more clipped as she spoke. "Fresh sheets?"

I thumbed over my shoulder. "There's a linen closet right across the hallway from—"

She stood to her feet and kept looking around the room. "TV?"

"The remote control on the bedside table rolls down a projector. From there, you can—"

"Kitchen?"

I drew in a deep breath. "Dalia."

"What?"

I tilted my head. "Okay, we'll do it your way. If I can guess the magical combination of things that will help you calm the fuck down, I get to join you while you do them. Deal?"

She rolled her eyes. "Whatever game you're trying to play, I'm not in the mood."

I walked over to her and placed my hands on her shoulders. She still refused to look at me, so I moved my head with hers until she had no choice but to give up the goose. However, when she finally stared me directly in my face, I didn't see anger behind her eyes.

I saw fear.

Unadulterated, chaotic fear.

"Fine," she said flatly. "Go ahead. Take your best shot."

And it was all the entrance I needed. "You're going to want to put on that little string bikini I see poking out of the top of your suitcase. Then, you're going to want to grab that book of yours that you constantly have stuffed in your purse."

She blinked. "How do you know—"

I placed my finger against her lips. "I'll take you out back, get you situated in our hot tub, and then I'll have Blade put together a little fruit and cheese board while I make up a nice pitcher of frozen margarita for you. You can relax out there as long as you want, and when you come back inside, I'll give you a full-body massage to help with the pain in your hip that I'm sure is constant."

She slowly backed away from my grasp before the edge of the bed caught her in the back of her knees. She fell to the plush comforter, bouncing softly as her jaw slowly dropped into her lap.

"How did you... How could... What..."

I backed up until I pressed against the wall opposite of her. "Take your time."

She glared at me before her shoulders slumped. "You guys have a hot tub?"

I barked with laughter. "Extra large, too. Fits all of us, if necessary."

"Kinky."

My smile fell into a grin. "So, you accept?"

"How could you have possibly known about my hip? Or the book in my purse? You've never even seen inside my purse."

God, I loved it when I was spot on. "It's written all over you, Dalia. One simply has to pay attention."

I wasn't sure what kind of reaction I expected, but when I saw those headlights engage beneath her splotchy black tank top, my cock tightened. I wanted to slip my mouth up that shirt and cling to those puckered tits of hers until she caved to me.

I cleared my throat and quickly pulled myself out of my trance. "Get into your bathing suit. I'll get everything else set up."

And as I made my way toward the bedroom door, her soft voice followed me.

"Is it safe for me to be outside, though?" she asked.

I peered over my shoulder at her. "It's safe anywhere as long as you're with one of us. Got it?"

She nodded. "Got it."

"Good. Now, take your time getting ready. Today is yours for the taking."

I closed her door behind me and couldn't help the smile that crossed my face. Goddamn it, the woman was a spitfire, and I knew I was in trouble. I paused for a moment, taking in how familiar it felt. Having a woman in that back room. Catering to her in order to get her to settle down. Walking her through the dangers of what she had unwillingly walked into, despite our best efforts to keep a low profile.

She even looked like Trishelle in a way, with that fiery red hair and those freckles that donned her body.

I only hoped things ended better with Dalia than they did with her.

"Blade!" I barked.

"What?"

I soared into the kitchen. "I need one of those fruit and cheese boards you're so fond of."

"Why?"

I gathered the ingredients for the pitcher of margarita that had been promised. "Dalia's going to relax in the hot tub for a while."

Lance chuckled and walked into the kitchen behind me. "Trying to play catch-up with me and Blade?"

I whipped around and my eyes widened. "You did not."

He shrugged. "What can I say? Orgasms calm the nerves."

Blade chuckled as he walked by, holding out his hand for a fist bump. Lance tapped his against Blade's, and I held my arms out while grasping the bottles of ingredients I hadn't set down yet.

"You're a fucking animal, you know that?"

Lance smirked. "Ain't got no other setting."

"And no," I said, turning toward the blender. "I'm not playing catch-up with you idiots. I've got my own way of doing things."

Blade shook his head. "Guess it's better than sloppy seconds."

"Hey," Lance said sharply.

I measured out the ingredients. "Third time is always a charm, fellas. Thanks for keeping her warm for me."

"Did you call the guys?" Blade asked, sliding one of his knives out of the wooden holder on the counter.

"Hold that thought," I said, putting the lid on the blender.

I pressed the button that started up the machine, and for a brief moment the whirring sound drowned out all of the bullshit the last few days had thrown at us. I hadn't even scrubbed all of the blood off my fucking boots from that evening, and here we were. Hoarding away a delectable woman in the hopes of keeping her safe.

Just like last time.

I turned off the blender. "You're good."

Lance didn't hesitate. "I called all of the guys while Dalia was outside digging her fingernails into my jacket. They're all on board with the plan to keep her here so she's safe."

"Good," Blade said.

I poured the margarita into the glass pitcher and walked it over to the freezer. "Did you tell them about the broken windows?"

Lance nodded. "They know everything."

"I can't fucking believe they know where she lives," Blade murmured.

I stuck the pitcher into the freezer so it wouldn't melt. "I suppose it's not that hard to figure out. All you need to see is her coming or going once, and that's it."

And when none of the guys answered me, my head fell back.

"Shit," I hissed.

"There it is," Lance said.

"Knew it would click over eventually," Blade said.

I turned toward our president. "They're stalking her."

Lance shook his head. "I think they started out by tailing us, and when they saw us heading toward the bar more than once, they decided to check things out."

"So, you're saying they saw us interacting with her, saw her flirting with us, and decided to stake her out, too?" I asked.

Blade sighed, turning to me with the food board or whatever he called it in his hand. "We got her into this situation."

"Then," I said and pulled the margarita pitcher back out of the freezer, "we get her out of it."

"That's the plan," Lance said, pinching the bridge of his nose.

Blade brushed past me. "By the way, any ideas on how to get our hands on that footage they've got? We have to get in front of that before shit really hits the fan."

I turned to face him "You mean, shit hasn't already hit the fan?"

"Wrong question," Lance said.

I rolled my eyes. "He's right."

Blade scoffed. "Then, what's the right question?"

"Pike?" Lance asked.

I plucked an aluminum straw from the cabinet and stuck it into the pitcher. "What the hell are they planning on doing with it?"

Lance pointed at me. "Bingo."

Blade opened the door with his hip. "I figured blackmail

was what we had settled on already. Especially if they're wanting to push us out and claim this town for themselves."

"Shh, shh, shh," I said as footsteps sounded above our heads.

We all went silent as Dalia's footfalls walked across the ceiling. We turned as she made her way for the stairs, and the soft plopping of her bare feet made me smile. Hearing her up and moving was enough for me to know how strong she really was deep down. Most people would have relegated themselves to a bedroom until the nightmare was over. Not her, though.

And when she came into the kitchen with a towel slung over her forearm in nothing but that green string bikini?

My cock cried out for mercy.

"A straw in the pitcher," she said as her bikini clung to her curves with all their might. "My kind of margarita."

I nodded toward the door. "Follow Blade. The hot tub's right out here. You'll have a great view of the lake while you're relaxing."

She sauntered past me, her curves moving with every step she took. "Sounds great. Thanks."

And when she found her way out the door with Blade staring at her ass, I tossed Lance a wink.

"Don't wait up."

Lance chuckled. "Trust me, I won't."

15

———

PIKE

"Thanks, you guys. I appreciate it."

I set the pitcher of margarita on the ground next to the edge of the hot tub and Blade bent forward to set his board down. His gaze roamed along Dalia's legs, slowing his descent to the ground before he released the food altogether. I watched him come back up, stalking her with that brooding gaze of his. And when he finally managed to turn himself away, he smirked.

"Have fun," he said, brushing past me.

"Oh, I will," I murmured to myself, holding my hand out to Dalia.

"You will what?" she asked as she faced me.

I wiggled my fingers. "Enjoy watching you relax."

She snickered. "Uh huh."

She slid her fingers against my palm, and I eased her down the steps. Her groan of relaxation bubbled through my body, hardening my already attentive dick. She submerged herself in the steaming water, her skin crawling with goosebumps as she sat down on the stone bench we had laid ourselves when installing the damn thing in the first place.

"Oh, this is paradise," she sighed, dipping herself below the water's surface.

It gave me time to shove my hand down my pants to rearrange my cock.

"Not getting in with me?" she asked, piercing the surface.

I watched her stand in the middle of the tub, water dripping down her breasts. Her string bikini tugged against her curves, and I found myself jealous that they were able to mold to her skin while my fingertips sat naked, and bare.

"Figured you wanted to relax after all the excitement," I said with a shrug.

She sat back down in the hot tub. "Well, someone promised me a full-body rub, and what better place to do that then with the relaxation of hot water all around us?"

I swallowed hard, feeling my dick leaking against my boxers. Fucking hell, was she serious? Did she have any idea what she did to us? To me? Yes, she probably did, hence that cheeky little grin on her face as she scooted over on the bench.

"Come on," she said, tapping the surface of the water next to her, "there's plenty of room for both of us."

I had to swallow again, but not because of nerves. I never got nervous, not even in the presence of sheer, unadulterated beauty. I had to swallow because the growl creeping up the back of my throat threatened to give me away.

And I was sure the last thing she wanted was yet another man pawing at her body.

"All right," I said, taking off my leather cut. "Give me a second."

While I didn't have a bathing suit on, I stripped down to my boxers and climbed in. How men wore those boxer-brief things, I'd never know. They were too tight. Never let the boys breathe. So, with my regular boxers flapping in the wind that kicked up, I eased myself down the stairs as Dalia turned over in the water, planting her forearms on the concrete edge.

"Ready when you are," she said.

I could have sworn I saw her stick her ass out just a tad. Just enough to drive me fucking wild. There was no hiding how hard my cock had grown. It was rigid with need, and as the jet bubbles kicked up, I watched them pop against her skin. The soft jiggling of her body with the movement of the water was too much to bear. My hands itched to slip between her thighs. My cock begged to sink against her walls.

It's just a massage, Pike. Get a grip.

I dipped my hands into the water, then crept them toward her. I started at her lower back, kneading and pressing my thumbs into the little butt dimples she had just above her juicy ass cheeks. They were so cute, and every single part of me wanted to kiss them until she demanded more.

"Mmmm, so good," she groaned.

She sighed as her forehead dropped to her arms and her body completely relaxed. She knelt on the stone bench, her legs frogging out with every stroke of my hands against her back. I worked my way up, paying close attention to either side of her spine, because Jesus fuck, her back was locked up.

"Do you get these often?" I asked.

"Hmmm?"

"Massages," I said as my hands made their way to her shoulders. "You're very tight. You should get them more often."

"I'm free every morning when I first wake up."

I snickered. "Don't tempt me with a good time, now."

"Hey, you're the one who started it."

Her giggle spread like wildfire along my skin. It made the hairs on the nape of my neck stand at attention. My arms followed suit, puckering so tightly that I had to stop and itch. This woman had crawled under my skin and made her home in my muscles. Every sound elicited a reaction. But after taking a moment to crack my knuckles, I got back to work.

"Shit."

"Ugh, right there."

"Jesus, Pike, where did you learn how to do this?"

I didn't even try to hide how stiff my cock had become. Every time it brushed against her ass, my balls jumped. Every time my hands ran up and down her fluid, soft skin, my cock thickened on the spot. I rolled my knuckles down either side of her back before placing my thumbs in those cute little divots at the base of her spine. Then, I pressed in and slowly slid them toward her sides.

"Keep, ugh, doing that," she moaned.

I continued with the fluid motion, and slowly, her body crept back against mine. Every time I shifted my pelvis away, she somehow found the length to elongate her back and shove that ass right into my groin once again. It got to the point where she was ready to push off the fucking edge just to find me, so I decided to lay it on thick.

Let's see how you like this, then.

I leaned into her, my cock settling between her ass cheeks as I dug my hands into her lower back. The groan that escaped her lips damn near made me blow my load against her, and I had to grit my teeth just to make it through.

"God, why does that feel so good?" she asked breathlessly.

"You're on your feet for many hours a day. That takes its toll after a while."

"You might be in trouble now that I know you can do this."

"Believe me," I said with a snicker, "I'd have no issues touching your body every single day, if that's what you needed."

She placed her cheek on top of her hands on the concrete. "That a promise?"

I surprised her and slid my hands along the globe of her ass.

She gasped softly, lifting it for my viewing pleasure as I leaned back long enough to take one of her thighs into the palm of my hand. I massaged in soft circles, making my way to her inner thighs before hopping to her other leg.

And when she whimpered, I knew I had her exactly where I wanted her.

"Yes," I said, massaging the inside of her other thigh. "That's a promise."

She moaned softly. "I'll—oh—hold you to it."

I couldn't stand it. I had to have her. I had to taste her. I had to feel her coming against my cock, or my mouth, or whatever part of me she wanted for her nefarious pleasures. However, I drew deep breaths in through my nose and kept my cool, even as my dick found the slit in my boxers.

Floating in the water like a bomb ready to strike.

"Pike," she said breathlessly.

I placed one hand on each thigh and dug the heels of my hands into her hamstrings. Jesus fuck, her body was completely locked up, and I knew it was, at least in part, due to the stress of the situation she had found herself in. She scooted her knees a little closer together, which damn near shoved her ass cheeks back into the palms of my hands. And as I continued to massage the backs of her legs, she bucked.

It was the smallest of movements, but she bucked that ass back against my hands.

"Pike," she whispered.

I knew what she wanted, but who didn't enjoy a bit of fore-play every now and again?

"Yes?" I asked cheekily.

"Pike, please," she whimpered.

I leaned toward her, pressing my hard-on back between her ass cheeks and heard her gasp. I placed my lips along the shell of her ear. I felt the jet bubbles kick back up, no doubt in part thanks to my wingmen who were, also no doubt, watching the show.

So, why not give them one?

"Please, what?" I whispered.

She drew in a broken breath. "I—I just—"

"Yes?" I asked as my hand roamed along the insides of her thighs.

She spread her legs more for me, sinking deeper into the water. "I just need—"

I lapped at her earlobe softly. "You need what, gorgeous?"

And just as my fingertips reached out for the pathetic scrap of fabric she used to clothe her pussy in that bikini...

"Pike," Lance said gruffly.

And I knew what that meant.

"What's up?" I asked as I froze.

"Huh?" Dalia asked lazily.

Lance's face had settled into determined stone. "You gotta come inside."

"Why?" she asked.

I pulled away from her and moved toward the edge closest to Lance. "What's going on?"

He thumbed over his shoulder. "Inside, now. Let the poor girl rest, for fuck's sake."

"No," Dalia whimpered.

I turned to face her and dipped my lips down, placing a kiss right against her temple. Then I whispered a soft promise in her ear that I knew she'd cling to for the rest of the day.

"Just a little taste of what's to come later."

"Promise?" she whispered.

I nodded and started out of the hot tub. "You have my word."

Her gaze bored a hole in between my shoulder blades as I climbed out of the hot tub. I wasted no time tucking my dick back into its confines before I scooped my clothes up from the patio floor. Lance tossed me a towel and I got it wrapped around my waist, and I stole one last glance over my shoulder at the lovely angel I had to abandon for reasons that I was sure were important.

But I regretted having to leave her.

She deserved more than that.

"Pike!" Lance exclaimed.

I rushed inside and tossed my clothes onto the kitchen counter. "What the fuck gives?"

"Our question's already been answered," Blade said.

It took me a second to register what he was saying. "Fuck."

Lance nodded and reached for his phone on the kitchen counter. "Come here, I've got a video to show you."

"Blackmail?" I asked.

Blade puffed out his cheeks. "I think it's worse, at this point."

What the hell was worse than blackmail?

"Here, watch," Lance said, handing me the phone.

The two men perched over both of my shoulders as I hit the white play button in the middle of the screen. But I already knew who I was staring at. The face it had been paused on.

It was Dirge, The Sentinel's President.

"Well, well, well," Dirge said when I pressed play, "what a tangled web we weave."

"Asshole," I murmured.

"Keep watching," Lance said gruffly.

"So, we seem to have a bit of a conundrum on our hands," he continued, the camera panning down.

"Do we know who's holding the—"

Blade cut me off. "Just shut up and watch it."

And when the camera finished panning down, I realized why.

"Shit," I hissed.

"Don't do it!" Phil exclaimed.

Somehow, they had gotten their hands on our newest prospect.

"Now that you understand who you're working with," Dirge said before he cracked his hand against Phil's face, "you've got two options. One, give us a slice of your operations, and your man here gets to live."

"It's a trap!" Phil exclaimed. "They're going to kill me an—"

Dirge punched him against his temple, and it was lights out for our man.

"Fuck," I growled.

"Or two," Dirge said, turning to face the camera again, "your man gets his cock staked on a piece of wood in the middle of town for all to see. We'll upend your operations. Expose your money-washing schemes. We'll chase you out like the dogs you are without a second thought. So, choose wisely."

"Goddamn it! Leave him alone!" I bellowed.

Someone gripped Phil's hair before holding up his bleeding face. Whoever the fuck was wielding the camera got a close-up shot of his crooked nose, and we didn't need a doctor to know it had been broken. My blood sizzled. My hand gripped Lance's phone so tightly that it cracked. And as a small splinter started at the side of the screen, Dirge's fucking face returned.

"Let this be a lesson for that little plaything of yours as well," he spat. "Give me what I want and get your man back or she's next."

"No!" I roared.

"Life's full of tough choices, isn't it?" Dirge asked.

The video ended and the picture returned to the beginning.

Where Dirge's fucking face stared directly at us, as if he had been watching us all along.

16

────────

LANCE

I snatched my phone out of Pike's hand before he did any more damage to it. But to be honest, I couldn't blame him.

"Who the fucking Christ are these assholes!?" Pike exclaimed.

"Easy," Blade said as he nodded toward the door. "She can still hear us."

"Well, I think she should at this point!"

"Can it," I said flatly.

I tucked my cell into my back pocket before I ran my hands through my hair. Who the fuck were these demon spawn who had rolled up onto our turf? There was no way any of this was a coincidence. No way in hell they had come after us. We had kept a low profile. Kept our mouths shut. We sent different men to wash money every single time so that no one could nail any one of us down.

So, why the hell had these fuckers come into town in the first place?

"We're missing something," I said as I slid my hands down my face.

"No fucking shit," Blade said.

"Our town isn't safe," Pike said, storming out of the kitchen. "They're not safe until every single one of those motherfuckers has been eliminated."

"Pike," I said.

"I'm ready for war," he said, panting for air. "I'm ready to take those motherfucks by the neck and just—"

"Pike!" Blade bellowed.

That stopped him in his tracks because Blade rarely raised his voice. "What?"

I sighed. "We need those deductive skills of yours. We have to try and get Phil back."

He straightened his back before he held out his hand. "Give me the video."

I pulled my phone back out. "You gonna keep a lid on it this time?"

"I make no promises."

I tossed him the phone anyway. "Do your best."

Pike scoffed as he opened up the video again. "Only if you let me do my worst when the time comes."

"We'll all get that time if we play our cards right," I said.

"Do we even know if he's alive?" Blade asked.

"One question at a time," I said.

I watched Pike's eyes as it flittered all across the screen. He replayed it once. Twice. Three separate times, and the entire time, he kept murmuring to himself. I walked over and peered over his shoulder, torturing myself with the image of Phil's bloody, lifeless face on that screen.

If the man had survived the kind of beating it was clear he had taken, it'd take a miracle and a half to patch him back up.

"I know where he is," Pike said, handing my phone back to me.

I snickered. "I knew you could do it."

"Where are we headed?" Blade asked as he strode up to us.

Pike raked his hands through his hair. "It's obvious they're in a warehouse. Judging by the state of the ceiling when the camera tilted up that way for a split second, it's been abandoned for a while. That narrows down where he could be. Assuming the guys are still in the area, which there's no reason not to think that because of how quickly they can access things, that leaves four main areas where Phil could be."

"And?" I asked.

"Right at the end of the video, there's a sound," Pike said, closing his eyes. "Took me a few times to pinpoint what it was, but it's the sound of a train."

I nodded. "They're on the south side of town, got it."

"Most likely near the main railway station. They've got a few abandoned buildings back there, and I'm sure one of them is where they're keeping Phil."

"Let's ride," I said, starting for the front door. "Blade."

"Yeah, yeah," he said with a sigh. "Stay behind with Dalia and babysit. I got it."

Pike scoffed. "If you consider that babysitting, then you didn't deserve the time you got with her in the first place."

Blade shrugged. "Not my fault you're already lovesick."

I whipped around and pinned him with a look. "You're the only one who's got the skills to defend this entire house if this is a trap to pull us away from her. You stay here, keep a lookout, and slaughter anyone who isn't us. Got it?"

Blade continued to stare Pike down. "Perfect. Just get him out of my face."

"With pleasure," Pike hissed.

"Good. Pike? You're with me. Tuck in the attitude and let's go get our man."

"If he's even still alive," Pike murmured.

I stepped in front of him and wrapped my fist up in his shirt. "Change the attitude or stay behind. We don't win anything with shit attitudes. That goes for both of you, too. Man up and suck it up. We're at war. Act like it."

"You're right," Pike said, shrugging off my touch. "My bad. Now, let's go. If Phil's still alive, we don't have much time."

"Lead the way," I said, following behind him.

I wanted brain matter spilled on the ground. I wanted necks broken and hearts being roasted over an open fucking fire so we could feed it to the animals of our woods. We couldn't get across town quickly enough. Mostly because we had decided that taking the car was the best route. Bikes were too loud, and if there was a body to haul back for a burial, we couldn't do that on our bikes either. We weaved our way through town, keeping off main roads and staying alert for ambushes as our tires rumbled over the train tracks.

Which signaled our arrival in Death Toll.

"Right," Pike said.

I blew through the yellow light and rubbernecked along my side of the road. We passed warehouse after warehouse, searching for any signs of bikes, people, or life. I waited for Pike's instruction. I waited for him to tell me when to pull over so we could search one of the many abandoned buildings that sat on that end of town. Death Toll was an apt description, since nothing sat on the south side of town except for the dwindling railroad system the town still used.

And even that was about to go under from the rumors I'd heard all across town.

"Anything?" I asked.

"None of these buildings match," Pike said.

"Maybe the inside doesn't match the outside."

He shook his head. "Not with the building Phil's in. Acoustically, there should be—"

I waved my hand in the air to shut him up. "Just tell me where to go. I know you've got this."

"Then, shut up with the idiotic suggestions and keep driving."

I let it slide, but it was the only time I'd allow it. For once, we had been caught with our pants down around our ankles, and it had been a while since we'd been attacked like that. Usually, we were the aggressors. The ones with the plan of action should things go south. So, playing catch-up and trying to get our bearings wasn't something we were used to.

We were all on edge.

But I needed them to hold it the fuck together better than they were.

"Is there anywhere else you can hear that train from?" I asked.

"Train whistles usually echo three to five miles out, further if it's a clear night. But that video wasn't taken at night, so we're working with a five-mile radius in the most perfect of conditions."

"Got a map?"

He pointed to his head. "Keep driving until we have no buildings, then we'll hit up the highway."

"The highway?"

He pointed behind us. "Death Valley's three miles from here. That's the next place to check."

"That's the most populated highway in the state."

"Which is why we're going to check and branch out from there. Keep driving, then we'll divert onto the highway with the ramp that's up the road."

With every mile that fell behind us, I grew weary. Phil was out there with no protection and no way to access us. He had only pledged our crew a few months back. He was a child in this world. We hadn't even issued him his own weapon yet because he hadn't passed his marksman training. The thought crippled me. I had left one of my men vulnerable to the elements, and there was a good fucking chance he was dead.

I'd never be able to live with it if Phil was dead.

What the hell was I going to tell his mother?

"Keep driving," Pike said. "Highway is about half a mile up the road."

"So, none of these?" I asked.

"Nope."

Easing onto the highway wasn't a difficult job but getting ourselves turned around so that we could patrol the back half of Death Toll was arduous. We had to go four miles out of our way just to make a fucking U-turn in a place that wouldn't draw attention, and every minute we wasted was another minute Phil was bleeding out somewhere.

"Stop!" Pike exclaimed.

I slammed on my brakes and horns blared from every direction. Tires squealed and cars wrapped around us as people flipped us the bird and told us to fuck off.

"What?" I asked, looking around. "What is it?"

But Pike simply pointed. "That's him, isn't it?"

I had to squint my eyes against the harsh summer sun to see what he was talking about, but when Phil's haggard body came into view, I pushed the gas pedal down as far as it could go.

"That's him, isn't it?" Pike asked.

"Let's get a closer look," I grumbled.

I veered my way toward the right-most lane of the highway, ignoring people screaming all sorts of obscenities at us. Some southern hospitality, right there. I didn't give a fuck, though, because the closer we grew to the lumbering, crooked figure, the more his features came into view.

"Holy shit, he's alive," I said breathlessly.

Pike rolled down his window. "Phil!"

He picked his head up and nothing but pain registered on his face.

"Phiiiiiiiiiil!" I bellowed, pulling off onto the right-hand shoulder of the highway.

Even before I got the car to a complete stop, Pike shoved his way out of the passenger's seat. He bolted toward Phil, who collapsed onto the grass just before Pike slid on his knees toward the man. I shoved my door open and took off, running as fast as I could toward Phil's crippled body. The sounds of the highway alone could have drowned out a child crying incessantly for its mother. But there was no containing the hemming and hawing of a man in pain.

"My God," Phil groaned as Pike tried to heave him up onto his feet. "I can't—I can't go—"

I grabbed his arm and tucked it around my shoulders. "On my count, Pike, you get him over my shoulders. Ready?"

"No, please," Phil begged.

"One," Pike said.

"Shit," Phil hissed.

"Two," I said.

Heaving him onto my shoulders peeled the most bombastic and blood-curdling scream I'd ever heard from a man out of his throat. My left ear rang with his shrieking as something warm and wet dripped along my neck.

"Get our doctor on the phone. And the guys. Get everyone to the bar now," I grunted, walking Phil back toward the car.

"On it," Pike said, pulling out his burner.

"Then get rid of the phone once you're done," I demanded.

"Yep," Pike said, dialing numbers.

"All right," I said, opening the back door, "just a bit longer, Phil. Stay with us. Keep your focus on my voice."

"My nose," he groaned.

"We'll get that fixed right up."

"My ribs."

I gingerly placed him in the backseat. Well, as gingerly as I could. But with the bruises and the blood that had caked its way all over his body, there was no way in hell we weren't moving him without some sort of pain spell. His eyes rolled into the back of his head. I hovered over him and tapped his cheek with my hand until he fluttered them back open. And as I steadied my breathing, I heard Pike instructing the doctor in the background.

"Just stay with us until we get back to the bar. There's so many good meds in store for you, boy."

Phil swallowed hard. "I'm—I'm sorry. They—had Mom, and—"

I narrowed my eyes. "They came to your house?"

"Ah!" Phil exclaimed, holding his stomach.

"Lance, we have to go," Pike said, placing his hand on my shoulder. "We don't have a lot of time."

I scooted out of the backseat. "Just stay awake, Phil, and that's an order!"

How the man survived, I didn't have a clue. But after racing back to the bar, the doctor injected Phil with morphine before attempting to move him. We came in through the back door, the guys all gathered around so prying eyes couldn't witness anything. And as I helped the doctor get Phil into the back room of our bar, he shooed us out behind the bar, leaving us all standing there, hoping for the best.

"Everyone!" I bellowed as I turned to face the filled bar. "Out! We are closed for today! Drinks are on us, just get your cards and get out!"

Mortar rushed out toward the crowd. "How long do you think they're going to be in there?"

Traeger made his way toward the door to usher everyone out. "It's neck-breaking time."

Even Riley growled, and Riley never said much of anything. "I'm ready to pump lead into every single one of those mother-fuckers. Who's with me!?"

The guys cheered, but when the doctor whipped open the door, he had a look on his face I'd never seen before. As the last person exited the bar, Traeger closed the door and turned off our neon "open" sign before throwing each and every lock.

I didn't like how any of this felt, especially with Blade alone at the clubhouse with Dalia.

"What is it?" I asked.

Dr. Higgenbaum thumbed over his shoulder. "He's fine. You guys can come see him."

I blinked. "What?"

The doctor sighed. "I mean, his nose is broken, yeah. But he's fine outside of that."

"What about his ribs?" Pike asked, rushing up to me.

The doctor shook his head. "They're not broken. They aren't even fractured. Bruised, sure, but not badly."

"So, where's his pain coming from?" Traeger asked, poking his head around my body.

"Poison," Dr. Higgenbaum said plainly. "He's been poisoned, but I've administered an antidote."

"He's going to be okay then?" I asked.

"It was a trap," Phil called out.

The doctor stepped off to the side and ushered us in with his arm. "He wants to talk to you guys."

I barged in. "Give us all a second, Doc."

"Sure thing," he said. "Anyone else want in?"

Somehow, we managed to squeeze every single one of the guys into that back room before Dr. Higgenbaum moved out to the bar to give us some privacy. Which was good, I suppose, because it meant we could all talk at once instead of relaying messages on unsecure phone networks.

"Feel free to make yourself a drink!" Pike called out to him.

"Did you say 'trap?'" I asked, hovering over Phil's head.

Phil pressed himself up with a grunt and Mortar rushed to his side. But Phil waved him off.

"Seriously," he said, swinging his legs over the wooden table we sometimes used as a hospital bed, "I'm bruised and my nose is throbbing, but that's it."

"That's it?" I asked.

He shrugged. "My stomach feels like shit, but Higgy said that's from the poison. Should flush out of my system in about twenty-four hours."

"But the blood," Traeger said.

Phil shook his head. "Most of it was fake. Funny camera angles. That sort of thing. It was a trap, you guys."

"How did you get to the highway?" I asked.

"They released me and told me to keep walking otherwise they'd kill my fucking mother. Can someone please go check on her?"

"I got you," Traeger said. "Mortar!"

"Already suited up. Let's go," the man said gruffly.

"Get us an update ASAP," I said as they made their way toward the back door.

"Absolutely. Phil!" Mortar called out.

"What?"

"Your mom got a favorite food or some shit?"

Phil drew in a deep breath. "That drive-thru taco place. She's all about the cheesy crunch shells."

"We'll get you that update soon," Mortar said.

"And no fucking my mom, Mort!" Phil called out.

I couldn't help but laugh because that was the kind of shit Mort did. He had always been a cougar-chaser. Even better if she had a kid or two. The laughter trickled through the guys until we heard them exit through the front door, and after the sound of their bikes faded into the distance, I turned my attention back to Phil.

"Did you see anything after they dumped you?" I asked. "What direction they went in? Who else was with Dirge? Anything like that?"

"No, you're not listening," Phil said breathlessly.

"Hey, you good?" Pike asked.

Phil went pale in the face, and I had to lunge at him to catch him before he collapsed back down into the bed.

"Someone, grab his feet!" I exclaimed.

Riley hopped to the task and shifted Phil's legs until we had him lying back down. The doctor came in to check his vitals, then instructed us to keep him laid down until the poison passed. He said something about it affecting his chemicals, or chemistry, and something about his brain. Balance. I didn't know. I didn't give a fuck. The only thing I cared about was the fact that Phil was alive.

He also had answers we needed.

"Hey, can you hear me?" I asked, hovering over him.

Phil reached up and gripped my jacket. "Distraction."

I blinked. "What?"

Phil swallowed hard. "It was a distraction. All of it."

Pike clicked his tongue. "Distraction from what?"

And that was when it clicked.

"Get back to the clubhouse. Now."

"What?" Pike asked.

I whipped around and fisted his shirt with both of my hands and heaved him up so close to my face that he danced on his tiptoes to keep himself steady.

"Find Blade and Dalia. Now!"

"You know," Dalia said, flopping down on my bed, "you're not much of a talker."

I ran my sharpening stone against my knife. "Nope."

"You hungry?" she asked, pointing to the half-eaten charcuterie board I had made for her.

"Nope."

"One of these sandwiches over here is for you."

"Nope."

"Thirsty?"

I peeked over at the barely-there margarita in the pitcher. "Nope."

"Are you going to say anything other than 'nope?'"

I grinned. "Nope."

She giggled, and it took everything I had to block out how angelic the sound felt settled against my ears. The last thing we needed was to get wrapped up in another tight pussy when hell was raining down on us. I'd heard the commotion downstairs. I heard Phil's agonizing cries. Thank fuck, they had found him alive.

But with those kinds of screams, I wasn't sure how long he'd be alive.

"Hey, babysitting isn't so bad," Dalia said. "At least you and I get to hang out."

I flickered my gaze toward her and continued sharpening my knife.

"Cat got your tongue?" she asked. "Because I've got a really nice candied B.L.T. that I tried to replicate downstairs in the fridge. Courtesy of a bit of inspiration from the other night."

My stomach rolled with a need for sustenance. "Did you make that potato salad that I keep smelling?"

"And here I thought you were only saying nope," she said, beaming with pride. "It's my mother's recipe. It's one of the few useful things she ever gave me."

I paused my sharpening stone. "Sounds like you and your mother had a rough relationship.

She leaned back against all the pillows. "That's just what I tell people. Sounds better than, 'I dicked around until it tasted good.'"

I tilted my head. "Then what happened with you and your mother?"

She shrugged. She did that a lot, and I didn't need Pike with me to know that she was masking some serious emotions with those shrugs.

"She left me on the side of the road when I was seven."

At first, I thought I hadn't heard her right. "She what?"

Dalia closed her eyes. "She got pissed that I kept sneaking food from the pantry when we couldn't afford all of the snacking I did, so she left me on the side of the road."

Maybe "serious" was an understatement. Who in the absolute fuck did that to their own flesh and blood? It made me sick. Whatever appetite I may have had, it got ripped away and tossed to the wolves. As I watched Dalia stare up at the ceiling, the tears glistened in her eyes before she blinked them away. The pain she carried in those curves of hers could tell stories ten times over, and it made my knives beg for blood.

Her mother's blood, specifically.

"Actually," I said, "I think I'll take that food now."

She bolted upright with a smile on her face. "You won't regret it. Here."

I took the plate from her and started with the potato salad. The flavors burst on the tip of my tongue, and somehow, she had gotten the potatoes to a point where they melted in the mouth. My eyes widened. I shoveled another large spoonful into my mouth before picking up half of the sandwich she had made.

And when I crunched down into it, my heart sank.

Jesus fuck, her candied bacon was better than mine.

"God," I groaned.

"Right?!" she said as she scooted to the edge of the bed. "It's great, isn't it? Took me forever to nail down the recipe. It's one of my favorite meals now."

I dipped the sandwich into the potato salad. "Consider it a favorite of mine now, too."

"Really?"

I nodded. "Really."

"You mean that?"

I stared her down and kept chewing. "Yep."

"I knew you'd like it."

"Though," I said, setting the sandwich down, "I could just be eating it out of courtesy. You *are* going through a rough time right now."

She barked with laughter. "There are many words that I associate with you, Blade. But courtesy isn't one of them."

"Really," I said, taking bite of the potato salad. "What words do you associate with me, then?"

She dangled her legs over the edge of the bed. "Quiet. Stubborn. Precise. Closed off."

"That's two words."

She smirked. "Technically, it was five. But I hear ya."

I shook my head. "I get why the guys want to share you."

"You do?"

"It's a bit more complicated than—"

It was the smallest noise, but it halted me in my tracks. I set my almost-empty plate down and held up my hand, silencing Dalia in her tracks.

"What is it?" she whispered.

I brought my finger to my lips. I closed my eyes and tilted my ear toward the door. Maybe I had simply misread a cue. Maybe the house was creaking. Maybe it had gotten windy outside. Maybe there was a storm approaching that caused one of the floorboards to—

TIP TAP.

"Come with me," I whispered, reaching for Dalia's hand.

"What's happening?"

I pulled her toward me and clapped my hand over her mouth. "You speak, you die. Understood?"

She nodded quickly as those wide eyes of hers teared up. I hated it for her. She was petrified, even though I knew she wanted to stay strong. I tore out of the bedroom and ripped the linen closet door open that sat adjacent to her room. I silenced my movements. I eased the door open and ushered her inside before slipping in and closing the door back behind me.

And that was when I heard it.

The soft pitter-patter of footsteps.

"What the hell is happening?" Dalia whispered, placing her lips as close to my ear as she could get.

"What was that?" a voice asked.

A gun cocked and my eyes widened. Without another word

spoken, I reached out and pushed the wall off to my right. It depressed inward and flipped to the side, exposing a narrow, hidden hallway that ran along the length of the house.

I beckoned for Dalia to take my hand, but she shook her head.

"I can't," she whispered.

"You don't have a choice," I whispered back.

"There. The room," the gruff voice said.

A tear trickled down Dalia's cheek and she peered through the slat of the door. Her entire body trembled. She shivered as goosebumps spread across her skin. Fear was taking over, erasing her ability to think clearly.

I took her hand and yanked her down the hallway.

"Come on," I hissed.

She fell toward me, and I cupped my hand against her mouth. I prayed with all my might that no one heard us as I dragged her down the hallway, away from the bedroom the men had already infiltrated. How the fuck had they gotten into the house? Where the fuck were the guys? Why had I not heard gunshots first?

She shoved me so hard that I stumbled backward, and it took all I had not to go crashing into the wall.

"You good?" I asked breathlessly.

She pointed at my face. "Do that again, and you're dead."

"If I hadn't done it, we'd both be dead. Now, are you coming or what?"

"Or what," she grumbled.

I reached for her hand, but she swatted it away. Whatever. I didn't care. If she wanted to die because she was too damn noisy, that was on her. But we had to get out of there before someone heard us.

"Follow me," I whispered.

"Can you tell me what the hell is—"

I craned my gaze over my shoulder. "If you don't fucking shut the hell up, Dalia, you'll get us both killed. Then, I won't be able to tell you how much I absolutely hate the idea of sharing you with anyone, much less Lance and Pike."

She snickered. "Well, you're just no fun."

"Yeah, yeah. Now, come on. Follow me."

Navigating our way through that house was a nightmare. Even though the tunnels ran parallel to the foundation of the house, we still had to slip out of the coat closet in the foyer to make a mad dash for the basement door. Still, we kept our feet light and our ears peeled, enabling us to navigate through the silent house.

Where the fuck was everyone?

"All right, down here," I said.

"The basement? Won't we be trapped down here?"

I grabbed her arm and tossed her down the steps. "Jesus, you ask so many fucking questions."

"Hey!" she exclaimed.

I closed the door and locked it behind me. I charged her, backing her all the way into the basement before I grabbed her wrist and pulled her against me.

"Let me go," she grunted, wiggling out of my grasp.

"What part of shut the absolute fuck up don't you understand?" I glowered.

She finally wrenched away from me. "If you'd just answer my questions—"

I wrapped my hand around her throat and pulled her close. "You really think your asinine questions are more important than our lives? Than the lives of my men?"

She gasped. "Blade, I can't—"

"Answer me," I hissed.

"No," she choked out.

I released her neck. "Then start fucking acting like it because you're starting to piss me off."

"Obviously," she murmured, rubbing her neck.

I walked over to the dresser in the corner and ripped open the bottom drawer. I pulled out the shotgun and checked to make sure it was loaded, then handed it to Dalia.

Who, of course, shook her fucking head.

"Take it," I said.

"I don't know how to shoot it."

I stalked toward her, picked up her hand, and slapped it against the gun. "You point and pull the trigger. That's it."

Footsteps sounded above us as Dalia took the gun from me. "Ammo?"

"Bottom drawer that's already sticking out."

"I just pop it open like in the movies, right?"

I blinked. "Jesus, we're going to die."

"Just answer my fucking question," she hissed.

"Yes," I growled, "just like in the goddamn movies, Dalia."

"Was that so hard?"

She lifted the gun and mounted it against her shoulder, and for a split second, she looked like a damn natural.

"Never held one?" I asked.

She rolled her eyes. "I may have grown up in foster care, but the streets raised me. So, announce yourself before you open that door again, otherwise I won't be able to show you why it'll be worth it to share me."

She made it hard not to like her. "Stand in that corner and aim for the door. Anyone other than us comes down those stairs, blow them to hell."

"Got it," she said as she backtracked.

I watched her stuff ammo down her fucking cleavage, and I swore to hell on high I'd never seen anything sexier. It took all I had to turn myself away from her and those bouncing tits, but I had bigger fish to fry. First, I had to figure out who in the fuck was trolloping like a goddamn show horse upstairs. Then, I had to figure out where Lance and Pike had gone.

"Stay put," I said, unsheathing my knives.

Dalia scurried into the corner. "Go. I got your back."

And as I made my way out of the basement, I closed the door behind me. I inched my way up the stairs, all the way to the top where the initial door to the staircase sat closed. Locked. Ready to be taken down once someone realized I had moved Dalia to the basement. There was no doubt in my mind that those asshats had found us. They were searching for Dalia, just like they said in their video.

So, I twirled my knives in my hands and readied them for death.

Just as someone started to pick the lock open on the door in front of me.

Come and get it, you bastards.

"Pike, you hear me?" Lance asked, soaring down the road back toward the clubhouse.

"Loud and clear," I said. "Phil?"

"Laying down in this helmet sucks ass."

"We got a faster way back home? Anyone?" Lance asked.

"You're acting like they're not already at the clubhouse," I said.

"If they're already there," Riley said as his voice came alive in our microphones, "then that's the card you play. They think you're not coming. Work with that."

"He's got a point," I said.

I hated having to think on the run, especially when people I cared about were in the crossfires. How the fuck had they snuck up on us like that?

"We're missing something," Lance growled. "Something important."

"For now, work with what you've got," Phil said.

"Any word on Mommy Dearest?" I asked.

"Not yet, but they haven't been gone long."

"Okay, so. Blade," I said and cleared my throat. "He'll shred at least three of them before he starts looking for other ways to get him and Dalia out of there."

"That's not good," Phil murmured.

"Why?" I asked.

"Because there were at least five different men with me in that warehouse."

"Fucking Christ," Lance hissed.

"You sure about that?" I asked.

"He looks pretty damn sure," Riley said.

Lance revved his engine and kicked it up a notch. "Come on, you can go faster than this."

"Talk to me, Phil," I said. "What else do you know?"

"I don't know. I can't be sure."

"Trust yourself, probie," Lance said curtly. "It's the number one rule you have to learn if you're going to be one of us. Trust what you heard and what you took in. You've been trained well. Blade doesn't let up unless he doesn't think you're worth it. So dig your heels in. We need you right now."

And with a heavy sigh, Phil started talking.

"When they had me tied to that fucking chair, I could've sworn I heard that Dirge dude talking about rallying men. Or gathering? He didn't say church, but it sounded like they were getting together for something."

"We have to get to that house. Blade's outnumbered," I said.

"Wait a second," Phil said.

"Spit it out," Lance said flatly.

"Lance, put in a call to the rest of the crew and have them follow Pike in. You and Pike split up, and—"

"I've already sent the text. At least six of them have already gotten back to me. They're headed there now," I said.

Phil chuckled. "Good, good. Make half of them go through the front and slash as many bike tires as they can along the way. Wrap the other half around the back and grab the filled gas cans we've got in the shed. Pour them into the hot tub and get those jets churning. You can funnel some of the guys into there and—"

I chuckled. "You maniacal freak. I love it."

"I do my best," Phil said. "Any chance Blade's already taken that girl of yours into the basement?"

"Most likely," Riley and Pike said in unison.

"Great," Phil said as his voice grew in strength. "Then you know where to find her—"

"That means she's cornered down there if anything goes wrong," Lance glowered.

"Then pick up the pace," Phil said. "But you can use the fact that we know they're already there to your advantage. That's the point. Don't try to trap them in the house. Set traps as you're going in so that when they get out, they're the ones that are cornered and taken by surprise."

"Let's get this man a cut when all of this shit is done," Lance said.

Riley snorted. "About damn time, too."

"Phil?" I asked.

"Yeah?"

"Get some rest. You did good. Let us know when you hear from Traeger and Mortar."

"I'll send them your way once I do."

"Thanks," Lance said, taking the hard left down the dirt road.

"Our engines are pretty loud right now," I said.

More roaring kicked up down the road and it made me wary. If they heard us coming, wouldn't they pick up the pace with the slaughter? Dalia was still in that house, and for all we knew—

"Good. Let them know we're coming. I want it to announce their death."

"All right," I said hesitantly. "But we should wait for them before we head on in. We're already outnumbered as it is."

If anything happened to Dalia, I'd never be able to forgive myself. We had gotten her into this mess, just like we had with Trishelle. She needed us in her hour of death, just like Trishelle. And even though I didn't know Dalia well yet, what I did know of her made me want to get to know her even more. I never thought I'd feel for another woman what I felt for Trishelle. The happiness and the excitement. The smiles that hurt one's cheeks and the feeling of my heart skipping beats whenever she smiled. Dalia had breathed life back into my shriveled heart. She had dug down into a part of my soul that had been hardened over with darkness when I had discovered Blade sobbing over Trishelle's body in the tub.

Yeah, sobbing.

"We have to get to her, Lance," I said.

"Don't worry, we will."

I hope Blade gave her a weapon, at least.

"Got an incoming call, patching you in," Lance said.

I held my breath as my microphone came alive along with Lance's voice. "You got us."

"So I came in the back way, and I don't see any movement in the house," Mongrel said.

We pulled off the dirt road and onto the gravel pathway that led right up to the clubhouse. But when we got there, we found a sight we never thought we'd see.

"Fuck," Lance hissed.

"Let me guess—no bikes," Mongrel murmured.

"Nope," I said, cutting the engine to my bike.

Lance did the same before he tossed his into the dirt. "I see two vans perched on the edge of the woods toward the west side of the property. Mongrel?"

He paused for a moment. "Got them."

"Get those tires slashed," I said when my head swiveled on its axis. "And see if they're unlocked. I'm curious as to what they're carrying in those damned things."

"Yeah, make sure they don't already have our fucking people in them," Lance growled.

"On it," Mongrel whispered.

I turned to face Lance. "Okay, so we have an idea as to how many are on the inside. Those vans only carry so many people."

Lance sighed. "There could still be at least half a dozen or so in there."

"And we've got that between the four of us, don't you think?"

Engines roared behind us as three more men skidded their bikes up toward the porch. They cut the engines and abandoned their vehicles as Mongrel came trotting over to us. I looked over at our president before I yanked my helmet off my head, then pressed the button on the side to disengage our Bluetooth connection. For all I knew, they'd heard every single part of that shit. And as the guys followed suit, we huddled up in the shadows of the trees.

"I have a feeling they're here for Dalia," Lance said, lowering his voice.

"The girl, yeah?" Mongrel asked.

I rolled my eyes. "You took out the tires on the van?"

Mongrel nodded. "Checked them, too."

Lance narrowed his eyes. "Why do you have that look on your face?"

He sighed. "They've got automatics in there, man. This is bad."

"Fuck," I growled.

"Okay, okay. Is there anything we can use in those vans?" I asked.

Mongrel grinned. "There's hand grenades, some ammo, a couple of guns they left behind, and a few bulletproof vests."

"Why does that sound like a trap?" I asked.

"Because it is. Scratch that," Lance said. "Everyone got at least one weapon on them?"

"Two," Mongrel said, showcasing his hips.

"Got a gun and a knife," Pike said.

"I've got my handgun. Guys?"

Everyone showcased their weapons, but it wasn't nearly the kind of firepower we needed to take on whatever the fuck was going on inside. It was eerily silent for an ambush. There was no movement in the windows, no screaming coming from the inside. Hell, we didn't even hear bodies dropping.

"Are we sure they're even in there?" I asked.

"Look," Lance said, placing his hand on my shoulder. "Blade is the only line of defense standing between those men and the woman we're protecting. She's gotten wrapped up into the shit unknowingly, and we swore to protect her at all costs."

Mongrel gnashed his teeth together. "I hate it when men fuck with women. Such a pussy move."

I nodded. "Exactly. So let's stick to Phil's plan then."

Lance turned to the rest of the guys. "Mongrel, you, Pike, and Lancaster take the back. Wrap around the edge of the house and stay in the shadows until you've got the shortest distance between yourself and that hot tub. Get the gasoline in there and get the bubbles going. Marky? Waylon?"

"Yeah?" the twins asked in unison.

"You're with me. We go in through the front and we make as much noise as we can. Shoot to kill, and keep your eyes peeled for Blade and a thick woman in a bikini."

"A bikini?" Marky asked.

Lance rolled his eyes. "Just do it. Everyone ready?"

I nodded. "Let's get this show on the road."

And just as I withdrew my weapon from my hip, I heard the most nightmarish sound. A sound I'd never be able to get out of my head. It echoed across the gravel lot and slammed against my chest before ricocheting through the trees. Birds scattered. The wind kicked up. The sky darkened as if the sound itself had summoned hell . A storm brewed above us as the siren sound held me hostage, filling my vision with red.

"Scratch the plan," Lance glowered as he withdrew his weapons. "We get in there and kill every last one of those Sentinels in sight."

Marky turned to face me. "Is that—"

"BLAAAAAAAAAAAAADE!" Dalia howled.

"Everyone get in the house," Lance roared as he broke out into a dead sprint. "Now!"

19

———

BLADE

I watched the door ease open without so much as a sound, and a smile overtook my face. I watched as The Sentinel in the red leather jacket stared down at me, a wild grin overtaking his features. I stilled my hands. I counted every single heartbeat that thudded against my chest. And the second he raised his gun to my head, I swiped up with my blade.

Feeling his skin weaken against the shining metal as his gun tumbled from his hand.

"Fuck!" the man cried out.

"Granger!" someone called out. "What's wrong?!"

The man stumbled toward me, and I simply held my knives out. With his wrist bleeding and his hand dangling from his wrist, I watched him stake himself on my knives. He choked on his own blood. The gurgling sound of his life flashing before his eyes filled me with a calm sense of relief. Footsteps clamored toward me and I counted their cantors. One was a little heavy on the left foot, two of them were heavy on the right. One of them scampered sort of the way I did, most likely their stealth guy. Then there was the lumberjack.

I counted five different footfalls, so I assumed there were at least six in play.

You know, just in case someone was as good as me in silencing themselves.

"Let's get to work," I said, tossing the dead man's body off my knives.

"Granger!" a man bellowed when he whipped around the corner.

I didn't even get past the top step before I slashed my knife across the man's face. He cupped his cheek and reached for his gun, but I cut through his belt like warm, creamery butter. His entire gun holster fell from his hip. I dropped both of my knives between his legs and yanked up as hard as I could, opening up his groin and spilling his life force between his legs.

"Two," I whispered.

"Get him!" one of the men commanded.

I stepped up from the basement staircase and readied myself for war. I twirled my body, kicking my leg out in perfect pirouette fashion as I fanned my blades through the man coming toward me. I dipped low, catching another set of feet before something hard hit the floor. I leapt through the air and came down with my knives, jamming them into the man's stomach before kicking myself up and slamming my feet into the gut of yet another man who attempted to come up from behind me.

"Is that all you've got?" I asked, landing back onto my feet.

"His knives! Get his knives!"

I yanked them from the dead body at my feet and turned around, jamming one of them straight into the top of a man's head. I watched the life flee from his eyes in a split second before he plummeted to the floor, and when I pulled my knife out, the sheer amount of gray matter splattered along my blade shivered me inside. My kind of fight if I were being honest. Brutal. Precise. Quick.

I whipped around and readied myself for yet another death. I threw my knives at the man charging me with two guns pointed right at my head. He cried out a deafening war cry that rattled the windows and echoed like thunder across the house. But the second my blades sank into his stomach, he fell to his knees.

"No. Oh, God," he choked out, falling face-first and shoved those knives deeper into his stomach.

A shadow moved to my left and I turned to face him, but I found not one, but two men approaching me. I turned to my right and found yet another man coming for me with what looked like a goddamn oozie trained at my head. I ran as quickly as I could, leaping into the air and throwing my feet over my head as bullets flew in every direction. And as I ripped my knives out of the man's gut, I landed on my feet before I flung myself into the hallway leading into the kitchen, only to slide into the boots of three more men waiting for me.

"Gotcha," someone said.

They grabbed my collar and yanked me up from the floor, but not before I stuck my knives out. Most of their movements did the work for me, and as I shredded through their skin, they dropped me back to the floor. Someone stumbled back, bleeding all over our precious marble floors as they cried out for help.

I scrambled to get to my feet before I saw the kitchen filling with Sentinels.

I needed backup, and quickly.

Less dead bodies means less clean-up.

"You're a dead man walking," one of the guys growled.

I sheathed my knives into their holsters. "Well, let's see what I can get my body count to before you complete the job."

I used his kinetic energy against the second man that lunged at me. I stepped off to the side and grabbed his arm, wrapping him back around before I slammed him into the wall. I heard a resounding crack before he cried out, and his gun tumbled from his hand. I kicked it off to the side before slamming my steel-toed boot into his gut and watched him plummet to the floor. Unconscious.

Someone wrapped their arm around my neck.

"I've got you now, you son of a bitch."

I grinned as I kicked my legs against the wall. I walked all the way up before kicking down from the ceiling, taking the man to the ground. I slammed him against his back, forcing him to gasp for air as another man hovered over me. He pointed a gun right at my forehead and I swore to hell, they were practically paving the way for their death.

As the man's arm loosened around my neck, I flung my legs in a roundhouse kick through the air. I snapped the gun out of the man's hand and it went off, and I rolled just in time for the bullet to strike the man on the floor who had the audacity to try and choke me out. He groaned in pain as his side poured blood onto the floor, and I leapt to my feet long enough to sucker punch the clumsy rat bastard in his gut.

And for the smallest of moments, I had a second to breathe.

How had these men crept up on me? I had to figure out how the fuck they had gotten into the house. I hadn't heard engines. Or footsteps. Or voices. Nothing. Not until they had gotten right up on Dalia's bedroom, which was another question altogether. How in the absolute fuck did they know where we had Dalia? It wasn't as if she'd been there for long in the first fucking place!

"I gotta train some more," I said breathlessly, making my way toward the stairs.

I took them, two by two, until I stood on my level of the house. I weaved my way back toward Dalia's bedroom, searching for any signs of busted windows in the bedrooms. Maybe they had snuck in through the multitude of guest bedrooms we had. There were plenty of windows in this place, thanks to our apparently defunct planning efforts, and as I got to Dalia's doorway, there was nothing.

No evidence of how they had gotten in.

No glass that had been shattered anywhere.

It was as if they had simply melded through the walls like a fucking villain in a sitcom television show.

So, what did that mean for—

"BLAAAAAAAADE!"

The blood curdling scream turned me on the balls of my feet. I sprinted back to the stairs, blood thrumming through my ears as my mind attempted to hold me hostage.

"BLAAAAAAAADE! HELP ME!"

She sounded so much like Trishelle, and as I worked my way down the steps, my mind won over. It yanked me back into another place and time. Where I had been someone else instead of the carcass of a human that was walking around. I leaned against the banister. I listened to her scream. And as I fought my brain with all my might, I lost.

"BLADE! PLEASE, HELP ME! WHERE ARE YOU!?"

"Trishelle!?" I called out, sprinting out of my bedroom. "Where are you?"

"Blade?! Someone?! Is anyone here?!"

"I'm coming, Trishelle! Just hold on!"

"Somebody plea-he-heeeease."

Her voice stopped me in my tracks. The echoing of the madness in her voice replayed over and over as I tried to steady myself onto my feet. Trishelle. She was in trouble. Those men had her, and she—

"BLADE, GODDAMN IT! WHERE THE FUCK ARE YOU!?"

No, that wasn't Trishelle.

That was Dalia.

"Dalia!" I bellowed as I leapt down the rest of the stairs. "I'm coming!"

And just as I turned toward the basement door, an arm came out of nowhere. My neck caught the brunt of the blow and flipped me, head over heels before I came down onto my back. I stared up at the ceiling, gasping for breath. I tried to roll onto my side, but something stamped down onto my hip.

Blurring my gaze as pain rocketed through my body.

"BLAAAAAADE!" Dalia shrieked.

"Da—Dalia," I choked out.

"Trishelle, oh my God."

"I'm so sorry," she said breathlessly.

The tub kept filling up with red. The water overflowed, hot and searing, as her stomach protruded through the tops of the bubbles.

"Trishelle, what have you done?" I asked breathlessly.

"I can't do this," she said weakly.

I fumbled with my cell phone to get it out of my pocket. "I knew you should've never come off that medicine. I'm calling—"

"Just let me be at peace," she whispered.

"Lance! Pike! I NEED HELP IN HERE!"

"Trishelle," I gurgled. "I'm—I'm sorry."

As Dalia's shrieks faded into the background, my vision tunneled. My lungs cried out for air that I couldn't give them. They'd kill her, and all because I couldn't focus. I couldn't do enough. I couldn't be enough. I failed her, just like I had failed Trishelle. Always looking over her, and never at her. Always protecting her, and never paying her enough attention.

We'd never be good enough for them.

"Dalia," I whispered.

And her screams were the last thing I heard before the world went black.

20

———

DALIA

I clutched the shotgun close to my chest and held my breath. There were so many sounds, and they all blended together to create what I was sure as the background soundtrack to Hell itself. Skin sliced and something gurgled. Loud thuds hit the floor above my head, and I knew they were dead bodies. All of them, with their lives ripped away at the drop of a hat. Or a knife, since that was what Blade seemed to gravitate toward. I squeezed my eyes shut before I talked myself out of that. I needed to see if someone came down those stairs. I needed my sight in case I had to shoot.

Footsteps faded away and the world stilled around me, but the sounds of fighting echoed off in the distance. Bones cracking and bodies dropping. Grunts, groans, and stifled cries for help. Tears streaked my face. Fear encompassed my entire being. I mounted the shotgun onto my shoulder, just for something to do. And as I held the heavy gun, pointing it toward the basement door, I stayed perched in that corner, in the little blind spot it afforded me.

"Come on, motherfuckers. I dare you," I murmured.

With every bone that crunched and every cough that sputtered into gurgling, it reminded me that Blade was the cause of it all. Blade was doing all of this to keep me safe, and in a weird way, it warmed my heart. He killed multiple men for me. But I wondered where Pike and Lance were. Had they gotten caught up in something? Had they been ambushed? Had they been at the house?

Jesus Christ, were they already dead?

All of a sudden, there was nothing. No bodies groaning. No thuds slamming against the floor above my head. No one gurgled on their own blood and no more bullets whizzed about. The chaos stopped just as quickly as it had started, and I looked down to see that I was still in nothing but my fucking string bikini.

"Well, that's just great," I murmured.

It felt like another world had descended upon me. Like I had been sucked into some sort of pocket dimension where none of the bullshit going on above my head existed. I inched my way out of the corner. I rounded to the middle of the entrance to the basement with the shotgun pointed directly at the door. I counted the amount of ammunition shells pressing against my tits. I stuffed at least fifteen of them down there, if not more.

But would I be able to reload the gun quickly enough?

"Come on, Blade. Where are you?" I whispered.

My arms grew tired, so I dropped the gun. I set the butt of it on the ground at my feet and rested my tired muscles. But a creaking sound coming from above my head leapt me back into action. I pulled the gun up from the floor and mounted it against my shoulder. The creaks above my head continued until a board shifted on the steps.

Holy fuck, someone was coming down the stairs.

And judging by the heavy footfalls, it most certainly wasn't Blade.

"Come on, Momma's ready," I glowered, aiming right at the door.

I didn't want to kill anyone, but I would. If it meant getting back to Blade, I'd do it in the heartbeat. It wasn't the first time I had leveled a gun at someone, and it sure as hell wouldn't be the last. And if Blade was hurt? God help whoever the fuck was about to come down into that basement. I hadn't even gotten a chance to truly enjoy the three of them. I wanted that chance. I wanted my moment with those men, and it was obvious they wanted theirs.

No one was ruining that for me.

Not even the brazen motherfuck that wanted to come after me.

"You've got this," I whispered to myself.

The doorknob on the door in front of me turned. I held my breath, steadying the gun against my shoulder as the door eased open. It didn't fling open with a grand entrance. No one hovered over me as they stood in the doorway like I had imagined. Instead, the door effortlessly fell open, revealing an outlined shadow of a much smaller person than I had anticipated.

In fact, the shadow wasn't much taller than me, and certainly not heavier than me.

My brow stitched together. I waited for the person to step into the light. I waited for them to reveal themselves, charge me, or draw a gun. Anything to give me a reason to pull the trigger. But instead, they just stood there.

Until a hand reached out and turned on the stairwell light.

"Oh my God."

Holy fucking Christ, I recognized that face.

"Hello there, Dee."

I finally released the breath I had held . "Micah?"

He clasped his hands behind his back. "I haven't been called that name in a very long time."

I lowered the shotgun. "Micah, what the fuck are you doing here? What's going on?"

And when he opened his arms, as if to showcase himself, I noticed the jacket he donned.

The red leather jacket.

"You're with The Sentinels," I said breathlessly.

He took a step into the basement. "You know, when I realized you were tangled up with these guys, it didn't really shock me. I mean, they're exactly your type."

I scoffed. "You mean, like you weren't?"

He waved his hand in the air dismissively. "The past is in the past. I've moved on from the little crush I had on you back in our foster home. But you've really stepped in it this time, and if you want your little boys to live, then you need to do what I say."

I picked the gun back up and leveled it at his chest. "Over my dead body."

He took another step toward me, and when he did, he straightened his back.

Which added about three inches to his stature.

"I can arrange that if you'd like," he said.

I wasn't afraid of much. After all, with the life I had led, we couldn't afford to be afraid. But Micah was terrifying. I watched him do some seriously fucked-up things back in our foster care home. One of the things foster kids did was they tried to make sure at least one thing in the house was theirs. For me, it was a kitty I had found on the side of the road. It took some convincing, and some serious chore time, but my foster parents let me keep it so long as I kept it fed and cleaned up after it. Of course, I had no way of knowing that the cat was pregnant at the time, and when I woke up to the chorus of meows beneath my bunk bed, Micah promised me he'd help take care of them.

Before I found him butchering one of the kitties in the bathroom one night.

"It was sick anyway. No point in letting it suffer."

"I always knew you were a monster," I said.

He walked toward me until his chest sat flush against the barrel of the gun. "And I always knew you were a cowardly whore. You can't pull that trigger. You already would have if you had the guts."

My trigger finger ticked. "Don't make me do this. There's another way out of this, Micah. I have sway with these guys."

He smacked the gun away from his chest and the force was so great that it pulled the damn thing out of my grasp. He rushed me, moving so quickly that I didn't have much time to react. And when he wrapped his hand around my neck, he moved and shoved me toward the stairs.

"Scream for me, whore. Scream as loud as you can."

"BLAAAAAAAADE!" I cried out.

I screamed so hard that it hurt my throat. Micah yanked me by my arm and I fought against him, scrambling to get back to the shotgun that laid there helplessly on the floor.

"BLAAAAAAAADE! HELP ME!" I exclaimed.

"Scream like the whore you are," Micah growled, fisting my hair.

He yanked me back so hard that it stumbled me off my feet. I went crashing to the ground, cracking my head against the wall. The world tilted around me. I heard Micah's heavy footsteps coming toward me before he yanked me up by my hair yet again and tossed me toward the shotgun.

"Go ahead," he said as he laughed. "Pick it up!"

"BLADE, GODDAMN IT!" I cried out hoarsely, reaching for the gun. "WHERE THE FUCK ARE YOU!?"

But Michael slammed his boot into the small of my back. "I wonder if that hip still hurts."

"No, no," I said, rolling over underneath his touch. "Please, whatever you want with me, just take it. But leave them alone. They have nothing to do with thi—oh my God!"

He slammed his heel into the hip I had dislocated when I was only thirteen years old. It was the first time Micah and I had ever fought, and it was over a date, actually. He wanted to take me out. I thought that was weird. So he shoved me down the steps and I slammed into the ground so hard that it fucking dislocated my goddamn hip.

That was how we ended up getting separated. When the hospital figured out what had really happened, the foster system split us up. Put me in another home to endure another round of survival tactics while Micah went to juvie.

At least, that was what I had heard on the streets.

"BLAAAAAADE!" I shrieked as the pain blinded me.

"You're doing such a great job," Micah said, grabbing my arm and yanking me back up.

I knew that if he got me off the property, I was fucked. If he drove away with me, they'd never find me. Micah was the definition of ruthless. He felt nothing. Loved nothing. Attached himself to nothing except his pride and his disgusting deeds. He had been proud of butchering that kitty. He had been proud of dislocating my hip. He had been proud stalking me all throughout high school, peeking around corners every time we dismissed just to catch a glimpse of me. It was why I had left. The second I found the money, I ran to another state and hunkered down. Somewhere I knew he wouldn't find me. And as he tossed me toward the steps, it finally hit me.

The Sentinels weren't after the guys.

They were after me.

And it made me wonder what in the hell they had done with Blade.

21

LANCE

"BLAAAAAAAADE! HELP ME!" Dalia exclaimed.

I leapt up all of the porch steps at once. I charged through the front door, with the world moving in slow motion all around me.

"BLADE, GODDAMN IT! WHERE THE FUCK ARE YOU!?"

I heard the exhaustion in her voice and panic gripped my throat. For the first time since Trishelle's suicide, I felt helpless. Scared. I felt like a little boy again, trapped in the middle of darkness and mist. My men trampled in behind me, leveling their guns all around my body as my head swiveled side to side, searching for the woman who had asked for none of this. Just like Trishelle had asked for none of it.

I didn't have to look hard for her, though. The second we all gathered in the foyer, I found that supple body of hers standing on her tiptoes. Her skin, reddened with exertion. Beads of sweat, sliding down her brow with those red, puffy eyes of hers giving away her predicament.

And behind her... was Dirge.

"Lance!" Dalia exclaimed.

I leveled my guns at the man's head. "Let her go."

"Lance," Pike murmured, "the bodies."

I turned my head toward him without taking my eyes off Dalia. "Look for Blade. He's here somewhere."

"You move," Dirge said as he cocked his gun, "and she dies."

"Lance, the stairs," Mongrel murmured.

I peered over Dirge's shoulder and saw Blade's hapless body sprawled out along the stairs. He was out cold, and his body looked like it had been dragged for some distance. His legs cocked themselves at unnatural angles. His neck had a massive ligature mark wrapped all the way around it. His arms jutted out with his wrists cocked at angles that made me sick to my fucking stomach.

The only hope I had was that his chest still moved with his breaths.

"He's alive, so let's keep it that way," I murmured back.

"Lance, p-p-please. I had no i—idea," Dalia choked out.

I shook my head. "I know you didn't. It's okay. We're going to get you out of this."

"What do you want?" Pike asked.

"I know what I want," I glowered.

Dirge chuckled. "So big and strong all the time. Doesn't that get exhausting?"

Pike eased his way out in front of me. "If we could just—"

"No!" Dalia exclaimed.

Dirge tightened his grip around Dalia's neck before he dug the barrel of his gun deeper into her temple. "If either one of you comes any closer, her brains go on this floor."

"Pike," I said, shaking my head.

He peeked over at me before falling back in line behind me. "What's the plan?"

There was no plan, though.

We had been properly ambushed.

Dalia's lower lip quivered and my lust for blood grew bigger than my entire body. It filled the caverns within me before shivering my core, holding my muscles hostage. I wanted to dismember that asshole and drop his body parts off at the houses of his men, just so they knew what happened when they fucked with us.

"Drop your weapon or she dies," Dirge said.

I tilted my head. "I thought the agreement was—"

"That was until your man moved. Now, drop it."

"Ah!" Dalia exclaimed before she gasped for air.

"Over my dead body," I growled.

"Just—do it," Dalia wheezed.

Had I heard her right?

"Dalia, this man, he's—"

Dirge placed his lips against her ear. "Why don't you tell him how you know me, yeah?"

My eye twitched. "You what?"

He relaxed his arm long enough for her to breathe. "I know him, Lance. Please, just do as he says because he will kill me. He'll do it without a second thought."

I looked over at Pike and realization crashed into him like a thrown brick. The missing piece. The missing link we had searched for this entire time. The fucking president knew her. Their president—their slimy, sleazy president—knew Dalia.

Our Dalia.

"How do you know her?" I asked.

"Lance, just drop your goddamn weapon!" she yelped.

"You know," Dirge said, sniffing her hair. "Dalia and I grew up in the same disgusting foster home, didn't we, sis?"

She whimpered, but he clamped his arm back around her neck and cut off her ability to speak.

"Dalia!" Pike said breathlessly.

I held my arm out and stopped him from charging her. We

were in a volatile situation without all the facts at our disposal. Which meant we had to listen to the person who had the most information to give.

Dalia.

"Is this true?" I asked, my gaze locking with hers.

Tears streaked her cheeks. "I didn't know. I didn't have a clue until he found me in the basement. I swear to hell on high, please, I—ugh, ngh, brp."

"Let her go!" I bellowed.

Dirge tilted his head and pinned me with that dead look in his eyes. "I can attest, she's telling the truth. She didn't know a damn thing until I finally exposed myself. No need to question whether or not you should've fucked her."

I snarled and gnashed my teeth together. "What do you want, douchebag?"

"It's Dirge, but I'll take it."

"Jesus," Marky hissed.

"Lance?" Dalia wheezed.

Dirge released his arm a bit. "There you go. Breathe, Dalia. Don't you pass out on me now, you've been so good."

"Is Blade dead?" she asked breathlessly.

My gaze flickered back toward the stairs, and I watched the smooth movements of Blade's chest as it puffed up and fell down.

Puffed up and fell down.

Up, and down.

Up, down.

But was it a question that was safe to answer? What if Dirge turned around and killed him? If I answered yes, there was a chance he'd take a bullet to the chest without having the chance to defend himself. But if I said no and Dirge knew I was lying, he may kill Blade anyway.

"Lance?" Dalia urged.

"My, my," Dirge said with a tsk. "The big, bad Lance reduced to this. It really is poetic, don't you think?"

"Shut up, Micah."

Mongrel chuckled. "Micah?"

Dirge's eyes widened and his arm tightened around her neck once more.

"Ah! No!"

"You're going to pay for that," he growled.

"Let her go!" Pike exclaimed, pointing his gun at Dirge's head.

"No, Pike," I said as I shot out my arm.

But Dirge did the unexpected. He moved his gun away from Dalia and pointed it directly at me.

Which was a turn of events I could stomach.

"Put down your guns, or Dalia here gets more than a bullet to her head," Dirge warned.

I watched as Micah's other hand moved from her shoulder down to her chest. Tears dripped down Dalia's chest as his hand slipped against the soft crest of her breast. His fingertips moved closer to her tits. She shivered in fear as choked groans fell from her lips.

I couldn't stop myself when I charged him, my vision bubbling with fury. No one touched Dalia. No one touched her without her permission. Especially the likes of him.

However, the sound of a gunshot halted me in my tracks.

"Stop!" Dalia screamed out as Dirge's bullet slammed right between her feet. "Everyone just fucking stop it!"

Dirge slowly brought his gun back up and leveled it at my chest. "You really are weak for her, aren't you? The big, bad Lance. President of the Shadow Boys. Reduced to a 'yes, boy' by a decent pair of tits."

Pike came up to my side. "If you don't let her go, I'm gonna—"

"I get it, though," Dirge said with a shrug. "I loved staring at her tits growing up."

"You're a sick fuck, you know that?" Dalia hissed.

My fists balled up at my sides and Dirge darted his tongue out. He licked Dalia's cheek, lapping up the tears falling from her eyes as she tried to pull away. Watching her struggle against that man solidified my thoughts. It brought everything into focus and rage consumed my body.

I'd take my time with Dirge.

And I'd make sure he was alive for as much of his death as possible.

"God—damn it," Dalia said breathlessly.

Dirge kissed her temple, even though she tried to dart away. "I'll taste more of you when I get you where I want you."

I shook my head. "You aren't leaving here with her, even if it kills me."

Dirge shrugged. "I'll take that deal."

"Dirge, NO!" Dalia cried out hoarsely, her voice fading in and out with her screams.

Everything moved in slow motion as I kicked off, getting myself a running start. Pike called out commands from the guys and I locked my stare with Dalia, registering the fear on her face. Her lips moved, but nothing came out. All sounds around me faded as I lunged forward, moving a step closer with every second toward the man whose body I wanted to torture for the rest of time. It wouldn't end like that. It wouldn't end with Dalia's dead body sprawled out for us to witness.

I watched Dirge point his gun at me, his trigger finger tightening against the trigger with only twenty feet between us to go. His lips moved, frowning in disappointment and anger as men poured out of the orifices of our clubhouse. They grabbed my arms. They kicked my legs out from beneath me. They tried to trip me up. They tried to prevent me from getting to our Dalia.

It wouldn't work, though. I grabbed their necks and slammed them into the ground. I curb-stomped those motherfucker's heads into the marble floor, their cries of mercy falling on vacant ears.

With every red leather jacket I dropped, my men followed suit, whizzing bullets past my body as I forced my way toward Dalia. It was an all-out war, and it wouldn't end until each and every one of them bled to death at my feet.

I thought I wasn't going to make it.

I thought *she* wasn't going to make it.

Until a shadow leapt up from behind Dirge.

"Move, Dalia," Blade commanded, swinging his knife through the air. "Now!"

And just as I held my arms for her, Blade sank his knife into Dirge's side, which was enough to dislodge the gun from his hand as it slid across the floor between my legs.

22

———

PIKE

The second Lance took off in a dead sprint, all hell broke loose.

"Everyone! Do your fucking worst!" I commanded.

We withdrew our weapons as throngs of red leather cuts poured from the hallway. They came in through the kitchen, rushing down the hallway as I took aim at every single one of them. Bullet after bullet left the chamber of my gun, and as I pulled a knife off my left inside ankle, I whipped it through the air just like Blade had taught me all those years ago.

I watched as a man dropped at my feet, choking on his own blood.

"We have to get to Blade," I said when I whipped around. "Mongrel, you and I will—"

"Uh, I think you need to turn around," Marky said with a nod of his head.

I whipped around and watched Blade soar through the air. He leapt like a wildcat in the night, his knife withdrawn, and his gaze locked with the back of Dirge's head. My jaw hit the floor as he cocked his knife to the side, aiming not for the man's head, but for his side.

"Move, Dalia," Blade commanded, swinging his knife through the air. "Now!"

He sank that knife right into Dirge's side and the man stumbled. His grip on his gun weakened, and as Lance continued charging the man, he slammed his fist right into the motherfucker's face. I watched as the gun slid through the air, discharging a bullet with the force of Lance's blow before it hit the ground and slid toward the side hallway.

"What's the command, Pike?" Mongrel asked.

Blade stood on wobbly legs, his body crooked as his face morphed into one of pain and regret. He stood on the steps, swaying from side to side before he fell down on his ass.

I'd never seen him look so haggard in all my life.

"Kill," I glowered. "That's your command."

It was an all-out war as bullets filled the air. Dalia ducked, covering her head and curling up into a ball at the base of the steps as Dirge faltered on his feet. I wasn't worried about him any longer, though. Blade's knives were long, and there was no way in hell that man was coming back from a wound like that. I turned toward the hallway and counted the shadows, popping bullets into the bodies as they rounded the corner.

I aimed for their head, sinking them to the floor with those lifeless eyes staring back at us.

And all the while, I kept my ears trained for Dalia.

"Gonna be a hell of a clean-up," Marky said as he pressed his back to mine.

I fired my weapon as we slowly started spinning. "Keep an eye on the hallway, it's packed with assholes."

He fired his gun. "Same with the kitchen, keep a lookout."

"Duck!" I exclaimed.

Marky and I hit the floor as an automatic weapon tore into the walls around us. A man started yelling as if he were in some sort of tribal warfare video game , and the trilling damn near deafened me. Never mind the fact that the plaster on the walls splintered and rained down onto the floor. Never mind the fact that windows had been busted, spreading broken glass all over the floor for mangled bodies to roll around on.

"Where the fuck is he?!" Marky exclaimed.

I rolled over onto my stomach, cursing the glass as it shredded my skin. "Found him!"

"Take him out!" Mongrel bellowed.

I aimed for the man's crotch as he clung to two automatic rifles. They bounced his entire body, as if he were in some sort of fucking Rambo movie, and his spread legs gave me the perfect shot. I closed my left eye and aimed down my sights. I drew in a deep breath, even with the world going to hell around me, and pulled the trigger.

Silence fell over us and the man hit his knees.

"My dick," he choked out.

Blood pooled on the floor between his legs and he bent forward, placing his face against the floor.

"Oh, God. My dick," he groaned.

Where's Dalia?

I hadn't heard her voice since the cacophony kicked up. Gunfire drowned out just about anything, and when I rolled over, I propped myself up onto my elbows. Blood splattered everywhere along the walls and the floor. I looked toward the staircase where Blade had been and I saw him dragging someone up the steps. Blood trailed behind the man who squirmed to get out of his grasp, and as I watched him disappear around the corner, he flipped his blade in his free hand before another body dropped at his feet.

Now, I understood.

Now, I knew why we had been so taken aback.

They had never been after us. Not by a longshot. They hadn't come into town to fuck with our businesses. They hadn't come into town wanting to shake down our friends. It had never been about us at all.

It had been about Dalia.

From day fucking one.

Dalia.

Holy fuck, where was Dalia?

"Dalia?" I asked and pushed myself to my feet.

A bullet soared by my ear, and I turned on a dime, holding out my gun in the process. A man in a red leather jacket wobbled on his feet, using the wall beside the basement door as a prop. His left eye had swollen itself shut. It looked like someone had broken his jaw. And as his weakened arm swayed from side to side, he pulled the trigger of his gun as many times as he could stand.

All the life drained from his face and he slid down the wall, leaving a bloody trail in his wake.

"Dalia!" I barked, spinning around.

"Where is she?" Blade asked as he trolloped back down the stairs.

I stumbled on my feet when I tried getting my bearings. I held my hand out, but there was no wall to support me. I fell to my side, feeling the floor connect with my hip before my hand slid against a sharp sliver of glass.

And when it ripped open my hand, it pulled me back into reality.

"Pike," Blade said as he dipped into my vision. "Where's Dalia?"

I shook my head softly. "I don't—I don't know. She—sh-sh—she—"

Blade helped me up and sat me in a chair off in the corner. "Sit. I'll find her. Do you need a gun?"

I popped out the magazine and saw it was empty. "Probably.

Blade looked around before he reached down and grabbed one of the automatic rifles. "Here, will that work?"

I scoffed, checking the magazine, and sure enough, there was half of one left. "Yeah, this'll do, I guess."

He patted my shoulder. "Good. Now, sit. I'll find her."

"You good?"

He stalked away from me while he twirled his bloodied knives in his hands. "Never better."

"Aaaaahhhh! Fuck you, Shadow Cunts!"

A man charged down the hallway that led into the kitchen and I picked up the rifle Blade handed me. I closed my eyes and aimed down the sights, then pulled the trigger and felt the blow-back against my shoulder. That fucking rattle stole my breath away. But all four of the bullets sank into the man's chest. He gasped for air and fell face-first into a pile of glass, and I flopped back into my chair as Blade peered over his shoulder at me.

"Thanks," he said with a nod.

I waved my gun at him. "Just find her."

"Blade?!"

The second I heard her voice, relief washed over me. I didn't see her, but I heard her. I heard her footsteps and listened to her cry out in consolation. I didn't have to see what was going on to know what happened. I knew Blade scooped her up. I knew she clung to him with all her might. And as I picked my head up, I focused on them just long enough to see Blade kiss the top of her head.

That made me grin.

Blade hadn't opened up to a damn person, much less a woman, since Trishelle's incident.

"Dalia!" I called out.

She whipped her head in my direction. "Pike! Oh, my God!"

"You okay? You hurt?"

Instead of answering me, she rushed me. She sprinted as quickly as she could across the foyer, stepping over piles of glass and leaping over dead bodies. Somehow, she had managed to get herself into a pair of sweatpants. Though, whose sweatpants they were, I didn't have a fucking clue. Did she own sweatpants?

Did I own sweatpants?

"Fucking hell," she whispered, throwing herself onto my body. "I thought for sure you guys were—"

I wrapped my arms around her as tightly as I could stand, which wasn't tight. But it still felt fucking amazing. Her warmth alone filled me with a second wind. Feeling her heart beating against mine reminded me that everything we had endured—every person we had just killed—was worth it.

"Are you hurt?" I murmured, kissing along her bare shoulder.

"I'm fine, I'm fine," she said as she pulled away and cupped my cheeks. "Are you hurt? What do you need?"

"You," I whispered.

"What?"

I gripped her hair and gazed into her eyes. "I need you, Dalia."

She smiled as tears crested her beautiful gray stare. "Well, you have me. Okay? You have me, Pike."

I wrapped my arm around her and she sobbed against the crook of my neck. She fell to her knees, scooting between my legs as her head slid off my shoulder. Down my chest. Over my stomach until it fell into my lap. Her tears drenched my jeans, and I threaded my bloody fingers through her hair, trying to give her some kind of solace.

Before another man ran out of the side hallway.

"Motherfuckers!" he roared.

I lifted my gun and unloaded five more bullets into that pathetic dickweed's body.

While Dalia clung to me for dear life.

"When will it stop?" she whispered.

I barely heard her question, but I still heard it. "Soon. It'll be over soon, pet."

"Dalia!" Blade exclaimed.

"Huh?" Dalia asked, picking her head up.

"If we go down today," Dirge said, pulling himself up from the floor, "then let there be fucking fire. Die, you spoiled fucking bitch!"

"Dalia, look out!" I roared.

Before I even thought about throwing her to the ground—before Blade even got himself into the air—Dirge pulled himself up from the floor. He cupped his side, still bleeding like a stuffed fucking pig, and reached for an automatic weapon at his side. How he even got it in the first place was beyond me. It wasn't the gun he originally had, but it didn't matter. With all the distractions and the men that had charged us, there were any number of ways he could have gotten his hands on that damned thing.

And when he aimed that barrel at Dalia, I did the only thing I knew to do.

I shoved her to the ground and stood.

"No, you fucking don't," I growled.

23

LANCE

I saw him bring his gun up and expected him to point it at me. After all, he apparently enjoyed saying my name more than the women I had fucked throughout my life. But when I watched his gun pivot from me off to the left, I heard Pike cry out.

"Dalia, look out!"

I didn't even have to watch. I knew exactly what was happening. So, I took off running. I turned on a dime and sprinted toward Dalia, pushing air through my lungs when all they wanted to do was collapse. I watched as the bullet zipped through the atmosphere, its trajectory, aimed right at Dalia's chest. And I wasn't about to watch another woman I loved die in front of my eyes.

After all, there were worse ways to die than saving a girl you care about.

"Lance, no!"

It was the last thing I heard before I stopped and spun around. As I watched the bullet barrel toward my body, I spread my arms out as something fell to my feet. I looked down long enough to see that Pike had tackled Dalia, barrel-rolling her out of the way, even as she reached out for me.

"Pike, he's going to get himself killed!"

I watched her. I watched the fear in her gaze and smiled at the fact that she could feel. It tore across my face, damn near closing my eyes as Pike scrambled to get her out of the way. Good on him. He knew what he needed to do. And even as she fought against him, flailing those gorgeous limbs of hers, I saw the passion. I saw the worry.

Emotions she'd be able to have now that she was safe.

"I've got you," I said as something slammed into my stomach.

"NO!" Dalia yelped.

My entire body got blown back, as if a goddamn mortar had hit me. Dirge's twisted face faded away as the ceiling came into view, and my vision dimmed. It tunneled into nothingness, holding me hostage and my back landed against something hard. Something cold. Something... unforgiving.

And as warmth seeped down my sides, I heard her voice.

"Lancey?"

Mom?

"Lancey-boy, where are you, kiddo?"

She sounded worried. Why did she sound worried?

"You leave my boy alone. Take whatever you want but leave him alone."

"Mom," I choked out.

The warmth of her lips as they touched my forehead made me smile. Her forehead kisses were the best. Heat encompassed me as she wrapped her arms around me, cradling me as tears streaked her cheeks. Why was she crying?

"Why are you crying, Mom?" I asked with a gasp.

"We need help over here!"

"Where the fuck is Dirge?!"

"Where are the rest of the fucking guys?"

Suddenly, the sound of a bullet made me jump. I buried

my face into my mother's bosom, seeking out her protection and she wrapped her arms around me. She held me close as another bullet popped off, and as she tipped to the side, I went with her, lying down with her as her lifeless gaze stared back at me.

"Get the jewelry," someone said. "I think we passed a gun cabinet in the hallway. Get those, too."

Robbed.

We were being robbed.

"Lance, can you hear me?"

Someone tapped my cheek. Or was it Mom?

"Mom?" I asked before I coughed.

Jesus, it was hard to breathe.

"Hey, El!"

I turned at the sound of my girlfriend's voice. "Abigail? Where the hell did you come from?"

I watched her slide in through the window of my grandparent's place. "Figured you'd want some company after today. You okay?"

I thought about the kid I had knocked out in school. "He shouldn't have been teasing you."

She snickered. "Well, you sure taught him a lesson."

"Yeah."

She sat beside me. "How long this time?"

I shrugged. "Three days."

"Long weekend. Nice."

"Tell that to my grandparents."

She cupped my cheek and turned my face toward her. "Thank you."

I shrugged. "It was nothing."

She pressed her lips to mine, and I had no clue what to do. After all, what the hell did a fourteen-year-old know about kissing? The coolest girl in school, and she pressed her lips to mine.

What did I do with my hands? Did I touch her? Did she want to be touched?

"Come on, El," she said with a soft giggle. "Put your hands on my hips."

And boy, did I ever.

"We need a doctor. Lance!"

"Dalia, come with me."

"No! We need a doctor! Someone help!"

"I'm calling Higgy now."

"Where the fuck is Dirge!?"

My cock twitched as I slid inside of her, our lips still connected. Abigail was beautiful, with hips that wouldn't quit and tits that blossomed much too early for her age. And I got her. I got to have her. I got to have all of her for the first time. Just like she got all of me for the very first time. It felt so good. It went too quickly. And as I gazed down into her eyes, she smiled up at me.

Before her face morphed into Dalia's.

"Hey there, handsome," she said, cupping my cheeks.

Her thighs molded to my body as my dick twitched inside of her. "I could go all night."

She giggled as she bucked against me. "You fucking better. I waited months for this."

I rolled her over and propped her up onto my cock. I staked her down, feeling her pussy walls vibrating around me. Her face kept changing— Trishelle, then Abigail, then Dalia. Back to Trishelle before her voice morphed into Abigail's.

"Love with all your heart, Lancey-boy. Promise me."

It all came so quickly, and yet seemed so slow. Everything flashed before my eyes. Graduation. My mother's grave. The judge that sentenced the robbers to life in prison for her death. Their obituary after paying off some guys in jail to make it look like an accident. That was my first ever splurge after joining up with the crew. That money sank into my palm and I knew exactly what I wanted to do with it.

A life for a life.

"I love you, Lancey-boy."

"Come on, El. Gimme that smile of yours."

"I'm sorry, Lance. I tried."

"Dalia," I whispered.

"I'm right here," she said as someone took my hand.

Her voice sounded so far away. "Dalia. I—"

"No, no, no," she whispered, stroking her fingers through my hair. "Save your strength. Just save it. You're going to need it when you're healing."

"There's something—"

"Shhhhh," she said, pressing her finger to my lips.

I had just enough strength to pucker my lips. To kiss the only part of her body I could reach. I felt weak. My toes went cold. I didn't hear bullets, though.

Was that a good thing?

"Kill her," the robber growled.

"Mom!" I yelped.

The warmth of her blood spilled onto my body as we laid there. I wrapped my arms around her, praying to any God listening that they breathed life back into her. I had no one without her. I had nothing without my mommy.

"Mommy, please," I said with a sniffle. "Please don't leave me."

"Lance."

"El."

"Boy."

"Motherfucker."

"Lance!"

"I love you, Lancey-boy."

"LANCE!"

I gasped for air, and everything came rushing back. My vision cleared. My heart leapt in my chest. And the pain.

Dear fucking God, the pain was excruciating.

"Lance! Jesus Christ, you've got to stay with me. You can't scare me like that."

I felt pressure on my gut as something wet pooled beneath my ass.

Why was my ass wet?

"Where's—where is he? Is he—did someone—"

"Enough!" Dirge demanded.

His voice echoed off the corners of the foyer as I stared up at the ceiling. Jesus Christ, the ceiling was vaulted all the way up to the third floor, and we somehow still managed to shoot specks of blood all the way up there. We'd never get this place clean. Not before the police got there, anyway.

"Hey, you still with us?" Blade asked, falling to his knees.

"Behind you," I said breathlessly.

He placed one hand on my gut, pressing down as hard as he could. The sheer scream that peeled from the back of my throat rattled my ribcage as he twirled his knife around and shoved it backward, staking the shadow I had seen charging him.

"Thanks," he said, ripping his knife out, before the body swayed and fell backwards out the front door.

"You'll pay for this," a voice growled.

Not just any voice, though.

Dalia's voice.

The explosion of a gun firing rocketed across the room, and it made me twitch. I hadn't twitched at anything in so fucking long, but I felt helpless. Like the little boy that held his dead mother in that closet while she tried to protect me from the robbers that had busted in. I laid there, feeling the life drain from my gut as Blade shredded his clothes and pressed them into my stomach.

"We need that doctor, you guys!" he exclaimed.

"Dalia," Pike said breathlessly.

"Die, you motherfucker!" she yelped.

Bullet after bullet zoomed across the foyer before nothing but the clicking of the trigger sounded. I lobbed my head off to the side, trying to see what was happening. Trying to see what the hell she had done. I watched Pike wrap his arms around her, picking her clear up off her feet. She dropped the gun to the floor, and I recognized the butt. It was red lacquer. The same color as those asinine red jackets those men wore.

Holy fucking hell, she had picked up Dirge's gun.

I followed Dalia's gaze, even as Pike tried to tuck her away in a closet. My arm flopped off to the side as someone rolled me over, and it gave me a perfect line of sight. I gazed into the cold, beady eyes of their president. The Sentinel's President. Dirge laid there, blood dripping from his mouth, and he looked almost... shocked.

Holy Christ, Dalia shot him.

She killed him.

For us.

"Atta girl," I said with a heavy sigh before the world went black.

24

———

DALIA

Everything passed in a blur. The bodies. The blood. The bullets. So much happened, and it was like my brain couldn't lock onto anything. Like it physically tried to shut down my eyes so that I couldn't take any of it in. Feeling Pike's arms around me angered me. He held me when I didn't want to be held. He rolled me away from Lance when we needed to take Lance with us. Why were we leaving him behind?

Watching that bullet sink into Lance's gut stilled something inside of me. Darkness overtook my heart as I clawed my nails against the ground, forcing my way out of Pike's embrace. My jaw quivered with fury. Rage consumed me as I pulled myself up onto my feet. And when I caught movement out of the corner of my eye, I turned to find him.

Micah.

That good-for-nothing bastard deserved to die.

"You'll pay for this," I growled.

It sounded like someone else's voice. Like someone else had possessed my body and taken control. I reached into the deep pocket of the sweatpants I had found when the gunfire first started because I felt exposed to the elements.

And as I jammed my hand into the pocket, I felt the butt of Dirge's gun Blade had knocked from his hand.

"Die, you motherfucker!" I bellowed.

I ripped that gun out of my pocket and turned the fucking thing inside out. I planted my feet and held it out in front of me, cocking it and pulling the trigger. The blowback shook me, forcing a shockwave all the way down to my toes. And when that bullet sank into Dirge's shoulder, I moved a little to the left and pulled the trigger again.

And again.

And again.

Until nothing else came out of the barrel except clicking.

Dirge collapsed to his knees as his stare went blank, and I refused to give him a second more of my time. I turned on my feet, dancing around Pike's outstretched arms and I lunged toward Lance's body. Someone had him tilted onto his side. His eyes fluttered closed before they bounced open, and I heard something about no exits.

I had no idea why, though.

The front door was wide fucking open.

"Lance?" I asked breathlessly, dropping to my knees.

He didn't answer me, though.

"Lance, talk to me. Please," I said as I laid down on the floor next to him.

"Dalia."

I ignored Blade's voice. "You did it for me once. I yelled, and you came back. Don't make me yell again. Just come back, Lance."

"Dalia, come here."

I shook my head. "Not until he says my name. Lance? Lance, can you hear me? Lan—what the hell?!"

"I'm sorry, Trishelle," he choked out.

"Let me go!" I yelped.

Someone grabbed my ankles and moved me. I dug my hands into the floor, feeling my nails ripping from their beds. The stench of metal filled the air as something soaked my chest, and when my legs were dropped, someone yanked me up onto my feet.

I found Blade staring at me with his hands on my shoulders.

"Why isn't he answering?" I asked.

"I need you to focus on me and stay calm. Are you hurt?"

I shook my head quickly. "There's blood, though. What's— how did it—"

I looked down at my hands and they were dripping. Little droplets splashed to my feet, dripping between the slats of my toes. The drag marks along the floor held my stare hostage as tears streaked my face. And when I found that the trail led back to Lance's immobile body, I couldn't breathe.

It was his.

Lance's blood was on me.

Shouldn't it be inside of him instead of on me?

"Dalia, focus on me. Lance needs you to focus," Blade said when he shook me softly.

My legs gave way beneath me, and Blade's arms wrapped around my body. He helped me onto the floor, scooping me into his lap as he held me close. Another set of hands stroked through my hair before the warmth of Pike's lips graced the shell of my ear. But all I could do was watch when the guys lifted Lance's body into the air.

As blood continued seeping from his stomach wound.

My head pivoted slowly around the room. Bodies, as far as the eye could see, littered the once beautiful marble floors. Blood splattered up the walls and on the banisters of the stair-case. Red foot tracks permeated around the foyer, marring the floors I had once found so shiny that I saw myself in them. Lifeless eyes stared back at me, begging for answers. Wondering who the fuck I was. Asking why the hell they had to die because of me.

But when my gaze found Dirge, laying there on his side with his legs spread, I froze.

Oh, God. I killed him.

"Dalia," Pike said as he gripped my chin and forced my gaze to his. "Can you hear me?"

I nodded mindlessly. "Why him?"

"What?"

I swallowed hard. "We grew up in—in the same—on—on the same—"

Blade rocked me softly side to side. "It's okay. Take your time. We've got you."

Pike searched my gaze. "Why he turned out that way and you didn't?"

My lower lip quivered. "Uh—uh huh."

Pike cupped my cheek. "Sometimes, my pet, people are simply born that way."

I knew he was right. I knew Micah had never been okay in his head. He always struggled. He always fought. He never once had a sliver of peace while we lived in the same house together. I never really knew what happened to him after we were placed elsewhere. They separated us, and all I remembered was feeling relieved that I no longer had to sleep beneath a boy who wet the fucking bed, even as a teenager.

I felt so bad for him. Even though I had every right to hate him. To want to kill him. To want to torture him just so he experienced the same kind of pain he brought everyone else. Even though I knew no one would hold it against me, I just felt so damn bad.

All of us kids deserved better than what we got.

All of us foster kids.

Including Micah.

"I'm so sorry," I whispered.

"Shh, shh, shh, it's okay. The doctor has Lance now, and everything is going to be all right," Pike said.

I leaned heavily against Blade. "I killed him. I'm a—a killer."

"Let's get her out of here," Blade said with a grunt.

My body rose into midair. "I killed him. I'm a murderer."

"You think she's going to pass out?" Pike asked.

"Not if I have anything to do with it," Blade murmured.

I had no energy to fight against his touch. It could have easily been me. With all the abuse we experienced, the locked refrigerators, and the beatings with switches for bad grades. My foster siblings begged for help as they were switched up and down the backs of their thighs. Our stuff constantly searched for drugs and weapons, like we were hoodlum criminals simply for existing without parents.

It could have just as easily been me standing on the other side of that gun with my lost mind guiding me.

It stole my breath away as my head fell back.

"There's blood on the ceiling," I said mindlessly.

If someone responded, I didn't hear it. I thought about all of the ways the blood could have gotten up there. Bullet wounds to the head. Knives being pulled out of stomachs. I envisioned things I had never once thought about, and it curdled my stomach as something warm encompassed my entire body.

"Am I bleeding?" I murmured.

"No, beautiful," Blade said and his lips kissed the back of my head. "It's just the bath water."

"Oh," I whispered.

I looked down and found myself clad in nothing but my bikini. Bubbling water crested my stomach, washing away my sins as the bubbles turned pink. Something moved behind me and I jerked, sloshing water over the edge of the porcelain tub.

Blade snaked his arms around my waist.

"I'm behind you, it's okay," he whispered.

I turned my head and found Pike perched on the edge of the tub, his leg completely soaked.

"Sorry," I murmured.

He simply shook his head, though. "No reason to be sorry."

"Want me to wash your hair?" Blade asked.

"Does it have blood in it?"

Pike nodded. "A bit."

I clenched my jaw. "Yeah, I guess so, then."

I looked around and found no blood in sight. No broken glass. No splintered walls. No holes from bullets in the cabinetry. The marble floors of my bathroom upstairs were pristine and shining. As if Hell itself hadn't just rained down on our world. Water poured over my head. It snaked down my skin, dragging the blood along with it as I watched the pink streams of bubbles trickle down between my breasts.

Then, I finally found the strength to ask.

"Where's Lance?"

Maybe I had dreamt it. Maybe it had been nothing but a fever dream brought on by stress. Those were a thing, right?

The tone of Blade's voice said it all, though.

"He's in the best of hands, Dalia."

I sank a bit deeper against him. "Is he dead? Did he—did he bleed out?"

Pike shook his head. "Not yet."

"Pike," Blade hissed.

"What? I'm not lying to her, even if it'll spare her. She deserves more than that after what she did."

I swallowed hard. "You mean, after I killed Micah."

Sometimes silence was answer enough, and when they didn't answer, I had mine.

"It could have easily been me, you know," I whispered.

Pike shook his head. "You're nothing like Dirge."

I scoffed. "All we did was try to survive, you know. You guys have no clue what we went through as kids. The beatings. The locked refrigerators. The starvation tactics when we got bad grades. Sleeping on the floor in urine-infested areas with six different cats and one litter box they all shared. Bedwetting that woke me up as it dripped onto my face. Micah's embarrassment when he woke up soaking wet. Mattresses that just got turned instead of—"

"Jesus," Pike said, pinching the bridge of his nose.

I closed my eyes. "I remember Micah being so fucking proud that he killed that kitty. He claimed it was sick, and he was doing it a favor, but I knew it was the same kitty that kept pissing all over his pillow when we were sleeping. It was... horrible. And yet—"

"Understandable?" Blade asked.

My stomach churned with nausea. It made me sick to even think about it. But we were kids. We were kids that got beat if we complained. Or if we said we were hungry. Or if we brought home bad grades. What the fuck was an eleven-year-old supposed to do with a bunch of kitties running around?

"I brought the pregnant cat home," I whispered.

"None of this was your fault," Pike said curtly. "And I'm not allowing you to think that."

Blade leaned me up and washed my back. "Lance has been in surgery for a few minutes now. We got a text just before we started running the bath."

My shoulders slumped. "Do you think he's going to make it?"

Pike reached his hand down into the water and took mine in his grasp. "He lost a lot of blood."

And that was when I lost it.

"Oh my God," I choked out as sobs poured forth.

I covered my face with my hands as Blade continued

washing my back. My chest jumped with my sobs when something heaved the water over the edge of the tub. Legs became tangled within legs as another pair of arms wrapped around me from the front, and as I leaned forward, I felt Pike's embrace as my aching lower back finally stretched itself out.

"There we go," Blade said, massaging my muscles. "Good as new."

"I'm so proud of you," Pike whispered before he kissed the top of my head.

But as I sat there in that bath, with bloody bubbles popping against my skin, only one thought crossed my mind.

"I'm sorry, Trishelle."

"Pike? Blade?" I said breathlessly.

"What is it, my pet?" Pike asked.

"What's on your mind, beautiful?" Blade asked.

"Who was Trishelle to you guys? Really?"

And my question stopped both of them in their tracks.

25

BLADE

I looked over at Pike and registered his cold, hard stare on Dalia's forehead. His body stilled. The hairs along his upper arms puckered, standing them on end. My heart felt as if it had turned to stone in my chest, and while the chaos of our men resounded downstairs, one question zipped through my mind.

Did we honestly need more trauma after what just happened?

"Guys?" Dalia asked. "Please. I think I deserve to know at this point."

Pike shrugged. "She's got a point."

Dalia's head fell against my shoulder. "Blade?"

She was right, though. She had been through too much with us. Endured too much. Seen too much. And with her life at risk every second she stayed with us, she deserved to know.

She deserved to know that she hadn't been the first.

"Trishelle was..." I began.

I heaved a heavy sigh as Pike picked up Dalia's legs. He placed them in his lap before picking up one of her feet and massaging it. I stared at the wall over his head. I locked my eyes with the frosted glass of the walk-in shower and tried to gather my thoughts.

How the fuck did I tell her about the first woman I had ever loved?

"We were... a family," I said.

Pike nodded. "Together for almost three years."

"The three of you?" Dalia asked softly. "With her?"

I nodded mindlessly. "She struggled. She was, you know."

"Troubled," Pike said.

"Troubled... how?" Dalia asked.

I swallowed hard. "Depression."

"Anxiety," Pike said.

"PTSD."

"She struggled with nightmares. A lot."

"She had a rough past."

Dalia snickered. "I understand that bullshit all too well."

My grip tightened around her. "She came to us in much the same way you did. She got caught up in something she wasn't supposed to, and we sort of overheard a conversation that pissed us off."

"She was being threatened," Pike said curtly. "Let's not mince words."

"Threatened? By who?" Dalia asked.

I ground my teeth together. "Her own father."

"Jesus," she said breathlessly.

Pike took Dalia's other foot into his hand. "We couldn't just turn the other way after what we had heard. I mean, the man threatened her fucking life over a goddamn botched dinner. How fucked up is that?"

"I would've killed him, honestly," Dalia said.

And she said it so plainly. As if taking a life wasn't the most wretched, yet incredible, thing you could do.

"We all have a darkness inside of us," Pike said, staring at me for much longer than I wanted. "And Trishelle was no different. She had a rough childhood, and it got spun into a rough adulthood."

"We couldn't walk away when we heard what had happened, so we told her we could protect her. If she came with us, we could get her away from her father for good," I said flatly.

It grew hard to hold back the tears as a knot formed in my throat.

"Needless to say, I think you pretty much know what comes next," Pike said, dipping her foot back into the soapy water. "The three of us got along well. Really well, in fact."

"It isn't hard to do," Dalia said, leaning deeper into my body.

I slid my arms around her and placed my forehead against the back of her head. "She got pregnant."

Dalia stiffened. "What?"

Pike sighed as he tilted his face toward the ceiling. "At first, we figured she had picked up a virus or some shit. Wasn't keeping much down. All that jazz. It sparked a depressive episode, and we figured it was better if she was under the care of a doctor."

"So, we called our doctor, and he proceeded to inform us that she was pregnant and experiencing hyperemesis gravidarum."

"What?" Dalia asked.

I cleared my throat. "Extreme nausea and vomiting while pregnant."

"She lost a lot of weight," Pike murmured.

"She was practically in a depressive episode during her entire first trimester," I said breathlessly.

Dalia stayed silent for a long time before she finally put the pieces together.

"She was pregnant with Lance's child, wasn't she?"

Pike and I nodded before I pushed myself out of the bath.

"He grew protective, as most men would. We fought constantly."

"He didn't like us touching her. Not when she was so bad off."

"So much fighting," I murmured, reaching for a towel.

Dalia's eyes lingered on my body before I caught her reflection in the mirror. I'd never forget her face, either. The sadness in her eyes. The pity strewn across her face.

I hated when people regarded me with pity.

"Sometime during her second trimester, she came off her depression medication," I said, wrapping the towel around my waist.

Dalia's eyes widened. "She did what?"

Pike shifted in the tub until he was behind her and gathered her into his arms. "Apparently, the doctor had informed her that her depression medication could be harmful to the child, so he switched her prescription. But she never filled it."

"Pike. You make it sound like it's her fault when you put it that way."

He shrugged. "In some ways, it was."

"Pike," Dalia said softly.

I shot him a look. "I was the one that first found her in the bathtub, two weeks shy of her third trimester."

Dalia looked up at me with tear-stained eyes. "She tried to kill herself, didn't she?"

I shook my head. "She didn't try. She succeeded."

Pike's tears silently dripped down his face as I looked back up at the ceiling. No crying. No tears. That was what I had been taught my entire life. Tears made one weak. Tears were something to exploit. Crying meant I had something to lose, and so long as I had something to lose, I'd always be a target in the lifestyle I had chosen.

And yet...

"She, uh," I choked out, "she slit her wrists. And—and there was so—so much blood."

"Blade," Dalia said as she stood up.

I turned my back to her and planted my hands into the bathroom countertop. "Lance took it the hardest, obviously. Blamed himself."

"We all did," Pike managed to say.

Dalia threaded her arms around my waist. "Come here, Blade. You, too, Pike."

I shook my head. "I'm fine. I'm fine. It's just—"

She reached around and gripped my chin. Even with those short, stubby little arms of hers, I felt the clench of her fingers before she turned my head. I rolled my eyes and shifted with her movements, because why the hell would I deny her what she wanted? She had just killed a man. Her life had been irrevocably changed because of us. Because of the situation she had been put in due to our presence.

Just like Trishelle.

And the baby.

A baby I would have loved as if it were my own.

"What?" I asked curtly.

She forced my gaze to stay with hers. "You're not okay, and that's all right."

I scooped her into my arms. I didn't want her to watch me cry so I tucked her head beneath my chin. Her curves molded to my strength, and a tear streaked all the way down to my jawline before tumbling to the top of her head. I heard the tub draining before Pike sloshed his way out. He ripped the towel from around my waist and wrapped it around his, and the entire time, I swayed softly with Dalia in my arms. I wanted to rewind time for her. I wanted to take her all the way back to the bar. All the way back to those cheeky little flirtatious movements and words she had once tossed at us.

It seemed like millennia ago.

And yet, it had only been...

I shook my head. "We should hear from the doctor any minute on Lance."

Pike walked out of the bathroom. "I'm gonna go check on the guys. See how the clean-up is going."

I kissed the top of Dalia's head. "How are you feeling?"

She yawned against my chest. "Tired."

I scooped her voluptuous body into my arms. "I can only imagine. Come on, let's get you in bed."

"But Lance?"

I walked her over to the bed. "Pike will come back with an update."

He nodded before he strode out of the bedroom. "Damn right, I will. Hold on."

I perched us on the edge of the bed before Dalia's shoulders shook. Her tears spilled against my chest, and I clung to her the way I had clung to Trishelle's bleeding body in that tub. I had crawled in with her, you know. Tried to scoop the blood back into her wrists. Good God, the gashes had been so fucking deep.

"I've got you," I whispered, rocking her side to side. "I've got you, beautiful."

Hearing her cry was one thing but listening to the change from crying to snoring broke my heart. She had cried herself to sleep, and it killed part of me inside. She deserved better, just like Trishelle. She deserved more from us, just like Trishelle. She deserved our protection, and our comfort.

She didn't deserve the bloodshed that had dropped into our laps.

"She's not like your mother, you know," Pike said as his voice came alive over my left shoulder.

I snickered. "I was an idiot to ever think so, too."

He walked over and patted me on the shoulder. "She'll understand. You know she will."

I leaned her sleeping body toward him. "Here, can you—"

"Of course," Pike said as he took her from me. "I got her."

My mind held me hostage as memories bombarded my senses. The endless amount of faces my mother brought back to the house while Dad was deployed. The numerous sounds coming from their bedroom upstairs while I slept on the couch, just trying to get away from it all. I remembered every face of every man she had ever fucked behind Dad's back without a care in the world as to what it did to him.

To me.

To our family.

How the fuck could I have ever equated Dalia to her?

"Jesus, there you guys are," Dr. Higgenbaum said as he charged into the room.

I shot to my feet and turned toward him. "Update. Now."

"Doc," Pike asked, tucking Dalia in bed. "Whose blood is that?"

Higgy clasped his hands behind his back. "Lance is stable."

Relief coursed through my veins, but I kept the stone-cold look on my face. "And?"

"Blade," Pike said.

I held my finger up to him and stared the doctor down. "But?"

"But," Higgy said breathlessly, "he's still in surgery. We've hit a point where he'll make it out, but what happens after is up to whatever God you believe in."

I didn't believe in God. "How bad is the damage?"

The doctor shrugged. "About as bad as you'd expect. He seized just before we got him intubated. We lost him once on the surgery table before we located the bullet and fixed the artery that it nicked."

Pike came over and patted my back. "It'll take more than a bullet to kill that stubborn dog."

"So you're saying there's a chance that he'll be stable, but not wake up," I said as the strength in my voice returned.

The doctor nodded. "After he's out of surgery, it's up to chance."

"Hey, Blade," Pike said, squeezing my shoulder.

I slowly turned to look at him. "What?"

"He's going to make it, Blade. He's got this."

But until he was coherent—until he woke up and got back to work—the crew was mine to command.

"Thanks, Doc," I said, brushing past him.

"Blade!" Pike called out.

I turned around and pointed at him. "Stay with Dalia. Don't leave her for a second. I've gotta go talk to the guys. Doc?"

"Yep?"

"Go make sure our boy wakes up."

With every step I took, more blood came into view. With every stride my legs risked, more bodies littered my vision. Our men moved as quickly as possible, hauling them out back and transporting them to every single dump site we had around town. Chaos rained down around us as men broke out plaster and paint, ready to clean up the walls and reduce the sight of war down to nothing but a slight altercation.

But when I found my way to the center of the foyer, everyone stopped.

"So?" Mortar asked. "How's Lance?"

I held up my hand to garner their attention and silence fell around me. Around us, really. I took a second to gather myself. To focus my thoughts and pull them away from the sleeping woman upstairs that deserved heaven instead of the hell we had introduced her to.

Then, I drew in a deep breath.

"Dr. Higgenbaum said that Lance will make it out of surgery—"

A raucous roar erupted around me as men clapped and whistled.

"But," I barked.

The silenced immediately, and the tension grew so thick that I could have sliced through it with a cold fucking butter knife.

"But," I said, putting my hand down, "he's lost a lot of blood. He seized on the table, and they lost him once. He's got a hell of a recuperation ahead of him, and that's if he wakes up from surgery."

"Is there a chance that he won't?" Phil asked.

I looked over at our prospect and saw how badly he struggled not to cry. "Yes, there's a chance he won't."

"What I wouldn't give," Traeger growled, "to resurrect that son of a bitch just to—"

I pinned him with a look. "Right now, we have bigger things to focus on. We've made a mess, and we'll have a hell of a lot of police officers to answer to with all of the gunfire that took place. C.U. Team!"

"Here," Traegar and Mortar said in unison.

They were the best at cleaning shit up, which was why they made up our Clean-Up Team. "You're in charge of the bodies. Plan F, and if that fills up, Plan N."

Phil and Riley stepped to the forefront when I volleyed my finger between the two of them. "We need your Burn-Up skills. We've got a lot of shit in this house that has been touched in ways the police will find if they step foot into this place. Plan C, and if we exhaust that avenue, Plan L."

"What about evidence?" Pike asked at the top of the steps.

I turned to face him. "Get the rest of the guys on it. We have extra furniture in our storage units. Get it out, get it placed, and help them disinfect what they can."

"On it," Pike said, charging down the stairs.

"Any other questions!?" I barked.

The men stayed silent as my back straightened. I had to focus. We all had to focus. We all had a job to do if we were going to get out of this without handcuffs slapped onto our wrists.

And I'd be damned if it happened on my watch.

"Then let's get at it!" I exclaimed and clapped my hands.

I watched as Traeger dashed toward the first body he found. He heaved the man up from the floor, with arms and legs dangling lifelessly along his sides. I tilted my head as I watched him march past me down the hallway. Heading toward the back door, no doubt. But, as the dead man's head bounced, it turned to face me.

I found myself face to face with Dirge's lifeless eyes as his spindly little body rocked with Traeger's movements.

Serves you right for touching what's mine.

"You'll be a great president some day," Pike said, walking past me with a shining new coffee table slung over his back.

I shrugged. "How's Dalia up there?"

He chuckled and walked to the table toward the living room. "Out like a fucking light."

"Good," I said with a nod. "She needs her rest."

"You should go lay down with her," he grunted, setting the table onto the floor in front of him. "She shouldn't be alone right now."

And while I agreed with him, I still shook my head. "The teams need help, so I'll float as necessary. How much furniture do we have to snag?"

He grinned. "We've got enough help on that front. But if

you want to drive one of those vans to the dump site, I know they won't object."

"Hell, no," Phil said, slapping a spackle trowel into my hand. "You've always been better at patching holes. You patch, I'll set up fans, and we'll have these walls painted within the hour."

That brought a grin to my face. "Time to put this place back together."

Pike shoved the table across the floor toward the living room opening. "One brush of paint at a time."

And as I looked up the stairs in the general direction where Dalia lay sleeping, I made a silent vow. A promise to her, as well as to myself.

I'll never keep you here if you don't want to stay.

But I prayed with all my might to a God I didn't believe in that when she woke up, she chose us.

Even if we brought nothing but death and destruction into her world.

26

LANCE

"Lance!"

I searched for the source of the voice, but it sounded so garbled. Like a botched radio translation from halfway across the world.

"Lance! Where are you!?"

I cupped my hands over my mouth. "I'm over here!"

"Lancey-boy."

I paused. "Mom?"

"Lancey-booooy."

I took off running. "Mom! Where are you!?"

"Get down!"

Something tackled me, and it felt like my face was dragged against a pile of rocks.

"God damn it. Mom!"

"Lancey-boy? Where in the world did you learn to talk like that?"

Something weighed my chest down, preventing me from breathing. Panic rushed through my veins. Voices swirled around me. Voices, nicknames, and people whose voices I hadn't heard in so long.

"Lancey-boy."

"Lance!"

"Tucker!"

"Sweetcheeks?"

I froze at the sound of her voice. "What?"

Someone tapped me on my shoulder, and suddenly I found myself standing up. Not laying down, not face-first in whatever gravel had chiseled its way across my cheeks. But standing.

In a hospital room.

"Sweetcheeks, look."

There she was, as beautiful as the day I first laid eyes on her. With chestnut brown hair and forest green eyes sat the mother of my child.

With bandages wrapped around her wrists.

"Trishelle," I said breathlessly. "Trishelle, what the hell did—"

"Look at how beautiful he is."

A chair slid behind me, knocking me clear off my feet. He carried me to her bedside, and as the sound of a child bombarded my ears, she tilted her arms down.

"He looks just like you," Trishelle said.

I couldn't pick my head up. I wanted to so badly. I wanted to look into her eyes. I wanted to stroke my fingers through her hair. I wanted to do so many things, but mostly I wanted to ask her why.

Why the hell had she done it?

"Isn't he perfect?" she asked.

I gazed down into eyes as deeply brown as my own. "He's amazing, Trishelle."

"Sweetcheeks?"

"Yeah?" I asked as I finally lifted my head.

And when I did, I saw her eyeballs bleeding.

"Trishelle!" I barked and shot to my feet.

"Why didn't you save me?" she asked as her head fell off her shoulders.

"Holy fuck!" I bellowed.

I scooped the crying baby out of her arms as blood poured from her wrists. It pooled onto the floor, gathering around my feet and filling the hospital room around us. I cradled my son—our son—in my arms, and as I backed toward the door, I watched her body fall into the pool of red filling the space around us.

"I'm so sorry," I whispered.

When I looked back down at our son, he changed. Morphed. Instead of an innocent, brown-eyed baby staring up at me, I saw Blade. Pike. Phil. Mortar. My men. Every single one of them. Those that had come and gone. Those that had come and stayed. They flashed upon my child's face like a nightmarish rewind as the blood climbed up my legs.

Filling up the room like a fucking pool.

"Trishelle!" I roared.

I sank into the blood. I lifted my child above my head as the floor opened beneath me, slowly swallowing me whole. The baby screamed. I cried out for Trishelle to help. But as the blood bubbled up my chest, something squishy beneath my feet gave way.

And I dropped our child .

"Why didn't you save us?" Trishelle asked.

"No, come on! Stay with me!" I bellowed, swimming through the blood.

The child's crying sounded so far away.

"You could have saved us," Trishelle whispered.

"Noooooo!"

I fell through the floor, the mess all around me drying up almost instantaneously as I fell through midair. My arms scrambled to cling to something. My feet dangled and flailed about. My stomach ripped itself into my throat, threatening to turn inside out before my back slammed against something hard.

And as I gazed up at a bloody red ceiling, I heard her voice.

"I'm so proud of you, Mister Man."

I closed my eyes. "I know you're not there, Mom."

Her warm hand cupped my cheek. "Just open those eyes for me, Lancey-boy."

I peeked an eye open and found her smiling face staring back at me. "Mom?"

"Come here, Mister Man. You've worked so hard."

I bolted upright and scooped her into my arms. I pulled her onto me, burying my face into her bosom the way I always used to do whenever I was scared. My body trembled. My muscles quaked. She slid her hands up and down my back, giggling like she always did whenever I held her a bit too tightly.

"You're making it hard to breathe, Lancey-boy. Why don't you let up a bit?"

I shook my head. "No."

I wondered if I was dead. If this was what the afterlife held for me. And as if she could hear my every thought...

"No, Mister Man, you're not dead. Not yet, anyway."

That picked up my head. "What do you mean, not yet?"

She smiled down at me. "I figured that would bring you out of your hidey-hole."

"Mom, what are you—"

She poofed into thin air before landing on her feet in front of me. She offered her hand. Her outstretched hand, free of the battle scars she accrued over the years from fighting her entire life.

"Walk with me," she said.

Her smile enticed me to stand. I took her hand, linking her arm with mine as her warmth radiated up my arm. Her smile lit up the stars as they blinked into being all around us. The room faded into nothingness, not that I could have told you what it looked like anyway.

My mother felt so real.

"How is this possible?" I asked as we walked.

"Watch," she said softly.

She waved her free hand in front of us and the dark, starry sky we walked upon molded and morphed. The blackness of the floor became the hard, scratchy carpet of my childhood home. The stained red couch in the living room faded into view, sitting in front of the massive box television set she had been so proud of fixing all by herself after finding it on the side of the road. I found myself staring out the back door, looking at the tire swing she had set up all by herself for me on my tenth birthday.

It swayed in the breeze that kicked up as the trees rustled around us.

"I'd almost forgotten about this place," I said mindlessly.

"Close your eyes and enjoy the moment," Mom whispered.

I did as she asked, and a faint beeping echoed off in the distance. Its rhythmic pulsing rattled my ribcage, and I could have sworn I felt something weighing against my chest.

But when I opened my eyes, it all disappeared.

"Is this heaven?" I asked.

She giggled as her head fell against my bicep. "My little slice of it, yeah. Are you hungry? I've got soup on the stove."

My stomach growled in response. "I'd love some."

She patted it kindly before flashing me that comforting smile of hers. "Come on, I've got that baked garlic bread you always loved."

"Lance."

A whisper on the wind. That was what it sounded like.

"Lance, wake up."

"Mister Man, you coming?" Mom asked.

I watched the tire swing tumble around in the breeze. Except, the trees weren't moving.

"Lancey-boy?" she asked.

I cleared my throat and turned around. "Coming, Mom."

I eased my way back into the house and slid the door closed behind me. I found Mom setting out two place settings at the small kitchen table that barely had enough room for my fucking arms. I chuckled as I walked over to the fridge. I grabbed her favorite drink, that nasty aloe water with the chewy bits in it.

"Got any beer?" I asked with a grin.

She swatted at me playfully. "Don't tell me you drink that swill. I thought I raised you better than that."

"Lance! Wake up!"

Dalia.

Holy fucking hell, that was Dalia's voice.

"She's beautiful, you know," Mom said, taking the aloe water from my hand.

I nodded and looked around the kitchen. "Yeah, she really is."

"Sharing her, though?" she asked as she cracked her drink open. "Since when is that a thing?"

I barked with laughter then reached into the refrigerator for a regular person water. "I guess some things just can't be explained."

"You've got that right," she murmured.

She patted my seat at the table and I couldn't move quickly enough to get there. That rhythmic beeping kept rattling on in the back of my mind as the fresh tomato basil soup called out to me. Mom ripped off a hunk of the garlic bread and set it on a plate at my elbow. She handed me the smallest spoon I'd ever seen in my fucking life, like a doll's spoon sitting in the palm of my hand.

"Really, Mom?" I asked. "Do I look like I can use this?"

She picked up her bowl and sipped from the side. "There are always other paths to take. Never forget that."

I stared at her for a long time as she continued sipping her soup. That beeping held me hostage before I finally managed to pull my gaze away. Nothing felt right, and yet everything felt as it should. From Mom's touch to Trishelle's screaming to the way I cradled our newborn son.

What the hell was happening?

I picked up the soup and brought it to my lips. Mom smiled at me from beyond the rim of her bowl as I tipped it up, taking the biggest gulp of my life. But the metallic taste caught me off-guard.

Rough, jagged, and jarring.

"What the fuck?" I asked as I coughed.

I sputtered soup all over my chin and had to reach for the hem of my shirt to wipe it off.

"I swear, you and that mouth of yours. You get it from your father, you know."

I wiped my chin off and spat the soup back out into the bowl. "Why does your soup taste like that?"

"Who said it was soup?" she asked.

I slowly looked over at her. "You said it was—"

My gaze dropped back down to the bowl and my stomach turned over onto itself. It wasn't soup. Not my mother's soup anyway. It was blood. A bowl full of it. The metallic taste lingered at the back of my throat as nausea encompassed me. It reminded me of the blood that had spilled all over the marble floors of the foyer.

"Dalia," I whispered.

"Lancey-boy?" Mom asked.

"Lance! Please!"

"Dalia," I said as I stood.

Mom stood with me. "Lance."

I stared her down. "Yeah, Mom?"

She walked out from around the table and cupped my cheek. "There's more than one path to take. Always remember that."

"LANCE!"

Mom faded away. Just like the hospital room. Just like Trishelle. Just like my son, sitting right there in my arms. Panic gripped my heart. My soul felt as if it were being ripped into two pieces. And as I reached out for my mother's fading hand, she sprung back to life.

"Is this what you really want, son?" she asked, linking our fingers together.

"Lance, please," Dalia whispered.

Her voice sounded so clear. So strong. Yet, so defeated.

"Why do I have to choose?" I asked. "Why the fuck do I always have to choose?"

She smiled softly and shook her head. "You and that language. It'll get you into trouble one of these days."

"Mommy. Please."

She cupped my hand within both of hers. "Mister Man, at some point in time, we all have to choose."

"No, Lance," Dalia said through her tears. "Please. I can't lose you, too. Just open your eyes. Open your eyes, and I can do the rest."

"She needs you," Mom whispered.

I pulled her into my arms and held her tightly. "I need you."

"Who said you were without me?"

My lower lip quivered. "I miss you so much, Mom."

She threaded her arms around me, even though she couldn't link her hands, and hugged me as tightly as I'd ever been hugged before. And in that moment, I knew.

I knew what I needed to do.

"I'll always be with you, Lancey-boy. Always."

"Lance, for the love of fuck, wake UP!"

"Guh-huuuuuuh!"

I gasped for air as my lungs cried out for mercy. Something slammed into my chest and wetness dripped down my shoulder. That incessant beeping continued to pound against my ears. Footsteps rushed around, muddling my train of thought as I tried to blink the world back into focus.

"Oh, my God. Lance. You're awake," Dalia said breathlessly.

I forced my arms to move. Even though they hurt. Even though they weighed two tons dangling from my fucking body, I managed to sling them across her body as she sobbed against my chest.

Her weight.

The whole of her beautiful, seductive, precious weight.

"I'm here, Dalia," I whispered. "I'm here, and I'm not going anywhere. I promise."

27

DALIA

I felt my shoulder shaking and my eyes snapped open. Disorientation clouded my judgment as something fuzzy worked its way into my view.

Then, those decadent blue eyes came into view.

"Lance is finally out of surgery," Pike said softly.

That was all I needed to hear, too.

"Lance!" I exclaimed, jumping up from bed.

"Wait, wait, wait," Pike said, taking my hand.

"Lance!"

He helped me to my feet as he took both of my hands within his. "He's still asleep. He got out a few minutes ago and—"

I gazed up into his face. "Is he alive?"

He nodded. "Yes, he's alive."

"Then, let me go," I glowered and wrenched away from him.

I took off down the hallway, making my way down the stairs. Blood rushed through my ears, garbling sounds together as men rushed around me, spackling walls and dragging furniture across the floor. How long had I been asleep?

Where the fuck was I supposed to be going?

"Dalia," Blade said.

He moved in the corner of my vision, and I whipped my head toward him. His long legs moved in my direction, and all sounds seemed to fade from my ears. I didn't like the look Blade had on his face. I didn't like the way he hovered over me as he cupped my cheek. His dexterous fingers stretched into my hair, tugging at the knots that had formed during my lazy nap.

"Where is he?" I whispered.

He nodded behind him. "Down the hallway, last door on the left."

I tried to move away from his grasp, but he gripped my hair and held me steady.

"Blade," I warned.

"He looks rough," he said, his head tilting off to the side, "so you need to brace yourself."

Footsteps came down the stairs and as I peered over my shoulder, I saw Pike standing in the middle of them. His gaze slid along my form, and that was when I realized just how crooked his body had become. He held himself up on the banister, as if exhaustion itself threatened to drown him where he stood. And when I turned back toward Blade, I didn't see darkness in his stare. Or apathy.

I saw worry.

None of it sat well with me, either.

"I hear you," I said.

Then, he released my hair. "Go. Higgy says he can hear us. Maybe."

"Maybe?"

He nodded mindlessly and his gaze locked onto something over the top of my head. "Yeah. Maybe."

It took all the strength I had to move, but when I did, I didn't stop until I came to the door with beeping behind it. I closed my eyes and drew in a deep breath when I raised my hand to the doorknob. Was I honestly ready? Was I ready to view whatever carnage sat behind the door?

No, I wasn't.

But I sure as fuck wasn't leaving Lance to do this alone, either.

"Lance," I said softly, turning the doorknob. "I'm here."

I pushed it open slowly and nothing could have prepared me for what I saw. His pale skin. His sunken in eyes. The absence of, well, anything. Tubes ran in and out of every orifice he had, and the beeping machines kept whirring and humming.

"Lance, wake up," I choked out.

Maybe if I asked him enough, he would.

"Lance! Wake up!"

A shadow moved in the corner of my eye and I whipped toward it, only to find a man dressed in a white coat with glasses sliding down the bridge of his nose.

"You must be Dalia," he said.

I slid my eyes down his form. "Doctor?"

He nodded as he held out his hand. "Dr. Higgenbaum."

I simply looked at his extension before turning back to Lance. "How did he do in surgery?"

"It was touch and go," he said before clearing his throat. "But he hung on."

My legs carried me to Lance's side, even though I didn't feel myself moving. "How long will he be out?"

"I'm not sure."

I snapped my head toward the doctor. "The fuck do you mean by that?"

He clasped his hands behind his back. "We've done everything we can for him, physically. He lost a lot of blood, and at one point in time, we completely lost him on the table. So opening those eyes of his is completely up to what his body chooses to do."

He looked so helpless. My knees were weak and I barely caught myself on the edge of the bed. Tubes up his nose forced oxygen into his lungs and I.V.'s in the tops of his hands forced fluids into his body. My toes tingled at the sight. Goosebumps spread along my body as I reached out and placed my hand on top of his heart. It was beating. Lance was alive.

And yet, it didn't feel as if he were alive.

"Maybe if I yell really loudly," I whispered.

The doctor chuckled, and I wanted to strangle him for it. "You could always try."

I drew in a deep breath. "Lance! Please!"

But the man didn't even fucking flinch.

"LANCE!" I yelped as I stood back to my feet.

I held my breath, waiting for him to move. Waiting for him to speak. Waiting for him to open those angry, brooding eyes and demand the neck of the man that had done this to him. My stare fell to his wound; to his torso, wrapped in gauze. I placed my hand over it and closed my eyes, conjuring the sight of a picture of Jesus my mother had hanging in the bathroom growing up.

Why the hell she wanted that picture staring at her while she took a shit was beyond me, but I needed that face.

I needed that power.

I needed that god to bring Lance back to me.

"Lance, please," I whispered.

My lips murmured with my prayer. If there was a god, and if he gave a fucking damn about what was happening on a planet he apparently created, then he needed to do something. Anything. I had done my part. I had eradicated the evil that threatened to pull my only living shred of family apart. These men had become my family. In the short time I had known them, my entire life had fallen into place. My wants. My wishes. My dreams. My fears. All of it culminated and swirled together, giving birth to the most insane of situations.

The most beautiful of situations.

"All you have to do is open your eyes," I whispered, curling my fingertips into the gauze wrapped around his body. "Just open those pretty little eyes for me, and I can do the rest."

"We all can do the rest," Blade said, his hand settling onto my shoulder.

I turned my lips toward his touch and kissed his skin. "Really?"

"Yeah," Pike said, wrapping his arm around my waist. "The four of us. Together. If that's what you want."

Tears slid down my tired cheeks and a smile crossed my face. "Did you hear that, Lance? The four of us. What a motley crew we are."

Pike chuckled. "Four peas in a pod."

"I hate peas," Blade murmured.

I nudged him softly before I whipped around to face the doctor. "Is it possible that he's got an infection?"

Dr. Higgenbaum slowly shook his head. "No. He's completely stable. The bullet has been removed. He's clear of infection for the moment."

"For the moment."

He nodded. "I'm running blood tests every hour."

"And when's the next one?"

The doctor smiled, but it was a painful smile. "Fifty-five minutes."

I slowly turned back toward Lance's helpless body. "Do we have guards outside?"

"The entire crew," Blade said.

"If he wants to wake up, he'll wake up," Pike said as he kissed my temple.

What the fuck did that even mean? I didn't have a clue, but

it didn't stop me from crawling into bed at his side. I wanted to feel him. I wanted to flood him with warmth. Maybe he was just tired. Maybe he needed someone to sleep next to him to make him feel safe. Maybe he just didn't feel safe opening his eyes.

"Lance?" I asked as I laid down beside him.

Maybe if I said his name the right way, in the right timbre, he'd wake up.

"Lance, it's me," I whispered.

I traced faceless pictures on his stomach and perched my head on his shoulder.

"Lance."

Pike reached for me. "Dalia, we should let him—"

I smacked his hand away before I pressed myself up onto my elbows, gazing down into Lance's immobile face.

"Lance."

"Pike's right," Blade said, sliding his fingers through my hair. "We've got a lot of work around here to do anyway."

I shoved myself up so far that I hovered my face in his. "Lance. Don't make me do it."

"Don't make you do what?" Pike asked.

I shuffled and moved around until I was on my knees. "You aren't leaving me a choice."

The doctor finally spoke up. "Maybe we should get her—"

I got right into Lance's motherfucking face.

"Goddamn it, Lance. I didn't kill that son of a bitch so you could die on me. You hear me? I didn't screw myself over for life and forever change the way I view the world so you could go soft on me now. I know you can hear me. I know somewhere in that addled brain of yours, you hear my voice. So, wake up. Wake up, Lance."

"We need to get her out of here," someone murmured.

"You take left, I'll take right," someone else said.

Their voices muddled together as their shadows hovered

over me, but I wasn't leaving the room. I wasn't leaving without hearing that man's voice.

So, I slammed my fists against his chest as hard as I could. "Lance! For the love of fuck, wake UP!"

"Guh-huuuuuh!"

"Holy fucking Christ," Blade said breathlessly.

"Move," Dr. Higgenbaum commanded. "Everyone move, now!"

I scooted back, but I refused to climb off the bed. "Oh my God. Lance. You're awake."

Jesus Christ, it actually worked.

I watched as the doctor shined a light into Lance's tired eyes. He checked all of the tubes and started to talk Lance through directions as he slowly removed one that had been shoved down his throat. Listening to that man gag was one of the most incredible sounds I'd ever heard. Seeing him move his hands, swatting them around as if there were an annoying fly buzzing about, brought such joy to my chest that I couldn't help but sob.

And the second the doctor moved out of the way, I flung myself onto his body.

I couldn't speak. I couldn't breathe. All I could do was cry into his shoulder as his body moved around beneath mine. His legs spread, accommodating the whole of my form as he grunted with effort. His arms blanketed me. His hands splayed across my body. Holding me, just like he always did.

"I'm here, Dalia," he whispered. "I'm here, and I'm not going anywhere, I promise."

"You fucking better not," I hissed.

"Good to see you back, my man," Pike said.

I heard the tears in his voice, even as Blade cleared his throat. "Welcome back."

"See?" I asked as I lifted my head, watching tears drip onto his face. "I knew you could do it."

"Dalia?" Lance asked breathlessly.

I cupped his cheeks. "Yes? What is it? Anything. Whatever you need."

His brow stitched together tightly. "Were you just... on top of me?"

Pike chuckled. "Yep."

Blade snickered. "Just needed the warmth of a good pussy, I guess."

Listening to Lance laugh felt like a miracle in and of itself. But when he coughed and sputtered, a straw came out of nowhere.

And I looked up to find Dr. Higgenbaum holding a cup of ice water.

"Drink this, it'll help with the dryness," he said.

I took the cup from him. "Thank you. For everything."

He gave me a soft smile. "It's no problem. I'm just glad he's awake."

"I've got you, okay?" I asked, turning my attention back to Lance. "Whatever comes our way, I've got you."

"We've got you," Pike said, stepping up behind me.

Lance stopped drinking long enough to speak. "And Blade?"

He folded his arms across his chest. "You know damn good and well I'm not going anywhere."

A grin spread across Lance's pale cheeks. "I see you've had a change of heart, then."

Blade shrugged. "What can I say? I'm a sucker for fierce women."

"Here, here," Lance said.

You know, before he coughed again.

"Drink some more. There's plenty of it," I cooed softly.

He studied me hard. I saw the gears turning behind those

eyes as he took a few more gulps of water. He drained the damn cup before his lips released the straw, and I set the cup off to the side on a table next to the bed.

I didn't have to wonder what was on his mind, though.

Because the second he asked the question, I knew I couldn't avoid it.

"You know about Trishelle, don't you?" Lance asked.

I looked over at Pike and he turned toward the doctor. "Give us a few, Doc."

"Come back in fifteen with more water, Higgy," Blade said as he stood to his feet.

The doctor reached for the empty cup. "I'll take my time."

I waited until the door closed. Until the doctor's footsteps receded all the way down the hallway, out of sight and out of mind.

Then, I turned to face Lance once more.

"Yeah," I said softly. "They told me."

He closed his eyes and I panicked.

"No, no, no, no," I said, tapping his cheek. "You don't get to close those eyes."

He snapped them open. "How much did they tell you?"

I placed my forehead against his and cupped the stubble on his cheeks with my palms. "Enough to tell you that you have to stop blaming yourself for someone else's actions."

He shook his head. "I could have—"

I kissed his lips softly, stopping him in his tracks. "Depression is hard, okay? It's a lifelong battle that started well before the three of you found your way into her world."

"I should have known that—"

I tapped his cheek softly and glared down at him. "You know as well as I do that not everyone makes it out of that battle alive. It's hell on earth, and what happened to her is not your fault."

"It was our fighting that—"

I captured his lips once more to shut him up. "She didn't come off her meds because of you."

He didn't say anything, and when he diverted his gaze, I moved with him. I refused to let him do this alone a second longer. I refused to let him carry this around. It was too much of a burden for something he had no hand in doing.

And I wouldn't let my Lance suffer in silence.

"She didn't. Come off. Her meds. Because of you," I said curtly.

His gaze returned to mine. "Then why did she? I don't understand."

I heaved a heavy sigh. "She probably thought that was best for the baby. Those medications can wreak havoc on things like that. Hell, any medication can. Have you seen those fucking commercials geared around women who took Tylenol and shit during their pregnancy? That shit is bonkers, Lance. Something as simple as Tylenol, and boom. Birth defects. Attention issues. Brain rewiring. All of it."

He swallowed hard. "Why didn't she tell us then? Why didn't she come to us?"

I had no answer for him, and I hated that. "I don't know, handsome. But you've got to stop blaming yourself for something she did. You're not the reason she died, Lance. You're the reason she lived for as long as she could, and you have to stop thinking otherwise because you know damn good and well, like I do, that if she loved you guys like I love you, she wouldn't have wanted that."

Silence fell all around us as Lance's eyes widened. His eyebrows rose clear off his fucking forehead, and I swear if they moved anymore, they'd hover in midair above his head.

Blade was the first to speak. "Did you just say—"

I held my hand up to him, stopping his words in their tracks.

"We can talk about it later. But you need to rest so that we can have that talk."

Lance lifted his hand and cupped my cheek. "Thank you, my angel ."

And at that moment, as I gazed around at my men and their shocked, cute little features, I realized there was nowhere else I wanted to be.

No matter how bad, how bloody, or how terrible things got.

"Now," I said as I slid off to Lance's side. "Where's that doctor with his water?"

28

PIKE

ONE WEEK LATER

"All right," Blade said, raising his hand, "church is in session. Let's take a seat."

All of the guys lumbered around, finding their chairs before they flopped down into him. It had been a hell of a week, and all of us were exhausted beyond measure.

Dalia had kept us going, though.

She kept a fire lit beneath our ass cheeks every time we felt like we wanted to stop.

"So," Blade said, easing himself into the chair at the head of the table. "Before anyone asks, Lance is doing well. Still recuperating. Still having to rest. But healing nicely."

"How much damage to our accounts?" I asked.

Blade licked his lips. "As you guys know, we had to pay a hell of a lot of officers to keep their traps shut on what happened here at the clubhouse, and it cost us all a pretty penny."

"How much?" Phil asked.

"Traeger?" Blade asked.

The man stood to his feet. "By my calculations, a little over one mil."

A sea of groans kicked up, and I had to admit, I wanted to

join in. It was more than we'd ever paid anyone in town, and all it had done was keep people's mouths shut and save our men from prison time. But it was worth it.

Especially since Dalia was one of the ones we had to protect.

"But there's some good news," Blade said.

"Thank fuck," Mortar murmured.

"I've got a buyer interested in some of our backstock, and the payday alone will replenish what we spent and get the rest of us through the back half of the year."

Usually, there were cheers and applause at that point. Maybe some high fives. Definitely some eager questions on how things might go down. But there was nothing.

Just a tired silence that draped over all of us.

"Well, don't rejoice at once," Blade said flatly.

I held up my hand. "Guys, I know it's been a hell of a past few weeks. I know we've all had a time trying to wrap our heads around the shit that unfolded, as well as what's going on with our president. So let's do him proud with this one. When he comes back, let's make sure he comes back with a clean slate so he can look forward. Not back."

Blade pointed at me. "Exactly what he said. So, who's interested? We can take a vote. All in favor of the transaction, raise your hands."

I'd never seen hands shoot up into the air that quickly, and it made Blade grin. For the first time in a fucking week, I watched that devious smile cross his face.

And I knew things would be all right.

"So, what's the plan? I know you've got one," I said with a smirk.

Blade leaned forward, placing his forearms onto the wooden table in front of him. "The buyer is a group of three individuals from out of the country. They're here to help start a new faction of their business, and they need firepower."

"What business are they in?" Riley asked.

Blade's eyes shimmered. "Let's just say they were burned by a dirty cop that got caught in some crossfire."

My eyes widened. "Holy fuck, Blade, are you talking about Griggs?"

He leaned back. "He's reached out and offered to pay a serious premium for the shit we've got. Anyone got any objections?"

I scoffed. "I've got a few."

Blade nodded slowly. "If I told you that Dalia was the one that floated the idea in the first place, would that make you feel better?"

Mortar snickered. "That's a hell of a woman you guys got there."

"Don't I know it," I murmured and raked my hands down my face.

"So?" Blade asked. "Are you really going to be the one to tell her that the deal she set up for us isn't going to go through?"

"Hell, no," I said.

"Then, let's start hashing out some details."

That church session was the longest in our history. We stayed there for four fucking hours figuring out how best to do this. I had no fucking clue how Dalia had managed to get in touch with Tommy motherfucking Griggs, or what kind of upper hand she used to bring his ass to the table. But after what she'd done for us— what she had done for Lance—the least we could do was trust her.

And after we were done setting things up with the purchase, Blade clapped his hands.

"Church dismissed. You have your orders. Now let's get to it."

As the guys scattered, I sat there across the table from Blade. He pinched the bridge of his nose as his shoulders slumped, and I wondered what he hadn't told us. The barrage of footsteps that lumbered down the hallway soon dissipated before they slammed their way out the front door, and the heavy afternoon sun blazed a trail through the floor-to-ceiling tinted windows of our third-floor conference room.

The clubhouse looked like it had never been touched.

But our memories knew better than that.

"Cat got your tongue?" I asked.

Blade shot to his feet. "She reached out to him herself."

I slowly stood. "That's a hell of a move."

"I still don't know what the fuck she told the man. She won't tell me. But she says the deal is solid, so I'm doing my best to trust her."

I walked over to him. "It's more than you've done in the past."

"She's earned it, don't you think?"

I patted his shoulder and squeezed it. "She's done more than earned it."

"Right," he murmured.

I walked over to the door. "Come on, let's go check on our patient. I'm sure he's driving her nuts right now."

"You sure it's not her driving him nuts? She's got him eating so clean that I'm pretty sure his second stomach is starving."

I barked with laughter as we made our way down the stairs. "She just wants him to heal up right. That's all."

"Yeah, and starve him in the process."

I nudged him playfully. "Well, don't almost get yourself killed and you'll never have to endure the torture."

"Thank fuck," he murmured.

And yet, that cheeky little grin of his refused to climb down off his face.

"Hey, hey," I said, walking into Lance's bedroom, "look who's up and about."

Blade walked in behind me and clocked Lance standing at the window. "You shouldn't be out of bed yet."

"Yeah," Dalia said as she stood to her feet from the chair next to the bed, "so tell that to him. He's being stubborn as fuck about needing help getting into the bathroom."

Blade chuckled and walked over to Lance's side. "Yeah, it's a man thing. I'll help him out. Come on."

Lance shot me a look. "Make sure she doesn't peek, will ya? She'll probably do it just to prove a point."

"What point?" Dalia asked, walking over to me. "The point that you're a stubborn fucking man whose dick I can suck, but not watch while I help you take a piss?"

I barked with laughter. "I'll make sure she stays right here."

As Blade helped Lance hobble into the bathroom, Dalia flinched by my side. I slid my hand into hers, interlocking our fingers and holding her at my side. I knew she'd never understand, but I got it. Dalia had seen him at his lowest, and he wanted to build himself back up. Show her he was still strong enough to do so.

Blade peered over his shoulder as he stood in the doorway of the bathroom. "We're good here. Why don't you two go and figure out what we're gonna do for lunch?"

"I'm not leaving him," Dalia said.

I wrapped my arm around her. "We'll order something."

"You can't order healthy food around here, Pike," Dalia spat.

I kissed the top of her head. "One pizza isn't gonna hurt."

"Hell yeah to pizza!" Lance exclaimed from the bathroom.

"When you're better!" Dalia yelled back.

Blade rolled his eyes before he closed the door, and I felt Dalia move again. Well, she tried, at least. I moved in front of her and placed my hands on her shoulders, staring into her face even though she refused to let her gaze meet mine. I clocked the bags beneath her eyes. The dark circles she tried to cover up using makeup that didn't match her skin tone. The crookedness of her stature.

I knew exactly why Lance was pissed.

"Not taking care of yourself doesn't help him," I said.

She didn't say anything. She just shook her head, like she could somehow shrug off how much she had neglected herself.

"You've already taken off work," I said.

She nodded, but she didn't look at me. Hell, she hardly moved, save for the nodding of her head in the first place.

"Did you find anyone to cover Lisa's shifts for you?"

Another nod, but no voiced guidance.

It broke my heart. "How are you doing, my pet?"

That made her look up at me. "As well as I can."

"Has anyone asked you that since everything happened?"

She rolled her eyes. "Honestly? I'm doing my best not to think about it."

I lifted my hand and tucked a strand of rogue hair behind her ear. "Take it from me, that's not a good strategy. You need to talk with someone about it."

Her lower lip quivered. "I knew him, Pike."

I brought her in for a hug and tucked her head beneath my chin. "I know you did."

She wrapped her arms around me and held me as tightly as she could. Which wasn't as tight as I figured she could have held me. So, I sat her down on the edge of Lance's bed.

"Talk to me," I whispered.

She drew in a broken breath. "I killed him, and I knew him, and every time I close my eyes, I see him."

I couldn't imagine what she was going through. Killing someone, I had done before. But killing someone I knew? Someone I had a past with? Someone I grew up with? I'd never done that before. That was completely different than simply defending what was yours from some nameless attacker. From some punk in the middle of the night that had chosen to disregard you while eyeing your woman. Hell, even that asshole in the alleyway meant nothing. I didn't lose one ounce of sleep after we splattered his brains all over that bar dumpster.

But if I had known the man? Grown up with the man? Understood why he turned out the way he did?

I wouldn't be okay, either.

"I've got you," I murmured, swaying us softly side to side, "I've got you, my pet."

"I'm—I'm so so—sorry," she choked out. "I never cry like this. I cry all—all the time, it seems, and I've never—I don't—"

I kissed the top of her head. "I'm glad you feel comfortable doing it with me. We're *all* glad you feel that comfortable with us."

She lifted her head and looked up at me with those puffy, tired, red eyes of hers. "I do, actually."

I crooked my finger beneath her chin. "Good."

I couldn't help myself. Even as her salty tears dribbled along her lips, I brought that mouth of hers to mine. It had been so long since I had tasted her. Ages, even. And as our tongues melded together, she blanketed herself over me. She crawled into my lap, straddling me as we sat perched on the edge of Lance's bed. My hands slid down her ass cheeks, cupping them. I pulled her toward my growing dick.

Jesus Christ, I wanted the release. I knew she needed it, too.

But just as I sucked on that plump lower lip of hers, Blade cleared his throat.

"It's your turn to shower him after he's done," he said flatly.

Dalia giggled then quickly moved off my lap, and I certainly didn't miss how she eyed my cock as it pressed against the zipper of my pants. "Yikes. Sorry about that."

I stood and winked down at her. "Duty calls."

But, I bent forward and pressed one more kiss to her lips before I stared deeply into her eyes.

"And don't you fucking dare apologize for something like that."

"Okay," she said softly.

I tilted my head as Blade came out of the bathroom. "Have you talked to Lisa lately?"

Her eyes danced between mine before they widened. "Oh, God. No, actually. I-I-I've been so... caught up in things."

I shoved my hand into my pocket and pulled out my cell. "Here. Call her."

She looked down at the phone for a while before she took it. "Thank you."

"Call them so I know how they are before I head into the bathroom?"

She shot her gaze back up at me. "Yeah?"

I smoothed my thumb along her cheek. "Yeah."

Blade walked up behind her. "Want some privacy?"

I was honestly shocked when she shook her head. "No."

I placed my hand on her shoulder. "Okay."

Blade slipped his arm around her waist. "We're right here."

And as I watched her dial her best friend's number, the phone started ringing.

Before she placed it on speakerphone.

"He-he—hello?" a hiccupping woman's voice asked when the line picked up.

Dalia gasped. "Lisa! What's wrong? What's happened to Brayden? Is he okay?"

"Dalia?" she asked. "Dalia! Oh, my God. Dalia. I—I have to —Brayden—"

She pulled away from me. "I'm coming. Wherever you are, whatever's happened—"

"Dalia," I said.

"No, no, no," Lisa said as she sniffled, "it's not like that. Dalia, the most wonderful thing has happened. I don't—"

That froze Dalia in her tracks and I looked over at Blade. He watched her like a hawk as that dastardly grin of his appeared on his face.

"Wait, what?" Dalia asked breathlessly.

"Does she know?" I asked.

"Know what?" Dalia asked as she looked up at me.

"No, she doesn't know yet," Blade said.

I whipped my head toward him. "You haven't told her?"

He folded his arms over his chest. "We've been a bit busy."

Dalia tilted her head. "Busy with what?"

"Who's that in the background?" Lisa asked.

Dalia quickly turned her back. "Nothing, it's nothing. Just... it's been a busy week."

"Dalia," Lisa said breathlessly, "someone covered Brayden's hospital stay."

I watched her back straighten before she slowly turned toward us. Lance chuckled from the bathroom as I heard water sloshing around, but Dalia didn't budge.

She simply stood there, staring up at us as tears dripped down her cheeks.

"Someone... did what?" she asked softly.

"I know!" Lisa squealed. "I don't even know what happened. Brayden is fine. It—the—the payment? Whatever— god, Dalia, I don't even wanna question it. What if it's too good to be true?"

Dalia tilted her head as she held the speakerphone to her mouth. "I'm so happy for you, Lisa."

She sniffled again. "It wasn't just payment, you know? I don't even know who did it. One minute, we were discussing treatment options for Brayden and his clotting disorder that I couldn't afford, and the next thing I know they were prepping him for procedures. I don't—it's like someone just…"

"Handed over their credit card?" Dalia asked as her gaze volleyed between me and Blade.

"Hey, don't look at me," Blade said as he held up his hands in mock surrender, "it was Lance's idea."

"Seriously, who's that in the background?" Lisa asked.

Dalia shook her head. "My God, I adore you guys."

"What?" Lisa asked.

"What?" Blade and I asked in unison.

Then, she turned her attention back to the phone call. "Listen, I have to go. But, why don't you, me, and Brayden go out and get some food tomorrow?"

"I'm not sure if he's up for going out anywhere, but you can certainly come over with things. We can hang out in the backyard while he plays video games and recuperates."

She wiped her tears off her neck. "Sounds great. I can't wait to hug you guys. I've been so worried."

"I can't thank you enough for covering my shifts. Did anyone give you any guff over it?"

She smiled softly as she closed her eyes. "No, no. It was taken care of. No need to go around checking on things."

"Thank you, Dalia."

"No," she said as her ethereal stare bounced between me and Blade, "thank *you*."

"For what?"

"You're welcome," I mouthed.

"No thanks needed," Blade murmured.

Dalia sniffled before clearing her throat. "For being the best friend that you are and giving me the best nephew ever, of course."

Lisa giggled. "I'll let Brayden know you're coming over tomorrow. He's gonna be so pumped."

"You tell him I'll be just as pumped."

"I will. What time will you head over?"

She shrugged. "Lunchtime?"

"Perfect," Lisa said, "I'll have something ready by then. Though, don't shoot me if it's a pizza. I may just order pizza."

"I want pizza!" Lance called out from the bathroom.

Dalia barked with laughter, and oh, how the sound melted over my eardrums. God, I loved it when she laughed.

"Seriously, who is that?" Lisa asked.

Dalia snickered. "I've got so much to talk with you about tomorrow. But, I promise you'll meet them soon."

"Them?"

"Yep. Them."

Lisa chuckled. "Well, I look forward to the stories. See you tomorrow, okay?"

"See you tomorrow."

"Love you."

"Love you, too."

And after Dalia tossed the phone back to me, Lance called out from the bathroom.

"We gonna get this show on the road now, or what!?"

"I have no idea what you guys did," she said as tears filled her voice, "but from the bottom of my—my heart—"

She tapped her chest as tears fell down her cheeks once more.

"Oh, God, you have no idea what you've done to that woman's life," she whispered through her tears. "You've—you guys—"

I walked over to her and pressed a kiss to the top of her head. "It's the least that we could do."

Blade came around as well, took her hand within his, and pressed a kiss to the top of it. "I'm glad they're all right."

"Me, too," she whispered as she helplessly wiped at her tears.

"If I sit on this toilet any longer," Lance barked, "my ass is gonna go numb!"

Dalia shook her head as Blade let out one of his rare little chuckles, and I drank in the moment. How full we felt. How good it felt to all be standing there, breathing and alive after everything we had been through. I looked over at Blade before we made our way toward the entrance to the bathroom. I peered over my shoulder, watching as Dalia mindlessly walked over to the massive window in her bedroom. She stood there, looking out over the horizon. Already trapped within the depths of her thoughts. And as I set my sights on helping Lance, Blade moved in Dalia's direction.

I grabbed Blade's arm to stop him in his tracks. His icy stare pinned me with a look. He tilted his head, his body completely turned toward Dalia. Was he ready to take her on? To take on another woman after what had happened with Trishelle? There were still so many things we hadn't figured out yet. Things we hadn't hashed out. Were we all ready to tackle it? Us? All four us of, and whatever it was we had built?

I didn't know.

But we were about to find out.

"Go easy on her," I murmured. "She's still reeling from what happened with Dirge."

With a nod of his head, he pulled away from me and I stood there in the doorway of the bathroom. I watched him take up a position next to Dalia, his gaze studying her as she stared straight ahead. For a moment, neither of them moved, almost as if neither of them knew what move to make. She caved, though. She leaned her head onto Blade's shoulder, and he sat there, his back straight with his hands folded in his lap. I held my breath. I waited for him to pull away or stand to his feet. Anything to put distance between his body and his feelings. He had been terrible about that shit since Trishelle's funeral, and Dalia deserved better than that. She deserved better from all of us after what she had done to avenge our lives.

But when I watched that cold-hearted man place a soft kiss on the top of her head, I knew we'd be all right.

All of us. Even him.

Eventually.

"All right," I said, turning toward Lance in the bathroom. "I'm not washing your dick, just so you know."

And hearing Dalia bark with laughter filled my heart with the comfort it needed. If she still had the ability to laugh, then she had the ability to heal.

Which was all I'd ever ask of her, so long as she kept me by her side.

"Hi," Dalia said softly.

"Hey."

She sighed. "How are you?"

I scoffed. "I want you to answer that question first."

She shrugged. "I don't know."

"Yeah, me neither."

She picked her head up. "Wait, you don't know how I am, or you don't know how you are?"

I pivoted my head to gaze into her tired eyes. "Both."

I'd barely been able to look at her all week. She had damn near broken herself taking care of Lance. Cooking our meals and keeping him on his medicine regimen. Her crooked figure and her half-hooded gaze broke me a bit more every time I looked at her. Every time I watched her grunt over the sink as she washed dishes. Every time I listened to her hemming and hawing as she limped around. All week, she had given too much of herself and not received anything in return, and I had no idea how to fix that. How to change it. How to take the weight off her shoulders so she could be free to rest the way she needed.

"Is it normal to feel this... empty?" she asked softly.

"Come here," I said.

I wrapped my arms around her and pulled her into my lap. I scooted myself back onto the bed until my feet pointed toward the wall and I gathered her in my arms. Her tears shattered my soul. The shaking of her exhausted body made me hold her tighter than ever. I wanted her to stop. I wanted her to save her energy for something she wanted to do. Maybe I could take her swimming in the ocean, or out on a bike ride, or across town for a picnic underneath a fucking tree.

Anything to get her out of that headspace.

Anything to get her out of this place.

"It's okay," I said, pressing mindless kisses to the top of her head. "Just get it out. That's important."

Sobs racked her body. Her beautiful, sensual, glorious body. She jiggled not with pleasure, but with pain. She shivered not with ecstasy, but with terror. It angered me. No woman as beautiful, as giving, and as selfless as her deserved the hell she had walked through since coming into our lives.

It took all I had to push Trishelle's fate out of my mind as I held her in my arms.

"Do you want to talk about it?" I asked.

She sniffled hard before laying her head against my chest. "Not much to talk about. I killed a man. Someone I knew. And it could have easily been me in that situation. I could've been the psychopath standing at the other end of that gun. I could've been—"

"No."

"What do you mean, no?"

I gripped her chin and forced her gaze to mine. "No, it couldn't have easily been you. I've heard the bits and pieces you say about him. I've heard about the cat he tortured, and the way he lusted after you even when you told him to stop. And you know what I think?"

"What?"

"It sounds like he had psychopathic tendencies well before all of this."

Her gaze searched mine, and the helplessness in them worried me. "Will I ever shake it? His face? Will I ever not see it when I lay down at night?"

I knew I had to tell her the truth, but I also knew she wouldn't like it. "The first one will always stay with you, unfortunately."

Her gaze slowly focused. "Do you remember the first person you killed?"

A heavy sigh left my lips. "Yeah, I do."

"Well, if you ever want to talk about it, I'm here. Okay?"

I snickered and tucked her head back against my chest. Her body had been destroyed. Her state of mind, mangled, and there she was, considering me before herself.

What the hell had any of us done to deserve such a savior?

"I owe you an apology," I murmured.

She paused. "For what?"

I closed my eyes. "For assuming you were like all the others."

"I don't understand."

I licked my lips and drew in a deep breath. "I intentionally created distance and kept you at arm's length because in the back of my mind, I had convinced myself that all women were the same. Selfish little motherfucks that didn't give a damn about anything but themselves."

I paused and waited for her reaction, but when it didn't come, I decided to press on.

She deserved an explanation for why I had been so shitty toward her.

"My mother was a serial cheater," I said, swallowing the knot in my throat. "Every time my dad deployed overseas, she'd parade men in and out of the house as if it were her full-time job. She didn't give a shit about what I saw or what it did to our family. All she cared about was the fact that she was lonely, and she didn't like being lonely."

"Jesus," Dalia whispered.

"And then, I met Laurel. She was my high school sweetheart, and apparently also a pro at sucking off the football players before a big game."

She wrapped her arms around my body. "Then Trishelle happened, and you found her."

I shook my head softly. "All of the women I loved... they all had these secrets. These—these things they did without my knowledge. They didn't care how it affected me, and they didn't care what it did to me. And I get it, Trishelle had demons. She had things she fought off in her sleep that no man could ever dream of. But..."

"But she still betrayed you in a way."

I grimaced. "I know that's not technically right. I know that what she did had nothing to do with us but—"

"But it still hurts, and she still left you behind. I get it."

My lips moved even though my brain came to a grinding halt. "When you started flirting shamelessly with all of us, I just figured you were the same. Wanting what you wanted when you wanted it without a care in the world, and I didn't have the energy to entertain it. I'm so sorry, Dalia. I'm sorry that I could have ever—"

"Blade."

"—equated you to such—"

"Blade, look at me. It's really important that you do."

I panned my gaze down to her perfect little face. "Yeah?"

She climbed up from her slumped position. She straddled my lap and her hands cupped my cheeks. Her gaze focused on mine, and at that moment, everything else faded away. Every nightmare. Every woman. Every terrible thing I had ever done to bring myself to that point. Every regret and every drop of blood that stained my hands ceased to exist as metallic eyes of hers held me hostage.

I wanted to be her hostage for all eternity.

If she'd have me.

"Dalia?" I asked.

She shook her head. "You never owe me an apology for healing from old wounds. Do you hear me?"

I nodded. "I hear you."

When her lips met mine, it stopped my heart in my chest. My hands traveled up her back, caressing her curves as my mind committed everything to memory. The way her tongue raked across the roof of my mouth awakened my dick. I wrapped her up and turned her over, placing her back against the bed as she spread those juicy thighs for me. I caved to her. All of her. Body, mind, and soul. And as my hands roamed over her peaks and valleys, I wanted to speak my truth to her.

But she beat me to the punch.

"Blade?" she asked softly.

I pulled back just enough to feel her breath pulsing against my lips. "Yes, beautiful?"

She kissed my lips softly. "I could never love any of you any more or any less than I already do."

"Goddamn it, you're perfect," I growled.

I slammed my lips back to hers and our teeth clattered together. Her legs locked around me as her pussy heated my clothed dick. That was it. That was all I needed to hear. She was mine. She was ours. And so long as I breathed in and out on a daily basis, she'd always be protected.

"Mine," I grumbled down the back of her throat.

She whimpered softly against my lips. "Mine. All of you."

"Let's get you out of these clothes, beautiful."

"Pike, you got some popcorn?" Lance asked.

I froze and Dalia's eyes popped wide open.

"I mean, I could go get some. You want a soda?" Pike asked.

"Hell, yeah. I'd love a fucking soda. This woman's got me drinking lemon water, for fuck's sake."

I wrinkled my nose and looked down into Dalia's face. "Lemon water?"

She playfully shoved me off her body while Lance and Pike slow clapped. I flopped onto my back, staring up at the ceiling as my dick protruded against my pants. I didn't even try to cover it. No use at that point. And as Dalia's giggles filled the room, a smile crossed my face.

"I never thought I'd see it, honestly," Pike said. "I just figured you'd keep fighting how you felt until she sat on your face one morning."

My smile faded into a grin as I shoved myself upright with my elbows. "Now, hold on a minute. I didn't know face-sitting was on the menu."

"Hey, I like face-sitting," Lance said behind me. "Are we making a schedule or...?"

Dalia's laughter filled the room around us, and the sound was so beautiful that it held me hostage. I stood to my feet and turned toward the guys, and their smiles surely matched my own. The sound was effervescent. Like cracking open a new soda and pouring it over a full glass of ice. I couldn't help but join her in her laughter as it bubbled up the back of my throat. And before I knew it, all four of us were laughing together for the first time in what felt like ages.

"My God, you guys are insane. You know that?" Dalia managed to ask.

"Insane for you," I said, my laughter settling down.

Pike patted Lance's shoulder. "He's all clean, so I'm gonna go order pizza. And Dalia?"

"Yeah, yeah, yeah," she said, waving her hand in the air. "I guess I can relax a little bit."

I watched Lance walk over to her. "Thank you."

She looked up at him. "For what?"

He stroked his knuckles along her cheek. "For taking care of me. Thank you."

She took his hand in hers and kissed every single one of his knuckles. "I didn't do a thing you guys wouldn't have done for me."

"Damn straight," I said then leaned against the wall.

Pike backed out of the room. "All in favor of three large three-meat pizzas, some breadsticks, and some soda, raise your hands."

Lance shot his fucking hand into the air so quickly, it almost knocked him off balance. I pushed off the wall and caught his arm as Dalia wrapped her grip around his waist. He stumbled back against the wall with Dalia's body falling against his chest and I tugged his arm to keep him steady so he wouldn't fall over.

And when she looked up into his face, her laughter started all over again.

"Man, you get a guy to eat a salad and he acts like he's dying," she howled.

Pike chuckled as he turned down the hallway. "Be right back!"

Lance wrapped his arms around her and I stroked my hand through her tangled, knotted hair. I searched for a brush and found one lingering on an empty bookshelf next to the bed, so I went to retrieve it. Dalia laughed into Lance's bare chest while I perched myself behind her, slowly stroking the brush through her hair. Her laughter filled the dark holes of my heart. Her warmth, bringing my soul back to life. Now that we had her— now that we were all okay—I couldn't imagine things any other way. Not any longer. Not when I had the heart of the most incredible woman sitting right in the palms of my knife-scarred hands.

I loved Dalia with everything inside of me that hadn't already died, and if she had it her way, I knew she'd piece me back together.

Just like she had done with Lance.

EPILOGUE
DALIA

Six Months Later

I paced the foyer as I waited for the guys to return. A double shift. I had worked a double shift at the bar, and they still weren't back. Even though the club had gotten back onto its feet, I always worried about them leaving for transactions. They had been gone for most of the night. Left at three in the morning and the sun had just crested over the front of the house. They had been gone for hours, and even though The Sentinels were completely out of the way, I still worried.

Until I heard the roar of their bikes down the road.

"Yes," I hissed and whipped around on my feet.

I rushed up the stairs and barreled down the hallway. I damn near sprinted into my room in nothing but my skimpy black lingerie and reached for the matches. I struck up one after the other, lighting all of the pheromone-laced candles I had purchased a few days ago in the hopes of surprising the guys.

I had damn near bought the entire shelf of them at the store across town, and I hoped they worked.

I hadn't felt their bodies against mine in a while.

"Dalia!" Lance boomed.

His voice was strong. Girded. Just like it had been before everything happened. It had been so long since I'd heard that kind of strength rushing through his body, and it puckered my nipples against my flimsy teddy top. I lit the last candle and tossed the matches into the corner. I'd clean them up later. At that moment, other things were on my mind.

Like being stuffed full of them all at once.

"Dalia!?" Lance called out.

We had done it. We had survived. With each call of my name in his voice, it reassured me that it was time. We were ready. All of us, together.

So, I drew in a deep breath. "I'm up here! I've got something for you guys!"

"Dalia?!" Pike said, their footsteps moving quicker. "Are you all right!?"

"She said her bedroom?" Blade asked.

"Yeah!" I said . "In my bedroom! Hurry!"

I'd never heard them move that quickly. They damn near tripped one another up as they soared down the hallway. I gave my hair one more good fluff before I rolled my shoulders back. I climbed onto the bed and perched on my knees, sliding them open before I took my position. I had practiced all night to get it right. I wanted the spread of my hips accented and my tits jutted out for the taking, and as their shadows came around the corner, Lance was the first face I saw.

And the way his jaw hit the floor brought me a flood of pride I'd never experienced in my life.

"Hey, guys?" Phil asked as he came down the hallway. "I thought we were having church up—"

Pike stuck his head into the room before his eyes widened. "Lance, call it off."

Blade stood behind the two of them and licked his lips. "No church. Not today."

Lance snapped his fingers at their newest inducted crew member without taking his gaze off my body. "No church right now. Tonight. Nine o'clock. Spread the word, Phil."

"Make it tomorrow morning. Nine o'clock," Pike said.

"Yeah," Lance said. "That."

Phil paused. "But—"

"Now," Lance barked. "Tomorrow morning at nine and not a second before. Go!"

And when Phil's footsteps receded into nothingness, a smirk spread across my face.

"Hiya, guys," I said in the most seductive voice I could muster.

Lance's face flushed with red. "Blade?"

The man tore off down the hallway. "I'll get the food and make sure everyone's gone."

"Pike?" Lance asked.

"I'll get the doors locked and head downstairs."

I tilted my head. "Downstairs?"

Lance stepped into the room with that devilish smile of his. "Don't worry, guys. I'll get her strung up."

I blinked. "Wait, what?"

Lance moved in the blink of an eye, picking my body up and tossing me over his shoulder. Giggles fell from my lips as I kicked my legs, and the candles flickered with my movements.

"Wait, wait, wait, the candles!" I squealed.

He spanked my ass, and it pulled a moan from between my lips.

"Oh."

He squeezed the skin he had spanked. "You're coming with us, sweet girl."

"Ready!" Pike called up the steps.

"Heading down now!" Blade exclaimed.

"I've got the package!" Lance bellowed, rumbling down the stairs.

I swear, the three of them sounded like three kids about to open presents on Christmas. I couldn't stop laughing as Lance carried me through the house. It felt like ages had passed since I had heard that kind of excitement in their voices. It had taken us so long to get past everything, and for a while there, I wasn't sure things would ever return to normal.

But this was better than normal.

Hearing their smiles was so much better than normal.

"Where are we going?" I asked.

Lance held me tightly as we descended into the darkness of the basement. "Ever wonder what's down here?"

"Only all the time."

"Well, you're about to find out."

When he dropped me to my feet, the guys gathered around me from behind. It took my eyes a second to focus in the darkness of the basement, but when they did, I found myself staring at some sort of wooden X.

"Has that always been down here?" I asked.

Lance's voice appeared in my ear. "Step toward it."

I did as he asked. "Now, what?"

"Now, keep moving until we tell you to stop," Blade said.

I peered over my shoulder and found three sets of hungry eyes staring back at me. I thought I'd had the upper hand. I thought that surprising them was the way to go. And yet, they had found a way to turn the tables. A way to catch me off-guard and remind me that, no matter what, I never really knew what was coming with them.

And it was one of the many reasons why I loved them.

"Blade, you take the left. Pike, you take the right," Lance commanded.

I turned to face them. "What does this—oh!"

Blade grabbed my wrist and pulled it over my head. "Hold still, beautiful."

Pike grabbed my other arm. "Come here, my pet."

They strapped me to that fucking thing before Lance walked up to me. He gazed down into my face and I tilted my head back as far as it would go. And yet, I still had to roll my eyes up to keep him in view. His leg reached out to mine. He kicked them open before Blade and Pike dropped down to attach my ankles to the fucking wooden whatever the hell it was.

And as Lance wrapped his hand around my throat, my body rose to the occasion.

"Surprise," he said, his voice dropping into his chest.

When Blade and Pike stood up, they backtracked toward the bed. I moved my eyes as much as I could while Lance pinned my neck to that fucking thing, and I watched Pike open a briefcase. He started pulling things out, but from where I was perched, I had no clue what the hell was in there. However, the second Blade popped open the caramel and chocolate sauce, the sweet, decadent smell filled the air all around us.

"What's in the briefcase, Pike?" I asked.

Lance used his fingers to guide my stare back to his. "Only good girls get that information."

I grinned. "Have I been a bad girl?"

Blade chuckled as he walked behind me. "Good work, Lance."

"Thanks," he said hotly.

"I think these will do nicely," Pike said .

With each toy he held up for me to behold, my eyes grew wider. There was a wand and a vibrator. A butt plug and a blindfold. There were all sorts of things I didn't recognize, like some sort of feather on the end of a stick and a circular looking thing with spikes on it.

It was Lance who slid his hand beneath my flimsy thong, though. "Let's see if I can't get her ready for us."

My eyes fluttered closed. "Oh, fuck."

His hand dipped between my wet pussy lips and his fingertips found my swollen mound. He circled them softly. Slowly. Teasing me as my legs quivered . My head fell back against the wooden cross thing and I tugged at my restraints, already needy for their touch.

"Here," Pike said, kneeling down. "I think I can help with this a bit."

"Hold onto that thought," Blade said, pulling something out of his pocket.

The way his blade hummed as he unsheathed it froze me in my tracks. Something teased my entrance, and the second it started vibrating, a desperate groan fell from my mouth. Blade tilted his head, eyeing me carefully as he slid the blunt end of the blade up my stomach. Up my breasts. All the way beneath my bra, until he pulled it forward and snapped the fabric.

Sending my tits plummeting to my body.

"Now, there's a sight to behold," Lance growled.

"In we go," Pike said.

"Fuck!" I cried out as his vibrator filled me.

He turned on the pulsing sensations as Blade's knife slid back down my body. Lance's fingers tickled my clit as his other hand held my neck hostage. My eyes rolled back. My muscles shivered and my body bucked .

"Hold still, beautiful, or you may get a sensation you don't like," Blade warned.

It was torture holding myself still. But when I heard the snap of my panties before the fabric fell away from my body, I almost came right then and there. I was exposed to them. My body, climbing up the mountaintop as they all watched me unravel. I bucked against Pike's toy. I slicked Lance's hand with my juices and Blade's knife came back to my neck. He walked around me, standing behind the cross and held that blade to my throat.

"Better hold still, beautiful," he purred, his voice dripping along the shell of my ear.

It was all too much, and before I knew it, my first orgasm crashed over my body.

"Oh, God!" I cried out.

"There is no God here with you now," Blade glowered.

My toes curled and my muscles locked out as pleasure sizzled through my veins. My pussy pulsed, pushing Pike's toy out and Lance removed his hand from my pussy. I lazily opened my eyes, half-hooded with ecstasy. And when I saw him lick my mark off his fingers, I fell helplessly against the cross behind me.

Blade tucked his knife away.

"My turn," he said, stepping out from behind me.

Lance stalked behind me and cupped my tits, tugging at my aching nipples. "Do your worst."

"Here," Pike said, passing something to Lance. "Let's get her other hole opened up for us."

"Wh-wh—what?" I asked breathlessly.

Lance chuckled. "Don't mind if I do."

He held the butt plug out in front of me. "Spit."

I gathered as much as I could into my mouth before doing as he asked.

"Good girl."

"Now," Blade said, brandishing chocolate sauce in one hand and caramel in the other, "where should my tongue start?"

He aimed them at me and squirted me down, damn near drenching me in the stuff. Lance pulled my ass cheeks apart, teasing my rosebud with the intrusion as his arm wrapped around my waist. If he cared that I was covered in dessert sauce, he didn't show it. If Pike cared that Blade had dripped any onto him, he didn't say anything about it. And as Blade's tongue ran along the expanse of my pulse point, lapping up the chocolate he had aimed down my body, I collapsed against the cross, dangling from my wrists as Lance popped the plug into my asshole.

"Shit!" I cried out.

"What a fucking view," Lance growled.

Pike chuckled and stood. "Press the button on the flat end. Let's see what it does to her."

"Huh," Lance said, his hand cupping the plug in my ass. "Interesting."

The second he pushed that button, the vibrations coursed throughout my entire body. My head fell back against the cross and I struggled to get myself upright. Blade stripped himself down, removing all of his clothes before devouring me with his mouth. He lapped along my tits and sucked random patches of my skin. He left hickies behind that Lance traced with his fingertips as he whispered nasty little nothings in my ear.

It was all too much, and as someone stuck their hand in between my legs once more, I felt myself climbing to the top again.

"Such a good little slut for us," Lance hissed. "I bet your pussy is begging for our cocks."

"Oh, fuck. Please. I want to feel you guys so much."

Blade chuckled against my right thigh as he knelt in front of me. "Trust me, we know."

"I'll get the bed ready," Pike said, rushing away.

Lance pressed his lips to my ear. "You ready to be our little cum dumpster?"

"Yes, yes, yes," I chanted.

"Mmmmm," Blade groaned, his tongue tracing languidly, "I don't think I can hold off."

Lance chuckled as he kissed my ear. "Then, don't."

"D-d-d—don't—Fuck! Blade!"

He dove his tongue in between my pussy lips and my asshole tightened around that plug. One of his fingers eased its way into my entrance, and as Lance continued whispering in my ear, I found myself overwhelmed.

"Such a dirty girl for us. Dripping with juices. Taunting us after work. You wanna be our little whore?"

"Yes," I moaned.

"Mmmm," Blade hummed, "delicious."

Lance lapped my earlobe. "You wanna take us all at once?"

"Oh, yes," I groaned.

Blade's tongue tickled the tip of my clit and it made me jump. My arms tugged at the restraints, and I did my best to place my legs over his shoulders. Anything to get closer. Anything for the release.

"Then," Lance glowered, wrapping his hand back around my throat. "Come for us. Be a good little bitch and cover Blade's face."

"Blade! Oh, holy fuck!"

My eyes rolled back as orgasm number two rumbled over my body. That tightly wound coil behind my gut popped and sweat dripped down the nape of my neck. Lance kissed along my bare shoulder. I collapsed with nothing but the restraints holding me up. And as Blade cleaned up the last of the syrup from my body, someone released me from the restraints.

I found my body floating through midair.

"Wow," I whispered.

Pike chuckled. "Trust me, we're not nearly done with you yet."

My back flopped onto something soft and comfortable, but

it didn't last for long. The second they rolled me over, someone worked their arm around my waist and hoisted my ass into the air. A smack came down against my cheek. Then, the other. And another. And yet, another still. It pulled groans from my lips and shot electricity through my veins.

I didn't even realize they were strapping me down again, until I tried to turn over and face them.

"What the fuck?" I asked breathlessly.

Lance chuckled as he perched behind me. "My, my, that plug looks decadent on you."

I felt his thick dick teasing my pussy folds. "Please."

"Please, what?" Pike asked.

I turned my head toward his voice and found both Blade and Pike standing there, completely naked with their dicks in their hands.

"Please, Lance, I want you to fuck me."

"Well," he said, lining himself up with my entrance. "Why the fuck didn't you say so, then?"

The second he plunged into my entrance, the world went blank. Someone tugged my tits, and I felt someone else's breath pulsing along my ear, but I couldn't have told you who. All I knew was his dick. All I felt was his command. His hands, spanking my ass cheeks. His voice, calling me his beautiful, perfect little princess. He spread me as if it were my first time. My walls collapsed around his cock, milking him for all he had as the bed banged against the wall with his efforts.

"That's it, Dalia. Come for us," Blade hissed.

"Such a good girl," Lance grunted.

"Fill her up," Pike said, gripping my hair and lifting my head. "Say his name when he does."

"Lance," I choked out.

"Fucking hell, so close. What a pussy she has," Lance grunted.

"Now," Blade glowered.

"Lance!" I cried out.

"Goddamn it, Dalia," Lance hissed.

He spilled into me, marking me as his own. I collapsed on the bed. His hands pounded into the mattress on either side of my body, and all I wanted was for him to fall on top of me. I wanted to be blanketed in his weight. Covered away from the world as I relished in our moment. But as I felt a lean, strong arm slide beneath my stomach, my hips were heaved back into the air.

Blade's voice echoed off the corners of my mind.

"You're dripping with him, and I can't wait to watch you drip with me," he whispered.

He teased my clit with his cock, and it woke me back up. Whether I had passed out or not, I didn't have a fucking clue. However, when he breached my entrance, my back arched. His length filled me to the brim, dropping my jaw and causing my nails to curl into the bed. He raked along that pebbled spot within my body so beautifully, and fireworks burst behind my closed eyes.

I heard nothing. Saw nothing. Experienced nothing, except the feeling of his dick raking against my walls. His pelvis, pounding into my ass cheeks and jiggling them for everyone else's viewing pleasure. I felt used. Tied down and filled for their own nefarious desires.

I never wanted it to stop.

"Blade, oh my God!"

"That's it," he growled, tugging my hair. "Come for me, my little princess. Show your king what he's worth."

"Fuck!" I cried out.

Ripple after ripple of desire rushed through me, holding me hostage as I collapsed against the bed. The leather bonds tugged at my wrists and his cock fell from between my legs. I had no strength. No control. Just my body, useless against them as they showed me exactly who owned every single inch of my being. My soul. My skin.

It was Pike who coaxed my head to the side and kissed my forehead.

"My sweet pet," he murmured.

I moaned. "Oh, Pike."

"Relax for me," Lance said, patting my ass.

I flopped on the bed as vibrations from the plug rattled my ribcage. I drooled against the stain sheets that stained themselves with the evidence of our debauchery. Oh, how I loved my men. My strong, valiant, capable men.

"Think you got one more in you for us, my pet?" Pike asked.

"She worked that double shift today," Blade said as something cool pressed against my skin. "She might be too tired," he said in a mocking voice.

I somehow managed to flutter my eyes open. "Anything for you."

His voice was wickedly luscious. "Good answer."

I braced myself for whatever intrusion waited for me. My body, shivering and in shambles, laid there in all its glory as Lance's massive hands gripped my waist. I heard him say something to Blade, but the world muddled around me as my body lifted itself, the restraints clanging together like chains in a dungeon.

That was where I was.

Their fucking dungeon.

"There we go," Pike grunted as he slithered beneath me. "You can lower her."

And when Pike's warm, comforting muscles blanketed me, I fell into his embrace.

"Hi," I whispered.

He nuzzled against my cheek. "Hey, yourself."

Lance's hand usurped my ass cheek. "Hold still, sweet girl."

I moaned and he pulled the plug out of my ass. My body felt empty, and I didn't like it.

"Put it back," I whispered.

Pike kissed the tip of my nose. "Sounds like someone wants to be filled up."

A set of thin, wispy fingers gripped my chin, pulling my tired gaze off to the right. I found myself face to face with Blade, his knees knelt against the mattress as his dick brushed my cheek.

"I've been waiting for that throat of yours," he said.

The bed beneath my knees dipped down before Lance's massive dick fell between my ass cheeks. "Ready?"

Pike eased the tip of his dick toward my entrance. "Ready."

Blade slid his thumb along my lower lip. "Open wide for me, beautiful."

I unhinged my jaw and stuck out my tongue, and the second his dick touched my mouth I felt Pike press up. His cock slid against my walls, pulling a groan from the back of my throat as my entire body tensed up. Something wet slid toward my asshole. Lance's hands pulled my cheeks apart and his tongue breached my forbidden hole. It all swirled around me, every sound and every sensation, and there were no words to describe how I felt.

Except for... loved.

"I love you guys so much," I said breathlessly.

Pike grunted as his pelvis bottomed out with mine. "I love you, Dalia."

Blade hissed as he slid his cock down the back of my throat. "Goddamn it, I love you."

And when the tip of Lance's dick breached my hole, I moaned around Blade's dick as my pussy collapsed around Pike's cock.

"You're perfect for us," Lance said with a grunt. "and I'll never stop loving you as long as you live."

Thrust after thrust, they claimed my body. Every hole, every inch, theirs for the taking. I fell against Pike, allowing them to mold my body to their lusts as they filled me to the brim. Back and forth. Side to side. Up and down, in and out. It all coalesced into a sweet, harmonic symphony that time itself had carved out for us. Their growls swirled around my head. Their hands held me hostage. My throat expanded and my pussy clamped down, which trapped Lance's dick in my ass.

"Fucking Christ," Lance hissed. "I'm coming."

"Just one...more," Blade choked out.

"Yes. Yes. Goddamn it, Dalia, here it comes," Pike grunted.

Feeling their cocks pulsing with their threads of arousal sent me spiraling over the edge. My body locked out. It held their dicks inside of my body as I lost all control of my faculties. My eyes rolled back. Fireworks burst behind my closed eyelids. My toes curled so deeply that my legs quivered, and for the life of me, I swear to hell I stopped breathing.

Just so I could drink it all in.

"Such a good girl," Lance murmured, kissing my lower back.

Blade pulled his limp dick out from my throat. "So beautiful with my cum dripping down your chin."

Pike slid his hands down my arms. "Let's get you situated more comfortably, yeah?"

I wanted to tell him that I'd never been more comfortable. More loved. More cherished in all my life. But all I could do was nod. The bonds around my wrists and ankles released themselves, and the guys piled into bed with me. Pike slid off to the side, turning me to face him as he stroked his fingers through my hair. Lance picked my feet up, settling them into his lap and he massaged the sore marks around my ankles.

Blade held me from behind, his head tucked against the crook of my neck.

"We have something for you," Pike said.

Blade picked his head up. "Did you remember to bring it down?"

Lance chuckled. "Nope, I bet he didn't."

I peeked a tired eye open. "What is it?"

Pike kissed the tip of my nose. "We can get it once we head back upstairs, but it's a key to the house."

Blade kissed my bare shoulder. "We want you to move in."

"If you want, that is," Lance said, his fingers massaging the ache out of my feet.

Tears of happiness streaked my cheeks as a smile took over my features. "You mean, I don't already live here?"

Lance barked with laughter. "She's got a point. Not like she's gone home much these past few months."

Pike captured my lips softly. "Well, now we can make it official."

Blade hovered over me to meet my gaze. "Will you move in with us, Dalia?"

I didn't hesitate to nod. "I'd love to. Honestly."

"Good," Lance said, pulling me to the edge of the bed.

I squealed when he scooped me into his arms, holding me against him. As he turned toward the steps, our naked bodies seated against one another, I heard the other guys clamoring behind us. I floated through the air, clinging to Lance and his strong form, reminding myself that he was all right. They were all right.

We were all going to be all right.

"Who's ready to take this show to the shower?" Blade asked.

I snickered. "Not sure I've got much energy to do that."

"That's okay," Pike said, snaking past me and Lance, rushing to open the door. "We don't mind putting in the work."

As we emerged from the basement, I took stock of the foyer. The pristine marble floors. The white-washed walls. The grand staircase leading up to the level Blade and I now shared. The windows that poured in sweet, rich ocean sunlight through the glass. The light blue accents made me smile. The black banister of the staircase reminded me of their leather jackets. And as we ascended, my life slipped into place.

Were we unconventional? Sure. Were we normal? Absolutely not. Were we perfect for one another in every way, shape, and form? Fuck yeah, we were.

"Here's to our future," I whispered, tucking my face into the crook of Lance's neck.

"Here, fucking here," my men said in unison.

The three big, brave, bold men who held my future in their hands.

Turn the page for a sneak peak at Twisted Flames!

Three bikers have me straddling the line between duty and desire...

As a DEA agent, I've always kept a distance wider than Smuggler's Bay between me and biker gangs like the Death Cheaters—until three of their members crash into my world and set everything on fire.

Suddenly, I'm caught in the crossfire between them and another MC that couldn't be more different—the Black Diamonds. The Death Cheaters despise those drug-running scumbags just as much as I do.

With my dark past and inked-up skin, I'm more like them than I'd ever admit—but they see right through my defenses and into my soul, despite the years that separate us.

Reid, the strong and silent type with bloodlust under the surface. Cash, the hothead who wears a playful mask. And Baron, the mountain of muscle with enough integrity to save them all. Each of them ignites something in me that I couldn't resist if my life depended on it—and it just might.

We may be the least likely of allies, but I know they'd do anything to protect me—even though I'm just as capable as any outlaw on a Harley. Because there's something fierce between the four of us, and no matter how much danger is hot on our trail, when I'm with them, it's a hell of a ride.

Twisted Flames is a complete stand-alone why choose motorcycle club romance. It is a part of the Twisted Intentions series, which features a new harem in each book. These books are not connected and can be read in any order.

"Do you really think I'm an idiot, Dee?" I asked as I slid my shirt over my head.

"Depends on when you're acting like one," he said flatly.

I sighed as I ran my hands down the front of my shirt. "Tucked in or no?"

"Does it matter what I think?"

I rolled my eyes. "Either pull your head out of your ass and get with the program or go away. But this is a prime opportunity, and I'm not wasting it just because we can't get Cap on the phone right now."

"Then don't ask what I think."

I lobbed my head over to look at my partner. The man that had held me down at the DEA ever since I took the field agent job they offered me five years ago. One random drug bust as a police officer right in the heart of our country's capital, and the next second, I applied for a DEA job that they practically threw at me. For five years, Dee watched my back. Trained me up. Covered for me when I did stupid shit because he knew it was for the greater good.

So, why the fuck didn't he have my back now?

"I take it there's nothing I can say to stop you?" he asked.

I threw the car door open. "Unless you wanna tell me why you absolutely can't stand the fact that we're about to pick up a massive lead in a case Cap has yet to bust wide open."

He leaned toward me. "You mean, a case *you* have yet to bust wide open. You know this isn't an official case."

I snapped my stare toward him. "It's back out on the street. I saw the logo. You know that that means, don't you? It means—"

"Someone has come in to fill the hole and continued dispersing the drugs that killed your brother. Yes, Angel, I know," he said flatly.

I stood and ducked my head back into the car. "Then, put some respect in your voice when you're talking about it."

When he didn't respond, I gave him one last chance.

"Sure you don't wanna come in?" I asked as I shoved the car door open. "It'll probably be one of the only times you can have a drink while on the job."

Dee pointed at me. "That."

"What?"

"That right there is why I'm not going in with you. This isn't a case for you. Right now, you're not on the clock. You're chasing a vendetta, and you're going to get yourself killed."

I blinked. "So, you're going to sit in the car while I get killed then?"

He gnashed his teeth together. "Just don't do anything stupid, Angel. Last thing I need is to haul your ass back to Cap and tell him what you did."

"What *we* did."

"Oh, no, this isn't my idea."

I stood up straight out of the car and stretched my arms over my head. "And yet, you're here with me now. About to listen in on a conversation that could blow this case wide open."

He snickered. "Trust me, with how heavy handed you

always are? The only thing you're about to blow open is a hole in their roof."

I grinned as I closed the door, and I made my way inside. Dee called out something from the car, but I didn't give a damn what he said. For once, we had a leg-up on the competition. On the crew peddling the same drugs that got my brother addicted. The drugs that destroyed his life. That took away his soul. A crew that I had found digging of my own volition in the late hours of the evening in my own damn bed because I was apparently the only person that gave a damn about getting that shit off the street.

I buried my brother with their drugs in his system.

And now, it was time for payback.

The rush of wind that fluttered my hair as I pushed the set of double doors open made me draw in a deep breath. The smell of fresh deep fryer grease had nothing on the warm scent of tequila floating through the air. Someone kicked on a blender, whirring together a drink for one of the patrons that hung themselves over a sticky-looking table.

The place was a dive if I'd ever seen one.

"What'll it be?!" someone called out.

I followed the sound of the voice. The trail of dulcet notes it left in its wake tugged my head around until I found myself staring at a grinning bartender. His stature towered over the bar as he stood there, shining a massive glass with the rag in his hand. He kept his gaze fixated on me as he threaded the stem of the glass through a roof-mounted storage unit, then slapped that damp rag right over his shoulder. His jet-black hair contrasted with his pale skin, and the bright background only served to amplify the deep green of his eyes.

It pulled me right up to the bar, and I cocked my hip to raise myself up onto a stool in front of him.

"What is that heavenly smell?" I asked as I put on my best innocent voice.

He chuckled as his head tilted off to the side. "House special. Lemonade margarita."

I pointed. "I'll have one of those. It sounds delicious."

He turned his back toward the mirrored wall of liquors. "Our extra crispy fries go great with it."

"Sign me up then."

"Order up!" he bellowed. "One large order, extra crisp!"

"Coming right up!" a disembodied voice off to my left yelped.

"So," the bartender said as he reached for a glass above his head, "don't think I've seen you around here."

I slid my gaze down his body. His chiseled jawline matched the pulsing muscles that stretched against his crimson shirt. It was a great color on him despite his pale complexion, and I had an awful time pulling my eyes away. Had he already made me? No, there was no fucking way. My shirt was much too thick to showcase the microphone taped to my chest.

Say something, you look like an idiot. "Didn't know the view was this good on the other side of town."

He chuckled, and the sound warmed me over like rich hot chocolate. "A woman whose poison is tequila deserves a good view before she forgets her evening."

I couldn't help but giggle. "You make a fair point. Tequila is one of those liquors."

"That," he said as he poured my drink into the glass, "and gin."

"Ah, you're a gin man."

"I'm absolutely a gin man. Keeps the Christmas spirit alive all year round."

I smiled. Genuinely smiled. "Christmas is one of my favorite times of the year as well."

"Order up!" the random voice called out from my left.

The bartender slid the drink toward me. "That would be your fries. Enjoy the drink, and I'll be right back."

And as the man turned toward my left, I couldn't help but watch his perky little ass while he walked toward the kitchen window.

Good God, the man was sexy as hell.

"You done staring?" Dee asked.

His voice came alive in my earpiece. "Don't tell me you like the view, too."

He snickered. "I can tell by the way you're talking. Be careful, he's already got you dropping your defenses."

I rolled my eyes. "It's just a drink and some fries."

"Uh huh."

"Here we go," the bartender said when he got back. "One large order of extra crispy fries. You want anything to dip those in?"

I smiled. "What do you prefer to dip them in?"

He winked at me. "Got a nice little dip in the back. It's usually just for the workers, but I'll spare you some."

"Ah, my hero."

He chuckled. "You stay put. I'll be right back."

Mm, mm, mm. I didn't even care if the sauce was shit. Watching that man walk away for a second time was very much worth the wait. My head tilted off to the side as his long legs bled up into a rotund ass that my hands wanted to—

"I'm proud of you, you know," Dee said.

I adjusted my glasses that held the camera through which Dee was able to view everything. And just like that, it hit me.

That man watched me stare down some other dude's ass.

"What's so funny?" he asked sharply.

I covered my mouth. "I forgot there was a camera on these things."

"You... forgot? Seriously?"

I kept giggling into my palm. "Completely."

"And you want to try and convince me that you're not distracted?"

That stopped my giggle in its tracks. "I swear, you're no fun. Since when did you become no fun?"

"Did you even hear me tell you that I'm proud of you?"

I paused. "Yeah, I did."

"Well, I am. After everything that happened, I would've put money on the fact that you wouldn't come back to the DEA. Suffering a loss like you did is hard on anyone. And then you came walking through those doors and showed everyone why you're the best at what you do."

"Yet, you're still questioning my every move."

"You can't exactly say you're unbiased toward this situation."

The second I located the bartender, I cleared my throat. "Well, well, what do we have here?"

The man with the piercing green eyes set a small container of what looked like yellowish goop in front of me. "It tastes better than it looks."

"You sure about that?"

He planted his massive forearms onto the table so that his eyes were level with mine. "I'm positive. Go on, try a bit. See what you think."

I eyed the sauce carefully and tried to figure out what was in it. Why the hell did it look lumpy? Relish. It could be relish. But who put relish in mustard? I bent down and sniffed it. For all I knew, I had been had and that shit was poison.

Then, Dee came to my rescue.

"It's honey mustard, sweet relish, horseradish, and most likely a twinge of ketchup for a bit of sweetness. You're fine."

So, I picked up a fry, dunked it, and tossed the entire thing into my mouth.

"Well?" the man asked.

Flavors burst against my tongue, and I couldn't hold back the groan working its way up the back of my throat. The sound split my lips, permeating the air between us as I leaned back against the barstool. I chewed slowly, enjoying this newfound sensation of horseradish, mustard, and relish. Such an odd combination, and yet my body wondered why the hell I hadn't thought of it sooner.

"Wow," I murmured.

"Yeah?" the man asked as he raised up. "I figured you might like it. It's definitely not for the faint of heart."

I leaned back up and reached for another fry. "Could use some hot sauce, though. The tang of that horseradish would do well with it."

He chuckled. "I'll give that a go next time."

I reached for my drink and pulled it toward me as I thought about my next move. I'd spent a great deal of time backtracking the inner workings of how this drug specifically came into the States and how it disbursed. It didn't take me long to figure out where the main hub of the drug was, and that was how I ended up in that bar. I mean, come on. A motorcycle crew taking over important South Carolina docks that just so happened to be stationed painfully close to the epicenter of the distribution city where my brother's white powdered killer came from?

Come on, no one was that fucking stupid.

The goal? To figure out where in the absolute fuck this crew was stationed. Out of all the scouting work I had done from my desk in D.C. and all of the traffic camera reports I had pulled, I couldn't piece together a pathway between them and wherever their homebase was stationed. The only promising lead I had gotten was a local telling me that some of the stretches of beach along the South Carolina coast were privately owned, especially with regard to the docks. All I needed was to get a bit of confirmation from one of their mouths, and I'd have enough to raid every single private beach along the coastline.

Either way, I'd find their fucking clubhouse.

That was what they called it, you know.

A clubhouse.

Sounded like a child's treehouse, if anyone asked me about it.

"Man, you weren't kidding about this drink," I said as I took another long pull.

The bartender pulled glass-bottled beers from the refrigerator behind him. "Glad you like it. If you need anything else, just let me know."

"Actually," I said as I picked up another fry, "I could use some advice."

"Trust me, I'm not that kind of bartender."

"I'm actually looking for somewhere, but I can't seem to find it. I was hoping maybe a local could help?"

"Tread carefully," Dee muttered in my ear.

"Oh?" the man asked as he turned around and placed the open beers on a circular tray off to the side. "Where are you looking for?"

I had thought about this conversation for days, ever since I had gotten Cap to sign off on allowing me to explore things further. No contact, of course, but what crew was ever taken down without a bit of rule-breaking?

Besides, it wasn't like anyone had fired shots yet.

"I need some... help," I said cautiously.

The man tilted his head. "What kind of help?"

I sighed heavily. "I'm trying to find my brother."

"Angel," Dee warned.

I ignored him. "He was last seen in the area, but no one seems to know anything about him. Or even seen him."

"How do you know he was last seen in the area then?"

I shoved my hand into the pocket of my jeans and pulled out the small locket. I unraveled the chain and pried open the small heart, revealing my dead brother's face. I stared at the picture for a little while, running my thumb across his beautiful face. So full of life, he had been. Such a lovely laugh.

Whoever owned those drugs now would pay for what they took from me.

"Here," I said as I handed it to the bartender. "Have you seen him at all?"

The man studied the picture carefully, but eventually shook his head and handed the picture back. "Sorry, but I haven't seen him around."

I sighed heavily as I clasped the locket closed and slipped it back against my thigh pocket. "Thanks anyway."

I felt his gaze hot against my forehead as I took another sip of my drink. "I could call around to the other bars. See if they've seen anyone matching his description. Maybe someone else has set eyes on him?"

"Really?" I asked breathlessly.

"Boy, you know how to pour it on, don't you?" Dee asked with a chuckle.

"Sure, it's not a problem. I mean, I can't guarantee anything, but it won't hurt to place a few calls."

"Do you want to keep the locket?" I asked as I reached into my pocket again. "Maybe it'll help if—"

"Well, well, well," a booming voice said behind me, "what do we have here?"

"Nothing that concerns you," the bartender said curtly.

I craned my head over my shoulder and saw a stalwart, scar-faced man standing behind me. The salt in his beard and at his temples contrasted the playful brown of his eyes. But the kindness in the bartender's gaze wasn't present in his.

"Hello," I said as I turned back to the bar.

"Goodbye," the bartender said as he slapped his rag down against the bar.

The man behind me grunted before he shuffled away, and I had to admit, the rush it gave me was outstanding. I had to draw a deep breath in through my nose just to calm the adrenaline coursing its way through my veins. This was the shit I adored. Hanging on by a thread. Teetering on the edge. And as I sat there, watching the bartender eye everyone in the bar above my head, the smallest part of me wished I wasn't working.

Because dear God, I wanted a slice of him.

"Looks like someone is a bit possessive," I said as I reached for another fry.

The bartender picked the rag back up. "Can't have my men getting caught up with the undercover cop sitting at my bar. I'm sure you can understand."

Dee's voice came alive in my ear. "Her cover's been blown, everyone! Go! Go! Go!"

And as the doors to the bar crashed in with agents that I didn't even realize had been there all along with us, I stared that man down. I watched that playful, boyish grin on his face slip into the most unsavory frown on the planet. My heart stopped in my chest. Agents lined the walls of the bar as guns were drawn and cocked. But all I knew was his glare.

His angry, powerful, brutally beautiful stare.

Want more? Twisted Flames is out now!!

ABOUT THE AUTHOR

Savannah Rylan is a romance writer that spends most of her time writing and reading. When not writing about sexy bikers and the women that love them, you can find her chasing around her toddler and two fur babies with her husband. She used to live in warm sunny California but has since moved to the East Coast where she has to deal with snow now, which she isn't too pleased about.

You can join her mailing list here!
Check out her website!

Box Sets

The Bad Disciples MC Box Set
The Road Rebels MC Box Set
Marked Skulls MC Box Set
Dead Souls MC Complete Collection
Black Hornets MC Box Set
The Lost Boys MC: The Complete Collection
The Callaghan Mafia Box Set
The Black Cobras MC
Dragon Riders MC
Dirty Misfits MC
Steel Scorpions MC

Series

Twisted Metal
Twisted Glass
Twisted Hearts
Twisted Flames

Bender (Steel Scorpions MC #1)
Angel (Steel Scorpions MC #2)
Goose (Steel Scorpions MC #3)
Viper (Steel Scorpions MC #4)
Reaper (Steel Scorpions MC #5)
Fangs (Steel Scorpions MC #6)

Brooks (Dirty Misfits MC #1)
Porter (Dirty Misfits MC #2)
Asher (Dirty Misfits MC #3)
Cole (Dirty Misfits MC #4)
Tanner (Dirty Misfits MC #5)
Finn (Dirty Misfits MC #6)

Link (Dragon Riders MC #1)
Bowser (Dragon Riders MC #2)
Ash (Dragon Riders MC #3)
Knuckles (Dragon Riders MC #4)
Sly (Dragon Riders MC #5)

Declan (The Callaghan Mafia #1)
Brody (The Callaghan Mafia #2)
Gael (The Callaghan Mafia #3)
Flynn (The Callaghan Mafia #4)

Cage (Dead Souls MC: Prospects #1)
Bear (Dead Souls MC: Prospects #2)
Saint (Dead Souls MC: Prospects #3)
Ryker (Dead Souls MC: Prospects #4)
Toxin (Dead Souls MC: Prospects #5)

Texas (The Lost Boys MC #1)
Stone (The Lost Boys MC #2)

Bronx (The Lost Boys MC #3)
Notch (The Lost Boys MC #4)
Diego (The Lost Boys MC #5)
Puck (The Lost Boys MC #6)
Frost (The Lost Boys MC #7)
West (The Lost Boys MC #8)

Jace (The Black Hornets MC #1)
Maverick (The Black Hornets MC #2)
Duke (The Black Hornets MC #3)
Colt (The Black Hornets MC #4)
Thor (The Black Hornets MC #5)
Jagger (The Black Hornets MC #6)

Knox (Dead Souls MC #1)
Grave (Dead Souls MC #2)
Brewer (Dead Souls MC #3)
Rock (Dead Souls MC #4)
Diesel (Deal Souls MC #5)

Girth (Marked Skulls MC #1)
Rodeo (Marked Skulls MC #2)
Abe (Marked Skulls MC #3)
Oz (Marked Skulls MC #4)
Dash (Marked Skulls MC #5)

Hawk (The Road Rebels MC #1)
Talon (The Road Rebels MC #2)
Snake (The Road Rebels MC #3)
Fox (The Road Rebels MC #4)

Gunner (The Bad Disciples MC #1)

Hunter (The Bad Disciples MC #2)
Tank (The Bad Disciples MC #3)
Glock (The Bad Disciples MC #4)
Marco (The Bad Disciples MC #5)